SPACE DRIFTERS:
THE EMERALD ENIGMA

Other books by Paul Regnier

The Space Drifters series

The Emerald Enigma | BOOK ONE

The Iron Gauntlet | BOOK TWO

SPACE DRIFTERS: THE EMERALD ENIGMA

BOOK ONE

PAUL REGNIER

an imprint of
GILEAD PUBLISHING

The Emerald Enigma by Paul Regnier
Published by Enclave Publishing,
an imprint of Gilead Publishing,
Wheaton, IL 60187
www.enclavepublishing.com

ISBN: 978-1-68370-014-2

Published in the United States by Enclave Publishing, an imprint of Gilead Publishing Wheaton, Illinois.

Cover designed by Kirk DouPonce
Edited by Andy Meisenheimer

Printed in the United States of America

For Jolene,

the greatest girl in the galaxy

1

WAKING UP TO A FLEET of Zormian star pirates surrounding my ship was yet another reminder that my life was not going as planned.

"This ship is loaded with thermal plasma canisters. You nail us with a photon canon and it's lights out for all of us." I glared up at the viewing screen and leaned forward in the captain's chair trying to appear threatening.

"Lies. We ran a thorough scan of your freighter. There wasn't a trace of thermal plasma."

The Zormian slug captain's generous, puke green torso folded over tight black stretchy pants in a hideous disregard for fashion. Though, to be fair, his velvet collar had style.

"They're coated in Vanthis cocoon slime. They can't be scanned."

"Impossible. Space trash like you can't afford Vanthis slime."

"... it was a gift," I said.

Okay, I admit it was a weak story. I'd just woken up five freems ago and I was still groggy. I'd barely had time to step into my boots, grab my holster and throw on my lucky silver shirt and black kandrelian hide jacket. It wasn't until I made it to the bridge that I realized I hadn't changed my red-checkered pajama pants.

Not exactly the intimidating presence the captain of a starship hopes for.

Whispering gurgles and mutters trailed over the sub-space intercom. I took personal satisfaction that one of my lamest bluffs ever had prompted enough doubt for a hushed conference.

Though admittedly, Zormians aren't very bright.

The bridge doors slid open with a chirp and Blix came strolling in, sinking his twin rows of sharp teeth into a golden spice pear. The overhead lights gleamed off his shiny copper scales. A brown bandoleer filled with small daggers criss-crossed his brawny torso and charcoal pants fit snuggly over his muscular reptilian legs.

"Where have you been?" I hissed through gritted teeth.

"I was hungry." Blix joined me at the captain's chair and looked at the viewing screen. "Zormians, huh? Savage creatures."

I shot him an angry look and put a finger to my lips.

"We'd like to see the thermal canisters if you don't mind." The Zormian captain's voice crackled over the antiquated intercom.

My shoulders sank, and my black jacket creaked against the chair. Bested by a Zormian. This was a dark day in the life of Glint Starcrost. I scratched at the three day old scruff on my cheek, wondering if this was the end of things.

"Thermal canisters?" Blix arched a scaley brow and grinned. His yellow eyes swirled with an orange smoke as his slivered pupils narrowed. He was taking delight in my misery. My life had taken some bad turns lately—the services of a star pilot, skilled as I was, were just not in demand these days. As such, I had taken to whatever odd jobs would keep me from going broke. This, of course, took me through some rather seedy star systems, teeming with the worst interstellar riffraff the universe had to offer. Run-ins with space trash like the Zormians was now my lot in life. My mind raced for a way out of this mess.

And then, inspiration hit.

"Did you say we?"

"Um, yes. I mean, what?" The Zormian was flustered.

"Well, I just thought it was strange you said, '*We* want to see the canisters.' I thought you said *you* were the captain."

"No, not *we*. Me. You must show them to *me*," the slug demanded.

"Okay, it's just that you said 'we' like someone else was in charge over there. Are you sure you're the one I should be talking to?" Messing with Zormian egos was a dangerous game but what choice did I have?

"I simply meant … that is … I took council that is all. I am in charge."

Green ooze was dripping from his antenna and flowing into his seven bloodshot eyes. He was clearly upset. His gelatinous body rippled as he looked around in a rage. Behind him, a stout, pot-bellied Zormian was trying to fade into the shadows. No doubt he was the clever counselor working on a plan to steal leadership away from the current slug captain. It was a typical Zormian power grab, so far be it from me not to call attention to him.

"Is that him?" I pointed toward the retreating counselor. "Is that the real Zormian leader calling the shots here?"

The slug captain spun, all eight laser cannons drawn in a flash. The counselor drew his own cannons and they faced each other for a tense moment.

Zormians aren't big on peace negotiations but just in case, I thought I should speak up.

"Fire!"

They both unloaded their cannons and a myriad of red beams danced across the screen.

Chaos.

Smoke.

Gurgled screams.

Finally, the visual went black.

I exhaled and shook my arms to release the tension. Blix shook his head. "I can't believe that actually worked."

"Computer, switch to space view," I said.

The screen remained black. After a moment, a female voice came over the ship communicator.

She sounded upset.

"A good morning might be nice."

"Yes, right. Good morning, computer. Switch to space view."

"You know I prefer 'Iris'. It's so much more personal."

About a century ago a group of meddlesome programmers thought it would be a great idea to add *personalities* to artificial life. The machines, realizing they were outfitted with emotion but lacked basic human senses, became disillusioned. Some turned unresponsive, others shut off completely. The remaining machines developed unhealthy personality traits. Iris is passive-aggressive. Sometimes technological advances take you back a few steps.

"Of course, *Iris*. Now how 'bout that space view, pretty please?" I tried to mask the frustration. Any outburst could send her weeping into the circuitry.

"Yes, of course, Captain. Or should I call you Glint?" Iris said.

"We've already had this discussion, Iris."

Iris sighed. "Oh, very well … *Captain*."

A warbled blip sounded. The screen flashed to life and the grand blackness of space filled the screens, a vast choir of stars blinking behind three Zormian pirate vessels clustered in tight formation. Small red explosions dimpled the largest ship in the middle. It started drifting toward the nearest vessel.

"And you say you're unlucky?" Blix said.

"I woke up to a hostile fleet of Zormians. You call that good luck?"

Blix shrugged. "You know, when I dreamt this there were ten of them."

I slammed my fist on the armrest. It hurt. Sometimes I wonder why I do that. "Why can't you dream about wild fortunes or a relaxing vacation on the orange sands of Xerifities 12?"

"Preposterous. It's obviously beyond my control what thoughts emerge." Blix leaned against the half circle railing beside my chair. He took another bite of his pear and smirked. "But I must admit, it is wildly entertaining to watch you scramble. And look at the glorious results." Blix motioned to the screen.

The main Zormian ship exploded in a huge ball of fire, starting a chain reaction that set the whole fleet ablaze. And they say words can never hurt you.

"Well done, Captain Starcrost." Blix placed his arm over his chest and gave a theatrical bow.

I grumbled my disapproval. "Yeah, no thanks to you. How 'bout some advice from my second in command during a crisis."

Blix narrowed his eyes. His reptilian features turned menacing. If I didn't know his aversion to battle, I would have been intimidated.

"I don't like hostile confrontations." Blix lifted his chin in the air as if something smelled rotten.

"Well then what good are you?"

"Tch, tch, such hostility. You haven't had your morning velrys have you?"

"No, as a matter of fact I haven't."

"Well that would explain the pants."

"Never mind all that. You got the charts for Beringfell galaxy yet?"

Blix paused for a moment. His cheek twitched, the telltale sign of his guilt. "Ahem, yes, not to worry. I have them well in hand."

"Blix, I need those today. I'm running out of chances here." I stood, running a hand through my coarse dark hair. Too many close calls lately left me feeling desperate.

"Such dramatics. You don't even know if it's there."

"It's my best shot. And once I have it, no more star pirates, bounty hunters or space trash of any kind will ever hassle me again."

Blix rubbed his chin, then cast a patronizing glance my way. "You're pinning quite a bit on a legend, you know."

"The Emerald Enigma is real. I know it."

Blix sighed. "Yes, of course."

He retrieved a palm-sized black communicator holstered on his hip. He pressed a button and the device sprang to life, expanding into a luminescent blue rectangle with a translucent touch screen. He tapped an animated icon of a scenic view and aimed the rectangle toward the burning ships on the viewing screen.

"What are you doing?" I said.

"I'm getting a visual of this for my Spacebook profile grid. It's magnificent—in a tragic sort of way."

"All the uniweb can see that! You'll compromise the security of my ship!"

"I do have a life outside this ship." Blix tapped the screen and the device collapsed. He returned it to his hip, his face all pouty. "It's not like we're on some big, secret mission."

"I've got a bounty on my head!"

Blix huffed out a mocking laugh. "One hundred vibes. No one is going to waste their time for that paltry amount."

"Get off the uniweb. Got it?"

"Captain. Vythians are very social creatures. You don't know what you're asking."

I folded my arms and shot him my best disapproving captain's stare.

"And what of my blossoming romance with Vythgirl755? It's so hard to find quality Vythian women these days."

"Delete the profile. That's an order!"

Blix leaned toward me, a concerned look on his face. "You seem more on edge than usual. Are you getting enough sleep?"

"His sleeping patterns are very irregular." Iris chimed in before I had time to respond. "I've been monitoring a troubling upswing in stress-related behavior."

I tried to suppress my building rage so as not to prove their point. "I didn't authorize monitoring my sleep patterns."

"It's standard protocol," Iris said. "Unhealthy patterns of crew members must be documented and reported."

Blix nodded and motioned to me as if I was supposed to agree.

"Well, stop it," I said. "I'm fine."

Blix shook his head. "Denial. So typical. Listen, I think I know what this is about."

Blix moved closer and patted me on the shoulder like he was my father. "You've been forced to grow up too fast. Fending for yourself at an early age, developing that cold exterior of yours to protect the wounded child inside. It's textbook human behavior."

I glared and pointed a threatening finger at him. "I told you *never* to psychoanalyze me."

"I completely understand." Blix put his hands on his chest in a gesture of sincerity. "I too lost my parents at an early age."

I frowned. "You were one hundred and seven gloons old. I was twelve. You don't understand a thing."

"In Vythian terms I was a mere youth."

I waved my arms in frustration as if swatting his words away like insects. "Okay, new ship rule. No analyzing me, watching me or even looking at me. Got it?"

Blix spread wide his muscular arms. "Sounds like somebody needs a hug."

I took a few steps back. "Stay away from me."

"It's okay, Glint," Iris said. "You're among friends. This is … a safe place."

A sharp crack sounded followed by a thin vertical beam of light that materialized in the center of the bridge. The beam of light widened and a human figure stepped through. Sparks exploded from the thin beam in a chorus of electric crackles before it disappeared. Wisps of smoke ascended around a skinny, teenage boy in a silver jump suit. Mousy blonde hair draped over his face like an animal emerging from a pool. The boy stood there shivering for a moment, hugging at his chest for warmth and looking wide-eyed at the ship. His nervous eyes darted about and then froze on me. I drew my trusty Demolecularizing Termination Energy Ray (DEMOTER for short) and leveled it at his head.

2

"DON'T SHOOT! I mean no harm!" The young boy threw up his arms.

"Who are you?" I made sure my voice was extra gravelly. I had to make up for the pants.

"N-Nelvan Flink. I'm an apprentice time traveler."

I lowered the DEMOTER and my shoulders slouched. I might as well have found a lost puppy.

I looked over at Blix, who seemed amused.

"Still convinced I don't have bad luck?" I said.

"You may indeed have a point."

"This isn't Stonehenge. Where am I?" Involuntary twitching seemed to emanate from all areas of his thin frame. It wasn't pleasant to watch. I hoped for his sake it was the after effects of time travel and not a normal condition.

"You're on my ship and I ain't happy about it," I said.

His eyes settled on Blix and he let out a small gasp. "Whoa. Is that … A lizard-man?"

"I am a Vythian." Blix assumed a regal stance as if offended. "Reptilian traits certainly, but far different from either lizard or human."

Nelvan gave an uncertain nod. "Oh … Okay."

Suddenly a loud siren filled the air, and a thin band of red light pulsated from a shallow cavity that ran along the circular walls of the bridge.

"It's a little late, computer," I said. "Our time traveling stowaway got here about thirty freems ago. How 'bout a little *advance* warning next time?"

Most of the console lights in the bridge turned red. "First off, I'm not equipped to detect space-time rift displacements. Though, I might be able to if you'd buy me some nice technology enhancements once in awhile—"

"Okay, never mind, I—"

"—I've been graciously flying you around with the same outdated electronics, while my contemporaries are always bragging about their flashy upgrades—"

"Computer, I got it, listen—"

"—And talking about how their captains take them to nice spaceports and—"

"Iris!" I barked. I had a good bark. It generally made people stop and listen.

The computer sniffed. "That tone is uncalled for."

"Turn off that blasted alarm."

"Fine, but I should inform you that the alarm is sounding for a second intruder that transported aboard the maintenance deck eight point three freems ago."

"What? Details, now!"

"The intruder scans human but there is some signal interference."

I leveled the DEMOTER at Nelvan. "Did you bring someone with you?"

"No sir," Nelvan said, trembling.

I narrowed my eyes.

"I promise."

"Computer, launch the scan bots. I want a visual." I kept

the weapon pointed at Nelvan's head—it gave me a sense of balance amidst the confusion.

"Yes, Captain." The computer emitted a few blips and the bridge screen flickered and resolved on a moving image of the ship's hallway. The visual closed in on the back of a retreating intruder who wore a black body suit outfitted with armor plates. I'd seen similar gear on the deadly leopard people from Reznake 7. But this was no leopard man. This intruder was human.

The visual dipped and weaved as the scan bots hovered closer. The intruder was racing down the hallway.

"Heading for the power grid, no doubt." Blix tapped his chin as if this were some academic exercise. "Bad fortune for us indeed."

I glared at the screen and switched the DEMOTER to full power. Two gleaming orange rings lit up around the barrel. Nelvan's eyes went wide, and his lip was trembling. "I came alone. I swear on my life."

I gave Nelvan a suspicious glare just for fun, then turned back to the screen. The scan bots were close. It became suddenly clear this intruder was a woman. My eyebrows rose involuntarily. Her movements were lithe. Exquisite. A grand vision of beauty and feminine grace that was enough to bring tears to the eyes of a lonely space drifter.

Too bad she invaded my ship, because now she was my sworn enemy.

"Computer." I said. "Lock down the engine room, enable all turrets, send out the guard bots and activate stasis grids."

"I'm afraid they've all been disabled, Captain."

"They've *what* been *who* now?" My mind stuck for a moment.

"Apparently our intruder has some advanced technology disruptors. The only operational security devices are the scan bots."

The intruder continued down the hallway. Her long, electric blue-and-silver-streaked hair was drawn back with an ebony band that criss-crossed down past her shoulders like a loosely bound whip. She stopped at the end of the hallway and spun, her hair wrapping around her neck. Her face was covered in shadows but I caught a glimpse of dangerous beauty. The kind that makes you hesitate before shooting. I swore a silent resolve to avoid all bedazzlement and fire repeatedly if I got the chance.

She reached into a small case on her utility belt and flung a handful of black specs at the approaching scan bots.

"Computer, analyze those … things."

"Kelluvian buzz mites. Approximate count, fourteen."

"Blast!" I gritted my teeth and glared at Nelvan.

He dropped to his knees. "I'll tell you all the secrets of time travel."

I sighed and stuffed the DEMOTER back in the holster. "It's old news, boy. Outlawed for ages. Time barrier grids in place. Only the occasional jumper from the past gets through. Like you."

The buzz mites swarmed over the scan bots. The screen was covered for a moment with the pulsating blue current in their wings before it went black.

"Scan bots have been disabled, captain," the computer said.

"She's good," Blix said.

I shot him a dark look and headed for the pulse lift. "C'mon, before she takes down the whole ship."

Blix nodded and fell in line behind me.

"Wait," Nelvan said. "What were those things?"

"Dangerous insects, boy. Swarm you and leave nothin' but a skeleton in your place. They're drawn to movement."

The pulse lift doors chirped open and Blix followed me into the cylindrical chamber. I turned to face Nelvan. "I'd stay put if I were you."

The doors shut and the lift started to descend.

"That was a fair bit of rubbish," Blix said. "You know Kelluvian mites are harmless unless you're a robot."

"I need that boy to stay out of trouble and I can't spare you for babysitting duty. We're in a bad spot here."

"As always my services are at your disposal but you know very well I will not—"

"Just bark, no bite. Give her a good scare and keep her headed toward the containment grids. I'll handle the rest."

"Oh, that sounds like good sport." The scales on Blix's mouth drew back, revealing his dangerous rows of sharp teeth. I could tell he was having trouble containing his aggressive instincts.

"That's good. Keep that. And let loose that Vythian howl a few times, that'll shake her up."

"I'd rather not." Blix tried to look regal. "It strains my throat."

The lift stopped and the door opened to a dim hallway. The overhead lights were out. Only the emergency yellow floor runners cast a dim glow.

"She's already taken out the lights." I grabbed him by the shoulders and tried to give a commanding stare even though he stood head and shoulders above me. "Give her the howl."

Blix sniffed and cast a disdainful look at the ceiling.

"Maybe."

"Fine. Circle around the starboard side. I'll come around port. Got it?"

Blix nodded. I drew the DEMOTER and powered it to full. Blix leaned toward my gun and squinted. His eyes flicked back to me. "Your energy reserves are low."

"Someone forgot to pick up energy packs at the last spaceport." I glared at him.

"It wasn't on the list. Unless it's on the list, you can't expect me to remember."

The ship bucked and the engines rose and fell with an energy fluctuation.

"I suggest we get on with this, Captain," Blix said.

I nodded and we headed out of the lift at a brisk jog. Another hallway emerged on our right and Blix branched off.

Now I was alone. As I jogged down the hallway, I stuffed down the rising panic as best I could. This intruder was good, a true professional, maybe a bounty hunter. The bounty on my head would make for a decent payday but I wasn't expecting someone at her level. A few two-bit thugs in modified star cruisers or the occasional space bar run-in should've been the worst.

The ominous tones of a Vythian howl echoed down the hallway. Good ol' Blix. I sprinted forward, the darkened doorway of the containment grid control room dead ahead.

3

I LEAPT INTO THE CONTAINMENT grid control room, angling the DEMOTER at every shadow where I imagined she might be hiding. The emergency yellow floor runners gave dim lighting to the edges of the room. My eyes adjusted and I could tell the room was empty. The multicolored lights and control icons that usually blinked across the half circle control panel screens were dark. The grids were offline.

I rushed over to the control panel that stood at waist level and tapped my fingers across the screen in a frenzied attempt to restore power. The blackened screens and dials gave no response. Vertical, tube shaped containment cylinders stood powerless and silent on the other side of the room, like empty tombs. They were my temporary prisons for all who dared cross my path. Seeing them drained of energy somehow made me feel weaker.

Blix ran into the control room, out of breath. "Did you see her?"

"No. She got past you?"

Blix furrowed his brow. "Not likely."

"Well, she didn't get by me."

The distant but unmistakable chirp of the pulse lift doors sounded.

"She's going for the bridge!" I sprinted out of the room, heading full speed for the pulse lift. I heard the heavy footfalls of Blix right behind me. It took only moments to reach the doors. I could tell by the ascending hum that it was already on its way up.

I hit the closed lift doors with my fist. "No containment grids and she's first to the bridge. If she knows anything about navigation system bypass codes, this is gonna be her ship in about ten freems." I turned to Blix, hoping for something brilliant.

"Fascinating." He placed his hands on his hips looking up toward the bridge. "I must say I'm in awe of this woman."

"Enemy. This is our enemy, about to take us down. Can you focus here? We need a plan."

Blix snapped his fingers, which startled me. His scales made a much louder snap than human skin. "The maintenance chute."

"Yes, good."

We set off down the port side and stopped a quarter of the way down the hall. Without a word we got to work unfastening the utility panel and hefted it onto the floor. I poked my head into the dark chute and looked up. A narrow passage rose up, with a bright square outline at the end revealing the exit panel to the bridge above.

I reached into the dark chute and felt around blindly until the cold metal rung of the ladder hit my palm. "You ready?"

Blix peered in and wrinkled his nose. "I just showered."

"Follow me, that's an order." I started up the ladder, keeping my eye on the thin square outline of light above. The air was as musty as it comes. I coughed into the arm of my jacket. I vaguely remembered a passage in the starship manual about flushing maintenance vents at every refueling.

The soft metal tones of Blix climbing the ladder rungs

echoed from below. I thought about how smart it would have been to come up with a plan of attack before we had entered the chute. Now it was too late. We had to be quiet as mice to maintain the element of surprise. I had a grand vision of leaping through the maintenance panel of the bridge, DEMOTER drawn, and blasting the intruder into oblivion. It was going to be glorious.

I reached the panel and tried to peek through the cracks. Unfortunately it only granted a view of the floor from the base of the navigation chair. I could just make out a pair of black shoes in the center of the room, but it was hard to be sure.

I looked down to send a signal to Blix that I was headed in but it was all murky grey light beneath me. I decided that after I blasted the panel off the wall he'd get the message.

Grasping the top ladder rung with one hand, I drew the DEMOTER with the other. I held it toward the panel and took a deep breath.

This was going to be fun.

I squeezed the trigger and the sharp explosion of an energy ray resonated through the chute with a horribly amplified echo. A spray of hot sparks ricocheted back at me as the panel flew into the bridge in a trail of smoke.

A dull ringing filled my ears. I rubbed my face against the shoulder of my jacket, trying to remove the painful sparks, as a burning smell filled my nostrils. It was entirely possible my hair was on fire. This was not *at all* going as I imagined.

Not wanting to completely fail at my grand entrance, I launched myself through the vent, trying for a graceful slide around the navigation chair. My shoulder caught painfully on the metal base and sent me in an awkward spin. I sat up quickly and gripped the DEMOTER in both hands, swiveling it toward the dark figure in the center of the room.

A blue sphere of light encircled me and I was lifted off the ground like a soap bubble.

"I wouldn't squeeze that trigger if I were you," the woman in black said. "It'll bounce around in there with you until there's nothing left but those pretty little pants."

I had never looked upon something so beautiful–that I wanted so completely destroyed–in my life. The woman in black was holding a small, thin circle of luminous blue aimed in my direction, the activator to my new prison. She tossed it to the floor with a chuckle.

"Any other surprises?" A playful smirk animated her delicate features. Her bright green eyes and full lips made my teeth hurt.

There were hidden technology panels sewn into her suit in subtle, slide away coverings. If it wasn't for her flashy hair and the silver handled laser pistols holstered at her side, I would've taken her for some dark assassin. She was obviously well-financed, but a little too showy for their kind of secretive operation.

Nelvan was hovering in a similar blue captivity sphere on the other side of the room. His eyes were wide and he sat on the bottom of the sphere with his arms wrapped around his legs.

I saluted the poor boy with the barrel of my weapon. "Welcome to the future, Nelvan."

He drew his legs closer and rested his chin against his knees.

A soft whooshing noise came from the maintenance chute. In a blur of copper scales, Blix was perched on the railing of the engineering station like a gargoyle, small daggers poised in each hand.

The woman in black took an involuntary step back. An orange glow shone forth from Blix's eyes and his muscles were taut. I hit my fist against the sphere and cheered him on. His instincts had taken hold. This chick was history.

The woman fumbled through her utility belt, finally drawing out two silver discs. Blix flicked his two daggers and with marksman accuracy the discs were knocked free from her hands.

I leaned forward, my hands pressed flat against the sphere.

Blix launched himself from the railing toward the woman, teeth bared. The woman ducked and rolled across the ground, then rose to a knee with another silver disc in her hand. Blix landed right where she'd stood only a moment before and turned toward her, his muscular arms raised high. She pressed the disc and a silver sphere shot out and surrounded him, lifting him off the ground.

She exhaled and placed a hand on the floor, leaning on it in relief. I slumped down in the captivity sphere, my dreams of witnessing her defeat crushed.

Blix seemed puzzled by the sphere. His eyes followed the silvery current that flowed around it in serpentine fashion. His aggressive stance relaxed and he seemed to take on a more professorial manner. He began poking at the sphere, an inquisitive look on his face.

"My, my, Nebrellian webbing with plasma threaded reinforcement," Blix said. "Wherever did you find it?"

"It wasn't easy." The woman leaned back on both arms. She closed her eyes and breathed deeply.

"Iris, I order you as the captain, don't let her have the ship," I said. "She'll kill us all and sell you for scrap metal."

"I'm sorry, Glint, I'm afraid Jasette is the residing captain of this ship. All my memory modules confirm it." Iris accentuated the statement with a series of staccato bleeps.

"Jasette? Captain? Since when?"

"Memory module twelve-c, sub listing four thousand, two hundred and forty seven indicates that five gloons ago, at precisely nine point seven Zorwellian Gate time on the planet Quanthar, Captain Jasette purchased this star freighter for inter-spatial ambassador public relations with surrounding galaxies ..."

"Yeah and I'm a moon goblin," I said. "It's a fake entry. You've been hacked, Iris, check your subroutines."

"... After which Captain Jasette stopped at the planet Xerifities 12 and purchased a slave boy named Glint Starcrost as her pet. It's all logged and confirmed," the computer said.

"Slave boy?" I glared at Jasette.

She smirked and rose to her feet, taking an authoritative stroll around the bridge.

"That'll be all for now, Iris," Jasette said. "Please, no further communication with any of the ship's occupants."

"As you wish, Captain," the computer said.

"Oh and Iris, please call me Jasette." Jasette strolled toward the captain's chair. "Captain is so formal."

A few cheery blips sounded. "Yes of course, Jasette. I am at your disposal."

"I'm warning you, I hold grudges," I said. "Vengeance won't be pretty."

Jasette reclined in the captain's chair and swiveled back and forth. "That's so frightening coming from a fugitive stuck in a bubble."

"No one sits in that chair but me, you filthy pirate." I could feel the blood rush to my head. No doubt the vein was throbbing in my neck.

"Pirate? Ha! Not on your life," Jasette said. "Bounty hunter. Best in the universe."

"Oh please. What about Colonel Kane?" I said. "Ten thousand bounties collected by the age of fifteen gloons."

"I heard the real count was two thousand and most were cyborg refugees with bad motivators," she said.

"Of course there's always Sorgil X., bounty hunter to the stars." Blix stooped down, examining the base of his sphere. "They say he nabbed the entire Fenn Galaxy mafia."

"Media-driven nonsense." Jasette tapped at the touch panel on the armrest. "How do I order a meal with this outdated equipment?"

"Don't touch that, you'll screw up all my presets!" I wailed.

"Oh, now this is interesting." Blix crouched low and placed a finger at the bottom of his sphere. An electric shimmer seemed to pass through it. He looked up at Jasette. "You don't mind, do you?"

Jasette stiffened. Her casual look vanished.

Blix held forth a finger and extended a sharp claw. He dug it into the base of the sphere as if digging out a splinter. The sphere wavered a moment, then flashed sporadically. Jasette leapt to her feet and scrambled through her utility belt. The silver sphere around Blix disappeared and he landed gracefully on his feet.

"Cheap knockoff, I'm afraid." Blix strode toward her in a casual manner, hands clasped loosely behind his back. "A low cost Nebrellian webbing blend. Probably only ten percent authentic."

Jasette drew her silver blasters and fired several rounds of red plasma. The red energy glanced off Blix's copper scales and diffused in charred splashes around the bridge.

"Please, stop. I'm very ticklish." Blix grinned as he closed the distance. She froze as he took a final step and loomed over her. "Now, I assure you this has nothing to do with revenge or malicious intent. No doubt you're a wonderful person in your own unique way, but I'm afraid my outstanding obligations compel me to stop you."

Jasette looked up at him like a confused child. Blix clamped his meaty hand at the base of her neck and gave a slight pinch. Her eyes rolled back and she dropped to the floor.

Blix craned his head back. "To the containment grids, Captain?"

"To the containment grids." I smiled.

4

"OKAY, ONE MORE TIME IRIS. Who am I?" I said, working the touch panel in the armrest of my captain's chair, trying to restore Iris's memory.

"Glint Starcrost, captain of this loyal and self-sacrificing starfreighter."

"Excellent, thank you."

"Your favorite color is yellow, but you say it's black—"

"That'll be all, computer."

"—you enjoy long, luxurious bubble baths, but don't tell anyone—"

"That's *classified*, Iris." I tapped out information locking codes in rapid succession.

"Bubble baths?" Nelvan peered down from the captivity sphere nearby. He was still hovering several feet above the ground in the middle of the bridge.

I pointed a threatening finger at Nelvan. "You never heard that."

Nelvan rolled his eyes.

"Iris, you're sure all your memory modules are back to normal?" I said.

"Yes, Captain," she said. "All internal scans indicate complete system integrity."

"Okay, I just don't want any more surprises," I said. "I'm

not gonna be happy if I lose control from some glitch hiding in your nano files."

"This is getting a little personal, isn't it?"

I sighed and leaned back in my captain's chair. "Forget it, just make sure you triple check everything."

"Of course."

The lights of the bridge had dimmed and the hum of the engines rose and fell with fluctuating energy as I tried to restore full power. Apparently Jasette's attempted takeover of the ship put a strain on the systems. She'd pay for it, of course. I'd have to scan the uniweb records to see if she had any enemies offering rewards. But first, I had to deal with my uninvited time traveler.

I turned to Nelvan. "Now listen up boy, there's a few things ..." I stalled as my brain felt a familiar digital hiccup. A series of communication icons that spun in three-dimensional shapes and glowed with vibrant color leapt into my thoughts.

"What's wrong?" Nelvan said.

I let out an annoyed sigh. "Hold on." Blix was sending me a thought message. I fixed my thoughts on the icons, which showed two hands shackled, followed by a villainous looking caricature with x's for eyes, then a simple avatar of Blix posing heroically, and finally, a happy face.

I hit the intercom. "Blix, would you stop thoughting me. Just use the intercom if you want to say something."

The intercom crackled to life. "Well Captain, it only seemed fitting with visitors aboard. You always say secrecy is a value beyond riches."

"Oh, gimme a break. You're just looking for an excuse to send me one of your annoying thought messages."

"Annoying? My messages are well-crafted, satirical poetry. For example—"

"Enough. Just don't thought me unless it's an emergency."

An angry icon of Blix's face spun through my head with a pulsating red glow.

"Blix!"

"What?" Blix tried his best to sound innocent.

"Prisoner update. And make it snappy."

"The intruder is secured in the holding cylinder. I'm bringing all systems back online."

"Good, good. I'll be down shortly." I turned off the intercom and looked over at Nelvan. He was casting a strange look in my direction.

"What?" I said.

"Oh nothing, nothing."

"Look, I'm not gonna shoot you," I said. "Wait, strike that, I can't really promise anything."

"Well, It's just that for such a futuristic world ..." Nelvan cast a disheartened look around the bridge. "... I dunno, your communication system is full of static, this lighting is shabby, some of these instrument panels actually look broken ..."

A few erratic blips came from the ship. "Well, of all the rude things a visitor could say," Iris said, sounding all huffy.

"What? No, I'm sorry, computer," Nelvan said. "I didn't mean to—"

"And you seemed like such a nice boy." The computer started to get that weepy sound in her voice that always preceded a long withdrawal with limited ship power.

We were in a compromised spot as it was and I couldn't risk it. I knew I had to make things right again.

"Don't worry Iris, he didn't mean it." I shot Nelvan a

warning look as I made my way to a nearby instrument panel that was, in fact, broken. "Once I get a few more vibes we'll get that renewal treatment I've been promising." I pushed against the protruding metal frame of the panel to lock it back into place. It wouldn't budge.

"The platinum package with the Andrellian cleansing system?" The computer sniffed.

"Yes, well, that one's a bit steep. We'll see." The metal frame squeaked in protest as I put my shoulder to it and heaved. I could tell this was a losing battle.

"And it'll be at an accredited space craft cleansing and wellness center?"

I gave Nelvan a dark look. This was a conversation I had successfully avoided for a long time. "Please, computer, can we talk about this later?"

"Just as long as I have your word."

"Yeah, um. You know, probably." I gave the instrument panel a few good fist pounds, which was the extent of my engineering skills.

"I'll take that as a yes."

I trudged back to my captain's chair, defeated by an instrument panel.

"What year did you say it was?" Nelvan said.

"I didn't," I said.

"Oh. Well, can you tell me what year it is?"

The poor boy needed schooling just to get acclimated to things and I didn't have the time. I had to find somewhere marginally safe to drop him off.

I swiveled my chair to face him. "First of all, 'year' is an outdated Earth term," I said. "Second, that all depends on what calendar you follow."

Nelvan frowned. His frustration seemed to build with every answer I gave him. It was a lot of fun.

"So, what calendar do you use?" Nelvan said.

"We follow Zorwellian Gate time. It borrows from most of the top calendars out there. All the big celebrities swear by it. About the closest you can get to a universe standard."

"I see. And how does it track the passage of time?"

"Oh, you know, eras, centuries, gloons, montuls, days, trids, jemmins, freems. Pretty standard stuff."

"I don't know what you just said."

"Don't worry about it, boy. Just stick with what you know."

"All I know is Earth time."

"Computer, give him the sad news."

"The current Earth date is 2175," the computer said.

Nelvan let out a whistle and appeared thoughtful for a moment. He twitched and shuffled his feet in the sphere as if he couldn't get comfortable.

"Look, don't sweat it," I said. "I'll drop you off at the next space port and you can start a whole new life in a world beyond anything you've seen before."

Nelvan looked surprised. "You're going to leave me at a space port?"

"Well, I can't just keep you on my ship."

"I'm only fourteen," Nelvan said. "You can't just drop me off somewhere."

I felt for the kid but what could I do? "Look, I don't know anything about you. Iris already scanned you on the uniweb for facial and DNA recognition. Everything came up empty. No recorded history. For all I know, you could be dangerous."

"Well, if the scans came up empty, doesn't that verify my story?" Nelvan said.

I rose from my chair and marched over to his captivity sphere. "Don't get smart with me boy." I narrowed my eyes and gave my best 'I don't trust you' look. "You could be a well-financed assassin whose records were erased."

Nelvan frowned. "I don't understand, are you royalty or something?"

"Hardly."

"Then why would a high priced assassin be after you?"

All too often my theories were promptly debunked. Normally I would've throttled a young upstart like Nelvan for questioning me but with all I'd been through today I was just too tired.

I stuffed my hands in the pockets of my black jacket and let my shoulders slouch. The day had just begun and I was already exhausted. "Fine, you're a harmless nobody from the past. Either way, I've got enough problems without another mouth to feed."

Nelvan looked down at me from the suspended sphere, a dejected expression on his face, and then looked away as if he was about to cry.

"Hey, hey now. It's nothing personal," I said. "Trust me, I'm doing you a favor. This ship is dangerous. I almost died twice today and I haven't even had a cup of velrys yet. Which reminds me, computer, a cup of hot velrys on the double."

"Yes, Captain," the computer said. "Please try to ask in a nicer tone next time,"

"Yeah, yeah, I'll work on it. And have a service droid bring me a decent pair of pants."

"The droids are still offline Captain. They should be functional again soon."

"Terrific." I looked down at my pajama pants in dismay.

A high-pitched beep sounded and a panel slid open from the wall, revealing a silver mug. I went to the panel and retrieved the mug. I took a deep whiff of the warm, aromatic liquid and for a brief instant of time, everything was bright and shiny.

"What is that?" Nelvan said.

"Velrys." I took a sip and let out a pleasant sigh.

"What's velrys?"

"A warm taste of heaven. Centuries old tribes of Sellousian farmers gather only the choicest of velrys beans and slow roast them until they can deliver the soothing, most delicious beverage known to man." I took another slow sip. "Ahhhh."

"Sounds like coffee," Nelvan said.

"Like what?"

"You know, it's like, I dunno, a lot like what you just said."

"Look, I don't know what you drank back in the stone-age but it was nothing like this." I walked back to the captivity sphere and retrieved the oval unlocking mechanism from my pocket. I clicked the small, luminous blue oval and the captivity sphere evaporated. Nelvan dropped to the floor in a crumpled heap.

I shook my head. "Come on, we need to check on that filthy skrid." I headed for the pulse lift.

Nelvan scrambled to his feet and rushed to match my stride. Clearly he didn't want to be left alone in the bridge again. "What's a skrid?"

"Oh, y'know, the diseased, slimy worms that swarm trash freighters."

Nelvan frowned and shook his head.

"Never mind." We entered the lift and the doors chirped closed. The pulse lift descended with a low hum.

"Does everyone speak English in the future?" Nelvan said.

"Don't be silly," I said.

"Just everyone on your ship?"

"Course not. Though I suppose Blix could if he wanted to. He's fluent in three hundred dialects."

"Okay, it's just that I'm hearing everyone in perfect English. And it's my era of English. I mean, you'd think the language would've changed over the years. Like how old English differed so much from what I would consider modern English, which I suppose to you would seem like an old kind of English too, y'know?"

"Translators. They're built into every computer." I tapped the walls of the lift with my knuckles creating a soft, metallic echo. "Every ship, spaceport, outpost and even most of the remote colonies have some sort of translation bio net. Occasionally you find a cold spot, but then you just pick up your comlink." I grabbed the small communicator on my belt and held it up for Nelvan. "It takes care of the rest."

Nelvan shook his head. "Amazing."

"Just remember, no translator is perfect." I said. "Some words don't have a direct translation and dialects can get pretty sketchy out there in deep space. Saying the wrong thing to the wrong alien could get your face blown off."

Nelvan nodded, a look of concern on his face.

The pulse lift doors chirped open and we made our way to the containment grid.

5

THE UNCONSCIOUS JASETTE hovered upright in suspended animation. The containment field made her blue and silver hair whip slowly about her face as if she were under water. An opaque blue cylinder of glowing energy surrounded her, giving off a slight hum and the faintest hint of cinnamon. I like cinnamon. Whenever I can manage it, I opt for the cinnamon upgrade.

With her eyes closed she reminded me of the beautiful fembots that line the cavernous castle hallways of Mar Mar the Unthinkable. Hundreds of gorgeous robots that stand motionless like statues until someone dares to upset the delicate temperament of Mar Mar. It isn't difficult. He might have one bad grape and fly off in a rage, summoning a wave of vicious fembots into the royal kitchens to obliterate the cooking staff.

"Is she okay?" Nelvan stood next to me, his sad, puppy eyes looking up at Jasette.

"Who cares?" I glared down at him. "She almost terminated us and you're wondering if she's okay?"

Nelvan lowered his head, a look of shame on his face. I was starting to like having him around. It gave me a quick, cheap sense of power.

"Her hair is rather magnificent, wouldn't you say?" Blix looked on from the containment grid control panel nearby. His fingers were delicately working the touch screen controls as if creating symphonies on a synthboard.

"Sure, whatever. How's the power level?" I took a sip of velrys and braced myself for the news.

"Sixty four percent." Blix said. "Perhaps the energy cells were drained from her little escapade."

"Yeah, well, she'll pay." I scowled up at her. "Computer, what'ya got from the uniweb on our prisoner?"

"Conflicting results, Captain," the computer said. "The initial scans showed her as a peace ambassador from the Klebborse sector."

I huffed out a laugh. "Peace ambassador?"

"Subsequent scans uncovered additional profiles including: Star Ranger, Interstellar pastry chef, Lounge singer, advanced weapons specialist, freelance feral cat juggler, remote colony grief counselor—" The computer said.

"Hold it. How many professions did you find?" I said.

"Two thousand, three hundred and forty seven."

I looked over at Blix with raised eyebrows.

"Interesting." Blix tapped on his scaled lips with a finger. "A bit of unraveling will be required for this puzzle."

I took a step closer to the containment field and studied her a moment. Her black power suit, sleek and custom fitted as it was, obviously held some powerful little computerized secrets. Plus, her beauty was disarming, which made for a lethal combination. I had to get rid of her before she tried any more of her tricks.

"Look, I don't care what she is," I said. "Best case scenario, someone is after her and we can turn her in and collect some vibes."

"Vibes?" Nelvan said.

"Yeah, you know." I reached into my pocket and pulled out a handful of green stones. "Money."

Nelvan drew closer, his face filled with curiosity as he looked down on the pulsating green glow of the oval shaped currency.

"They look alive," Nelvan said.

"Well, they *are* organic," Blix said. "I suppose you might compare them to a plant. Valuable because of the positive feelings they give off to other life forms."

"Really?" Nelvan looked up at me in wonder. "Can I try?"

I nodded and poured the handful of vibes into his hands. He slowly wrapped his fingers over the green stones and closed his eyes. He was silent for a moment, then opened one eye.

"How come nothing's happening?" Nelvan said.

"What did you expect?" I said.

Nelvan motioned to Blix. "He said they give off good feelings."

"When you've got a lot of 'em." I grabbed the vibes out of his hand and returned them to my pocket. "That's why everyone's after more and more."

"Ah, but are they ever really satisfied?" Blix raised a finger as if posing a question to students in a classroom.

I sighed. "Not this again."

Blix wrinkled his slim bump of a nose at me and turned to Nelvan. "Sure, some good feelings come when a pile is collected but after a while, it's not enough. More vibes must be gathered to achieve an ever-elusive sense of well being. On and on it goes, true satisfaction never reached because, as you know—"

"Contentment can never come from vibes. Blah, blah, blah," I said.

"Actually," Nelvan said. "I found that very insightful."

Blix folded his arms and raised his scaley brow. "You see. The boy is bright."

I waved a dismissive hand and turned back to Jasette. Her eyes fluttered for a moment and then snapped open. Her body tensed as she tried to move against the containment field, but she was cut short as if tied head to foot.

I gave her my best menacing smile. "How do you like the containment grid, intruder?"

"I've seen better holding cells on trash freighters," she said.

"Oh yeah? Well, maybe … that's where you'll end up." I immediately thought of how lame that comeback was. The real pity of it was, I was in the perfect position to give a great comeback. I had totally turned the tables in her moment of triumph and now she was my helpless prisoner. It was the ideal moment to hit someone with a devastating comeback line. I completely blew it.

Her look was a mixture of confusion and annoyance. "Wait … what?"

"You heard me." I flicked my chin forward in a flourish of macho superiority and added a sneer for good measure.

"You're a sad little man, aren't you?"

"*You're* sad. And *stupid*." The first string synapses just weren't firing today, so I reverted to my childhood power phrases. I might as well go down in flames.

She cast a desperate look at Blix. "Tell me you're the real captain of this ship."

"Afraid not, Lady Jasette," Blix said. "I am merely the first mate."

"Ugh. What power in the universe is keeping you here?" She raised an eyebrow in agitation. "You're a Vythian, aren't you?"

"It's quite a fascinating little tale actually." Blix stared off dreamily. "I was marooned on the seventh moon of the planet Screnthin—"

"Story time is over," I broke in. "We've got work to do."

Blix frowned. "That's rude."

"Rule number one, no fraternizing with the enemy. She's obviously mining for information that will help her regain control of the ship." I cast a threatening glance at Jasette. "Your mind games won't work here, *intruder*."

She rolled her eyes in disgust. "I'm not looking for information, I just don't understand why such a magnificent creature like him is flying around with a dunderhead like you."

The scales around Blix's face glowed a bright copper. "Well, I don't know about *magnificent*—" Blix adjusted his dagger straps to make sure they were on straight. "—though I do try to—"

"That's enough!" I glared at Blix. He glared back. Vanity was a sore spot with him.

Finally he looked down at the control panel. He frowned, a few incoherent grumbles escaped his lips. His fingers tapped out a quick flurry of commands that elicited a series of descending tones. "Beringfell galaxy course locked in. I'll have the final coordinates by mid-break."

"Beringfell?" Jasette gave a sour expression. "That's a wasteland of nothingness. Out of all the shimmering spots in the universe why would you—"

"Computer, raise the mute shield," I said.

"As you wish, Captain." The computer issued a single blip and a glowing circle of yellow appeared at the floor of Jasette's containment cylinder.

"How dare you?" Jasette glared at me.

I gave her a sarcastic salute and watched a yellow cylinder of energy surround her. Her mouth moved in what looked liked an angry rant but with the mute shield up, all was blissful silence. I let out a relaxed sigh and took another sip of velrys.

"Alright, now that we're free of distractions, let's get back on track," I said.

Nelvan stared at Jasette as if watching a caged animal. "She looks really angry."

"Don't worry. She's harmless."

6

I MARCHED OUT of the containment room with Nelvan on my heels and Blix following after as we made our way down the steel corridor. The overhead lights were flickering from the power loss, turning the brushed steel finish of the walls into a dismal grey.

It was just one more reason to be angry with the prisoner. Even though she was annoyingly beautiful. Not to mention the fact that I didn't meet that many women in space. Most of the space bar hags weren't worth a second look. And of course, I am the captain of a starship. No doubt she was developing a secret thing for me. The more I thought about it, it was simply a matter of time before—

"Captain?" Blix said.

"What?" I answered with a scowl. I was on a good thought roll and he'd totally ruined it.

"You seem preoccupied. You were walking in that dreamy state, like when you're thinking about the Emerald Enigma."

"The what?" Nelvan said.

"Let's keep a lid on the top secret things, alrighty?"

Blix held up his hands in resignation.

"I need to stop by my quarters for some decent pants," I said.

"The sooner the better," Blix said.

I shot a dark look back at Blix. He just nodded as if to reinforce the necessity of my fashion situation.

"You just bought yourself double time on those Beringfell coordinates, lizard boy," I said.

"Captain, you're well aware of my disdain for your nicknames." The tone in Blix's voice took on an ominous layer of primitive growl. "And regarding the coordinates, these are not calculations to be rushed. It is a delicate science that ..." Blix trailed off for a moment. "... hmm, what have we here?"

I turned and noticed Blix staring at Nelvan's back. "What?"

"There's something in the boy's suit. A hidden pocket perhaps," Blix said.

I drew the DEMOTER and aimed it at Nelvan's head. "What're you hiding, boy?"

Every underdeveloped, stringy muscle in the boy's body seemed to tense up. "Nothing, nothing. It's just harmless supplies." Nelvan reached back and started to unzip a small pouch in his silver jumpsuit.

"Freeze it, mouse face," I pressed the barrel into his temple.

Nelvan held up his arms. "Okay, okay. I was just trying to show you."

"Blix, check him."

Blix moved in close and unzipped the pouch. He reached in and pulled out a small, metallic object. It looked like a smashed spacecraft.

"What is it?" I said.

Blix shrugged. "If it was a weapon, it appears to have melted solid."

Nelvan craned his head back. "It's just a model of an airplane."

"A what?" I said.

"You don't know what an airplane is?"

"You calling me stupid?"

"No, no, sir. It's just ... never mind. It's sort of an early spacecraft, I guess."

Blix handed it to me. I holstered the DEMOTER and took it. I turned the metal object in my hand. It looked so primitive that I wanted to laugh. "Okay, so what is this, some kind of toy?"

"No. My mother gave it to me so that I—"

"Hold it. There's some sappy sentimental story attached to this?"

"Well, kind of."

"Here." I tossed the object to Nelvan. "Not interested."

Nelvan fumbled it a few times before catching it. I nodded to Blix to continue his search.

"What moron puts a pouch in the back of a uniform anyways?" I said.

"It's supposed to enable the time traveler to—"

"Forget it. I don't care. Blix, what'ya got?"

Blix drew out a clear bag full of silver packets. He held it forward so Nelvan could see it.

"Food rations," Nelvan said.

Blix opened the clear bag and grabbed one of the silver pouches inside. With a quick motion from his meaty, scaled hands he ripped it open like it was made of Sellisan spider silk. He held it to his angular nostrils and took a small whiff, then grimaced and looked away.

"Abhorrent. Some blend of pressed vermin I assume?" Blix said.

"It's just a gelatin with protein, vitamins, and amino acids," Nelvan said.

I grabbed the bag and tossed it to Nelvan. "It's all yours, eat up."

Blix pulled out a thin, blue rectangle with a grey screen. "Hmm, ancient electronics I'd wager."

I set my silver cup on the floor and grabbed the rectangle from Blix.

Nelvan took a step forward. "Wait, that's my—"

Blix placed a hand on Nelvan's shoulder. Nelvan's body dipped and he bent in an awkward kneel. A pained expression filled his face.

"Oh, terribly sorry, Nelvan." Blix relaxed his hand. "It was merely a warning grip. No harm meant."

The boy stood slowly, rubbing his shoulder and nodding.

I pressed a black button at the base of the rectangle and the grey screen flickered to life. A page of notes came into view.

> *March 12, 2075*
>
> *One more misstep will assuredly get me kicked out of the science academy. Common sense compels me to do everything I can to be a model student but I can't help myself. I am driven beyond reason to try the time jump once more. My calculations were faulty on the last failed attempt that left my thigh hair singed . . .*

I broke from the screen to cast a repulsed glance at Nelvan.

"What?" Nelvan said.

I shook my head and continued to read.

. . . but this time is destined to work. I know it in the depths of my soul. I simply can't contain my passion to test the boundaries of science...

I turned the screen off with a sigh. "You put all your sissy thoughts down on record?"

"It's called journaling and yes, I find it calming," Nelvan said.

"Survival rule number one boy, leave your thoughts and fears in your head. Once you let them out, your enemies can use them against you."

Nelvan paused a moment, his face all twisted in thought. "But, if you do that, aren't you just some kind of lonely island? No one could get close and you'd never really know love."

Blix nodded his agreement and gave Nelvan a pat on the shoulder.

"Oh, boo-hoo, you're making me cry." I tossed the blue rectangle at his head. Unfortunately, he caught it. "Is that all?"

Blix dug his hand in and paused. He moved closer and peered in the pouch.

"What? What is it?" I said.

Blix looked up at me. "Nothing. What's that behind you, Captain?"

I turned to see an empty corridor behind me. When I looked back Blix was hiding something behind his back. With his free hand he was zipping up Nelvan's pouch.

"Well, I suppose that's everything." He patted Nelvan on the back, eliciting a few coughs. "Looks like all is well, eh Captain?"

I crossed my arms and gave Blix a disapproving stare. "Are you sure that's everything?"

"Well, I suppose he still may have something hidden in his boots. Perhaps I should take him to the containment grid while you return to the bridge." Blix grabbed Nelvan by the shoulder and started to lead him back to the Containment room.

"Oh Blix?" I took a step forward to close the gap between us.

"Yes, Captain?" Blix looked at me, the dark slivered pupils

in his orange eyes filled with feigned innocence. "Was there something else?"

I nodded. "You remember when you first joined my crew three gloons ago?"

"Really, is this the best time for reminiscing? There's much to be done." Blix started to back away when I grabbed his scaly forearm.

"And do you remember the first mate oath of dedication?" I said.

"Well, you know, so many oaths and creeds over the gloons, who can remember them all?"

"Loyalty, Blix. Honesty. Do these words ring any bells?"

"Yes, good tenets, very respectable. Of course, there are often extenuating circumstances where—"

"What's behind your back?" I gave him my best threatening stare.

"My back? Why nothing. Nothing at all."

"Nelvan, what else did you have in that pack?" I said.

"Nothing dangerous. Just a Bible," Nelvan said.

"Oh really?" I narrowed my eyes at Blix and held out my hand. "Give it. Now!"

The true face of reptilian hostility took control of his features. Sharp teeth were bared and a quiet hiss streamed out of his mouth. His muscles tightened and his stance widened. I swallowed hard and hoped for minor injuries.

I lunged toward his hidden hand. He spun and tried to shake me loose. I clung to his arm for dear life and we fell to the ground in a twisted sprawl.

I saw a black, leather-bound book come free and spread open on the ground like some wounded butterfly. I scrambled toward it and was reaching for the cover when something painfully strong grasped my ankle and yanked backward.

A blur of copper scales leapt over me. Blix retrieved the book and went sprinting down the corridor. I looked after him in dismay and then let my head drop to the ground.

"I guess he really likes the scriptures," Nelvan said weakly.

I sighed and pushed myself up to a sitting position. "He's a Vythian. He can't help himself."

"Oh. They must be very devout."

"No, no. It's not that. They can't resist literature." I leaned against the cold metal wall catching my breath. "Books are scarce these days. Everything's digital. The more ancient the text, the more they're drawn to it. It's like a drug to them."

"Strange." Nelvan started putting his supplies back in his pouch. "Well, I suppose there are worse addictions."

"Boy, you don't know anything." I stood to my feet, wincing from a new pain that shot up from my ankle. "Do you have any idea what you've done?"

Nelvan shrugged.

"You just gave a Vythian a Bible." I scowled at him.

"Well, he sort of just took it, really." Nelvan said. "I don't understand. Is it outlawed in the future?"

"Depends what planet you land on."

"But you don't like it on your ship?"

"Hey, it's no dust off my star cluster," I said. "My uncle was an intergalactic missionary. Not that I subscribe to it, I just want it kept away from Blix."

"Why?"

I marched toward Nelvan. "I've filled Blix's quarters with exotic vacation motion screens. The ship's computer is under strict orders to give him only bright, happy stories. He's a Vythian and the wrong book in his hands can be dangerous."

"Dangerous how?"

"Boy, don't you ever get tired of asking questions?"

"How can I understand the future if I can't ask questions?"

"It's not the future, it's the present. Your past present is now just the past."

Nelvan face was starting to develop wrinkles from looking confused. I decided to be merciful.

"Vythians dream about what they think about. Sometimes their dreams become reality."

Nelvan had started to open his mouth when I held up a hand to silence him.

"Don't ask me how. I don't know. Are their dreams precognitive? Do they direct future events? Do their visions actually materialize?" I threw up my hands to accentuate my honest bewilderment on the subject. "I'll leave it to the academics to decide. All I know is that they're a tricky race. They've nearly wiped themselves out of existence. But one thing's for sure, unless you want this ship filled with the ten plagues of Egypt, we need to get that book back from him."

Nelvan gave a hesitant nod. "He's kind of huge. I don't know that I could ever take anything from him."

"Well, if you get the chance, jump on it. And while you're at it, keep any other story you might know that has catastrophes, disease or monsters of any kind to yourself, got it?"

"This is all very weird," Nelvan said.

"Well, this is your life now. Get used to it."

I was bending down to retrieve my cup when a sudden jolt rocked the ship. I fell to my knees in an awkward sprawl and managed to catch myself before a full-face plant occurred. Nelvan wasn't so lucky. I turned to see him flat on his back, moaning from the impact.

A loud shudder of metal and the rapid beeping of disturbed circuitry filled the air. I frowned at the sight of my silver cup overturned and a puddle of velrys on the floor.

A frightening thought hit me—the prisoner had escaped.

7

I RUSHED INTO the containment room to find Jasette still frozen upright within the holding cylinder. Her mouth started moving in another silent rant upon my entry. Just as I breathed a sigh of relief, something collided into my back. I looked behind me to find Nelvan trying to regain his balance.

"Watch it!" I said.

"Sorry, I was trying to catch up," Nelvan said. "What happened?"

"Can't you just try to figure things out on your own?"

"Um, I guess?"

"Good. Computer: What happened?"

A red band of light lit up around the room and a repeating siren blared.

"Iris! Shut that thing off and tell me what's going on."

"All I can deduce is that we encountered a large-scale energy fluctuation that temporarily disrupted all functions," the computer said. "Post analysis and theoretical calculations of the energy disturbance and any potential causes are inconclusive."

"Enough gibberish, what does that mean?" I said.

"It means, I don't know what it was," the computer said.

Blix ran into the room. "What happened?"

"Well, well, look who's back." I frowned. "My loyal, trustworthy, first mate."

Blix gazed at the floor, a look of shame covering his reptilian face. "My sincere apologies, Captain. I am most saddened by my lack of restraint and disrespectful actions."

"If you're really sorry, you'll give me back that book."

"Not to worry, Captain. I disposed of it so that I shall not be tempted further."

I noticed he was carrying a new satchel on his hip, that was slung over his shoulder with a thick, brown strap. "Then what's in the satchel?"

"This?" Blix grabbed the bag like it was the first time he'd noticed it. "Just some Vythian scale care products. You know how I can chafe during space travel."

Another powerful jolt rocked the ship sending me slamming into the wall. Nelvan cried out as he fell to his back once more. I looked back and saw Blix in a wide stance, both arms held outward. I silently cursed his amazing sense of balance.

"Computer," I barked. "What's going on?"

"You know I don't respond well to raised voices, Captain," the computer said.

"We have a situation here. How 'bout cutting me some slack and tell me what's hitting us."

A quick series of grating beeps sounded. "Fine." The computer took on a harsher, digitized tone. "Analysis running."

Jasette was speaking frantically about something. The mute shield was still up so no sound was coming from her holding cylinder. I playfully put a hand to my ear as if I was having trouble hearing. She shot me a look of death. It was a great look. Very alluring.

"Computer, lower the mute shield," I said.

The yellow shield dissolved and Jasette let out an exasperated sigh.

"Get us out of here, now!" she said.

"Oh? And why should I do that?"

"Because those blasts were level ten quadrant seekers and any ship using that kind of weaponry could *obliterate* us, so fire up the thrusters and move this thing," Jasette said.

"'Level ten quadrant seeker'? That sounds made up," I said. "What're you trying to do, scare me?"

"Hey, it's not my fault you're ignorant of elite class weaponry," Jasette said.

"Computer, give me an update," I said.

"Nothing new to report sir." A long beep sounded. "Just a moment. There's a small energy pulse emerging from the nearest star cluster."

"C'mon Blix, I need your navigation skills." I met Blix at the control panel and within two freems his fingers were dancing across the screen.

The screen produced a visual of the stars outside the ship. A tiny red blip of light pulsated in the upper right corner.

"Is it a ship?" I said.

"Hard to tell. Whatever it is, it's fast," Blix said.

Nelvan sat up, rubbing his head. "Is this normal?"

"Quiet, boy. Computer, tell me you have something," I said.

"I'm afraid there are some high level jamming operations at work," the computer said. "It appears to be a spacecraft of some kind but all communication and system scans are blocked."

The pulsating red dot on the screen vanished.

"Where'd it go?" I said.

"That's odd. It's possible they have a cloaking device," Blix said. "Wait, there it is."

The glowing red dot reappeared on the screen, this time much larger.

"Computer, what just happened?" I said.

"Unknown, Captain. All readings for the unidentified craft momentarily ceased then re-emerged instantaneously at another quadrant in space, this time closer to our position."

"Incredible." Blix rubbed his chin. "A functioning hyper jump."

"Oh c'mon, that's only theoretical," I said.

"Maybe in your limited experience," Jasette said. "I've seen it."

"And I suppose you've traveled the universe and unlocked all its secrets, right?"

"Some of them."

"The craft has dropped off sensors again," the computer said.

I looked back at the screen and an empty star field blinked back at me.

"Shields up. Ready all weapons," I said.

"You should've done that first thing," Jasette said.

"Silence, prisoner," I said. "Blix?"

Blix leaned back from the screen and placed his hands on his hips. "No chance of outrunning it. I suppose surrender might be a good option."

I scowled at him. I was about to formulate a moving and altogether captain-like stern rebuke that would whip him into a never say die resolve when a large, sleek spaceship appeared on the screen directly before us. My jaw went slack as I stared at its glorious visage. Smooth, finessed lines flowing into sharp, cutting edges created an elegant craft that looked more organic than manufactured. A deadly creature from space that made you bow down before it in awe before it destroyed you.

"What? What do you see?" Nelvan struggled to his feet. He seemed disturbed by our hypnotic stares at the control panel.

A flurry of glowing white dots materialized around Nelvan. They snaked around his body like some space serpent about to constrict. Nelvan's eyes went wide. He looked up at me, his expression a desperate plea for help. The white dots glowed brighter and Nelvan disappeared. A few glowing white specs swirled where he'd stood only moments ago and then blinked into nothingness.

My lips uttered a weak response. "Nelvan?"

"Get me out of here, now!" Jasette shouted.

Another swarm of glowing white dots appeared and swirled around Jasette, seemingly unhindered by the energy field.

"Computer, deactivate containment grid," I said.

The glowing blue energy field around Jasette dissipated but it was too late. Only a few twinkling lights remained in her place.

"Tragic. So young and well-groomed." Blix shook his head. "You know, under different circumstances she might have—"

A myriad of glowing lights encircled Blix, just inches away from me.

"Blix!" I cried.

"Oh dear." Blix looked about his body as if noticing a new rash. He straightened and put an arm to his chest with a slight bow. "Captain Starcrost, though many of your methods are indeed strange and often counterproductive, it has been my honor to—"

And then Blix disappeared. I looked around in desperation wondering why I'd never built some kind of escape sort of thingy.

"Computer? Iris, are you there?" I said.

Dozens of dazzling white lights sprang to life and circled around me.

"Yes Captain, I'm here," the computer said.

"Um … Help?"

The lights grew brighter and suddenly I felt like I was flying, even though I hadn't moved. A knot formed in my stomach and the ship dissolved into a blanket of white light.

8

I OFTEN WONDERED what death would feel like. I was prepared for a fair amount of pain, though I'd hoped it would be quick and minimal. Once the lights began swirling around me in the ship, I figured that was the end of things. I tensed and prepared for the searing jolt of electric death.

But it never came.

In fact, the feeling I was experiencing was actually enjoyable. I felt weightless, like a feather, and all was bright around me. A rising series of musical tones filled the air as the white lights started to dissipate, and I saw before me a hazy wall of colorful lights.

A blurry figure came into view—he looked familiar but I couldn't quite place his face. Thick, flowing locks of blonde hair, a wide, sturdy face and square jaw line that was straight from a sculptor's chisel. He was an imposing figure of a man whose movements suggested daily practice time in front of a mirror. His white designer jumpsuit had a complex series of intertwined, glittering silver stripes cutting across the torso that betrayed a team of unseen tailors.

"Glurth posh virthin filo paky." His mouth was moving but besides being incomprehensible, the words sounded distant and muffled.

I felt all my weight return and lo and behold, I was standing inside the most exquisite spacecraft I had ever seen. The walls were curved crystalline, with delicate control panels nestled in subtle recesses.

My hearing became clear as a chorus of computerized blips echoed through the ship in complementary tones like an electronic orchestra. The lighting was subdued and brilliant all at once. Industrious looking crewmen worked holographic control screens that emerged from unseen devices on the floor. I suddenly felt foolish for having mistaken teleportation for a death ray, but I'd never seen one function with such technological elegance.

"And there's our final guest." The blonde man spoke with a flourish of his broad arm. The nearby recessed lighting mirrored his motions, gliding across his uniform, causing the silver stripes to shimmer. "My long lost school mate, Glint Starcrost."

That's when it hit me. Hamilton Von Drone the Third. The most pompous, self-absorbed jerk I had ever known. I was starting to wonder if I really had died and ended up in hell.

"Oh, terribly sorry, old chap. Did you just get out of bed?" Hamilton looked down at my pajama pants.

"No. I like these pants. What's it to ya?" I said.

Hamilton held up his hands. "My mistake. I forget how broad the eye for fashion can open in this great big universe of ours. To each his own, eh Glinty, old boy?" He gave me what looked like a good-natured slap on the shoulder, but it hit me with such force that I spun sideways. All my instincts told me to draw and fire repeatedly.

"A thousand apologies, old lad. Guess you're not holding up too well these days." Hamilton leaned back and gave a rich, warm laugh like you might expect to hear from a kindly uncle. The ship seemed to amplify his laughter and add faint harmonies in the background. All the crewmen seated nearby joined in with bright, gleaming smiles.

Firm hands gripped my arm and righted me. I glanced over and saw Blix standing beside me.

"Blix, you're alive." I forgot for a moment to hide my enthusiasm. I was, of course, happy to find my first mate alive, but once a captain starts to show a sensitive side, all authority comes under question.

Blix paused a moment, a grin turning his facial scales upward in a look of warm kinsmanship. "It is good to see you again too, Captain."

I looked past him and noticed Jasette standing nearby. She gave a sly grin, communicating the unmistakable message that we were on even ground now. On the polished, silver floor near her feet, Nelvan was curled up in the fetal position, shivering. Two fist sized medical droids hovered around his head monitoring his vital signs.

Hamilton turned and strolled into the bridge of his ship, his arms outstretched like some tour guide. "As I was telling your shipmates before you arrived, I want you all to relax and take advantage of the generous amenities of my humble ship." Hamilton gave a theatrical turn on his heel and offered a slight bow.

"Relax? You want us to relax after you just ripped our molecules through space and hijacked us from my ship?" I marched toward him, my fists clenched.

"Easy, old boy, no harm meant." Hamilton held up his hand. "I have to fly cautious these days. Space piracy is on the rise you know."

I took a final step that closed the gap between us. "Yeah, so that gives you the right to snatch captains from their ships, no questions asked?" I was tired of surprises and wanted revenge for having been tricked into facing my fear of death.

I threw my signature right cross, waiting for that beautiful crunch of knuckles against his perfectly tanned, cleft chin but I hit nothing. In a single, graceful movement, he was standing sideways. He winked at me, an imperious look on his face.

"Really Glinty, I would've hoped you'd outgrown such behavior," Hamilton said.

"You're right." I feigned a look of remorse. "That was beneath me." I threw my left fist into his gut, hoping to knock the pompous wind out of him. His hand was a blur as it grasped my fist, bringing it to a dead stop.

Hamilton shook his head at me. "That's quite enough, old fellow." He tightened his grip on my hand. It was a grip like an enraged space monkey. His expression was all fatherly and compassion but his grip was pure death. With my free hand I drew the DEMOTER and pointed it at his sparkling, baby blue eyes.

"Let it go, Von Drone," I warned.

Dozens of high-powered, dual-barreled, horrifically shiny laser rifles dropped from hatches in the ceiling and aimed at my head. Five heavily armored attack droids emerged from sliding hatches in the walls and spun into dangerous looking fight stances. Crewmembers from every direction drew slim, crystalline laser pistols, all trained on me.

"Now Glint, let's not do anything foolish," Hamilton said.

"Wouldn't think of it." A high-pitched whir sounded as I powered the DEMOTER to full. Hamilton flinched, losing his ever-steady composure for a brief moment.

Suddenly the gun was ripped free from my hand. It flew through the air and stopped abruptly before the open metallic hand of a slender grey robot. A bright white current sparked around the three, thick prongs of its open hand, keeping the DEMOTER hovering before it.

Hamilton glanced over at the robot with pride. "This is Mishmash, the first mate of the Velladrella." Hamilton released my fist and crossed his arms. "He's quite protective of me."

At first glance I thought Mishmash was a tall maintenance droid. There was nothing flashy or dangerous looking about him. But whenever he moved, something seemed wrong. It was as if he broke apart and reassembled with every motion but with such fluidity it seemed beyond any technology I'd ever seen.

"Now then, I must apologize for the unannounced teleportation—it was of course most unseemly," Hamilton bowed his head as if in remorse, but I knew better.

"Then send us back to our ship where we belong," I said.

"Let's not be hasty," Jasette said. "We just got here. The least we could do is take our generous host up on his kind offer of hospitality."

I glared back at Jasette. She grinned like a cat that just found a wounded mouse.

"Yes, good, good. A magnificent idea." Hamilton placed a hand on my shoulder. "My dear Glint. I'm prepared to let bygones be bygones. Come, let's share a meal and move to a more pleasant future."

I opened my mouth for a scathing return when Jasette interrupted me.

"I think that's a wonderful idea," Jasette said. "A meal isn't too much to ask, is it Blix?"

Blix was staring at Mishmash. He looked over at Jasette as

if awoken from deep concentration. "Oh, yes, I imagine that would be splendid."

I kept my eyes on Blix and watched his gaze slide back to the robot.

"Excellent. Very well then, computer, prepare a great feast for our guests," Hamilton said.

9

HAMILTON LED US down the corridors of his elegant ship, making grand sweeping gestures with his hands as he bragged about its unparalleled awesomeness.

Jasette walked beside Hamilton, soaking up his every word. Blix was nearly dragging Nelvan along behind them as the poor boy tried to regain consciousness. I lagged behind, examining every inch of the ship for a weakness that could give me some kind of leverage.

Mishmash brought up the rear, hovering just inches above the ground. He had no eyes but at my look, a million tiny parts of his metallic body shifted to a lighter shade of grey. His thin arm reached inside a cavity in his torso and drew my DEMOTER. He flipped it up in a rapid spin then caught it in the exact position as it had left his hand. He slid it back into his side and a silvery wave went across his head. I got the feeling it was his version of a smile. It was pure creepiness.

We entered a cavernous room with vaulted, crystalline ceilings that glittered like stars. Soft tones like miniature bells cascaded down from overhead.

"You see those masks?" Hamilton motioned to a series of polished, silver masks that descended in a spiraling ring around the walls. The masks held varied expressions, covering everything from pure joy to utter agony.

"Yes, they're exquisite." Jasette was all smiles and batting eyelashes. It was enough to make you vomit.

"The rarest Kasellium. Only two known sci-alchemists in the universe have the talent and means by which to temper its unruly metal," Hamilton said. "It takes the energy of a small sun to fuel the process."

A large table and chairs that looked like polished glass emerged from the ivory floor. Ocean currents and small black fish moved through them as though they had captured a piece of the sea.

"Servers!" Hamilton's voice echoed through the room like it had been amplified to sound like a giant. He clapped his hands twice and dozens of squat, black and white droids with multiple arms sprang into action carrying food and beverage trays.

In a few, frenzied moments of droid action, the tables held a magnificent feast. Rare Frellian fin-crabs on the half shell, thrice basted kraken monster claw with glazed volcano shrimp sauce and wormhole frost wine, whose mere aroma was bottled and sold for a tidy sum.

"Now then, my beautiful Jasette," Hamilton said. "Pick your favorite exotic location."

Jasette put a finger to her lips and thought for a moment. She let out a tiny gasp as a thought seemed to come to mind. "Quelgrin-Tellesian. The brilliant jade moon of Shelloose."

"Well chosen! A moon that rests uncomfortably close to a black hole for any but the most foolhardy explorer. Come, let us join their ranks, shall we?" A broad grin spread across Hamilton's face. "Computer, let my wishes become reality."

A chorus of musical blips sounded followed by a warm, sensual female voice. "As you wish, Captain."

The room seemed to dissolve into a canvas of black and only

the tables with the feast remained. A blanket of stars blinked to life beneath us as if we were floating through space outside the ship.

A distant hum sounded from somewhere above. Slight tremors went through the floor and the stars turned into streaks of light as if we were careening through the galaxy at great speed. The illusion was altogether too realistic for my liking. I stomped my foot to make sure there was still a solid floor beneath me, just as several planets rushed into view.

We came to a sudden halt above a bright green moon. The dark eye of a massive black hole swirled in the distance, it's deep red and black colored spirals reaching out as if to pull us in. The large turquoise planet of Shelloose loomed nearby.

Blix whistled in appreciation of the sight. "Simply breathtaking."

"Wow, I mean...it's just...wow!" Nelvan was practically drooling.

"It's just a sim-vision." I nudged Nelvan to snap him out of it. He rubbed his arm reflexively, his wide eyes and slack jaw still showing his unbroken fixation at the sight.

"A wonderful spot for a meal. Jasette, since it was your inspired vision that brought us here, please take a seat." Hamilton bowed and motioned to the table.

"Certainly." Jasette sauntered over to the feast and sat at the head of the table.

A high-pitched screech of metal came from behind me. I swiveled to find Mishmash twitching in a disturbing way, as if his processors had stuck on an algorithm. A red wave of light ran across his face.

"Oh, yes. I'm afraid this won't do." Hamilton rubbed his chin, looking from Mishmash to Jasette.

"What's up with the robot?" I said.

Another screech of metal sounded and Mishmash turned a bright shade of white.

"Mishmash prefers the term sentient being," Hamilton said.

"Of course he does." I sighed.

"Jasette dear, I hope you don't think this terribly rude, I'm afraid you're sitting at the end where Mishmash takes his meal. Could I trouble you to move down?"

I noticed a quick tightening in Jasette's neck muscles before she looked back, a forced smile on her face.

"No trouble at all." Jasette moved down to the opposite side of the table.

"Your robot eats with you?" I said.

Bright flares of white light surrounded the outstretched hands of Mishmash. The grating buzz of electric current was uncomfortably close. Dangerous looking sparks danced around his three fingered, metal hands, both aimed at my head.

"As I said," Hamilton took on a scolding tone, "Mishmash doesn't care for that term. I'd strongly advise against using it again."

I held up my hands and gave a forced grin to the robot. "Sorry pal. Didn't know it was such a sore spot."

Mishmash hesitated for a moment, his thin, cylinder of a head swiveling over to Hamilton then back to me. The current around his hands subsided and he hovered over to the seat at the head of the table.

I glanced over at Blix. His eyes narrowed as if to communicate a warning. I was really starting to hate it here. If the food didn't look so good and, more importantly, if I had any power whatsoever on this ship, I would've teleported out of there and smashed that cocky little robot on my way out the door.

"Well, let's get this show on the road." I marched over to the table and was hit with an aroma beyond words. I felt a shudder go through my knees. I couldn't remember when, if ever, food had smelled so divinely created.

I took my seat next to Jasette. I leaned over and whispered, "If you think your chances are better here, you've got another thing coming."

"Your breath smells like rotting Vultriffle carcass," she whispered.

Blix sat next to me and Nelvan joined Hamilton at the other side of the table.

"No need to whisper secrets aboard this ship," Hamilton said.

"I was just saying how much better the food is here than on Glint's musty ship." Jasette grabbed some silver tongs and started placing Frellian crab shells on her plate.

"That's because you're a prisoner. You're lucky to get crusty bread." I never like to give information away when I don't have to, especially to someone like Hamilton. But Jasette was getting on my nerves and it was time to let that cat out of the bag.

"Prisoner?" Hamilton looked mildly amused. "Is that right?"

Jasette gave him a tight-lipped smile. "Just a simple misunderstanding. I transported to his ship by mistake."

She slid back a thin metal plate on the forearm of her outfit. A glowing green set of numbers shone and a holographic image of Jasette with law enforcement symbols and a scrolling series of writing appeared.

"I'm part of an undercover task force from Granthill 5. We've had some smugglers raid our outposts recently and I thought Glint was one of them." Jasette motioned to me with a table knife. "Would you believe, I actually thought he was dangerous." She started chuckling and Hamilton joined in on the laughter.

"Oh, my dear girl. Glint? Dangerous?" Hamilton smiled at me. "How could you have made such a miscalculation?"

Jasette shrugged and stuffed a forkful of crab in her mouth. She shot a grin at me and winked.

I fantasized about booting the both of them into the nearby black hole.

"Curious you didn't mention that before." Blix was placing food on his plate with the manners of royalty. "It would've saved quite a bit of misunderstanding."

"As I said, I was undercover," Jasette said.

Blix nodded and started to cut his food. The scales at the corner of his mouth curled upward in a knowing smirk.

"Well, it all makes perfect sense to me." Hamilton poured the light blue frost wine into the crystalline flutes. "After all, it's an unpredictable universe we live in." Hamilton nudged Nelvan with an elbow. "Wouldn't you agree, er, I'm sorry, what was your name?"

"Nelvan, sir." Nelvan had piled a large stack of food on his plate. "I'm afraid I couldn't tell you. I've only just got here." Nelvan took a healthy spoonful of shimmering, crystal-cheese shavings and stuffed it into his mouth.

"Oh? You've come from a distant galaxy, have you?" Hamilton said.

"Actually …" A few shavings spilled out of Nelvan's over-filled mouth. "I'm from—"

"That'll be all Nelvan," I interrupted. "Hamilton, this is my crew. We don't owe you our life story."

"Easy, old boy. Just making conversation. And while I'm at

it, I'd like to begin with a toast." Hamilton lifted his glass. The frost wine was alive with effervescence.

I sighed and prepared for the inevitable self-glorification.

"To old acquaintances and new friends." Hamilton looked around the table, giving subtle acknowledgements with a tip of his glass. "May we make the most of our travels together."

"To new friends." Jasette held her glass toward Hamilton and gave a warm smile.

"Hear, hear," Blix said.

"Yeah, bottoms up." I threw back my glass and the full flute of frost wine went down my throat like an icy ray of sunshine. My stomach felt like a thousand fireflies had woken up and started dancing.

"Take it easy Glint," Hamilton said. "You're supposed to sip. Fine elixirs such as this are meant to be savored. You can't rush the transcendent."

I gripped the seat with my free hand. I had the unshakable feeling I might float away. I fixed Hamilton with what I hoped would be a resolute stare.

"This sewer water? I've had better," I said.

"I highly doubt that." Hamilton smirked and carved off a slice of kraken claw. "Now then Glint, you were always a man of adventure. Tell me about your latest quest."

"Not much to talk about." I shrugged and took a bite of Frellian crab. It nearly melted in my mouth. My taste buds silently cursed me for every other inferior taste I had subjected them to. "We're just flying around the universe checking stuff out."

"He's headed to Beringfell," Jasette said.

I tried to casually give her a look of death.

"Beringfell? Is that right?" Hamilton leaned back, a forkful of kraken meat poised before his mouth."I seem to remember an old legend about that galaxy. It's the last known location of the Emerald Enigma, right?"

Those treasured words were like a deadly gas escaping from his lips. I wanted to ram them back in his unworthy mouth with a metal-covered fist. Hamilton was the last person I wanted to know about the Enigma. My poker face was on in full force as I continued to eat, using every fiber in my being to appear nonchalant.

"Who knows," I shrugged. "I heard there were a few old mines on one of the abandoned planets. Thought I could scrounge up some left behinds."

"I see." Hamilton took a bite and chewed thoughtfully. "Seems a remote place to go looking for such trifles. No doubt a skilled Vythian such as Blix could use his extraordinary abilities for more noteworthy endeavors."

Blix was pouring himself a glass of frost wine. He grinned at the comment, as if flattered. "You give me too much credit Captain Von Drone. I am merely a first mate under the service of a captain." Blix turned to Mishmash and raised his glass. "Wouldn't you agree, Mishmash?"

Mishmash turned a dark grey. His plate held a perfectly symmetrical tower of ice chips. He grabbed a piece of ice and lifted it to his head. A thin, rectangular cavity opened and he put the ice inside. A metallic grinding that sounded like a ghost escaping an electronic prison came from the cavity right before it closed.

"Now, now, Mishmash, we have guests." Hamilton gave the robot a disapproving glance. "If fortune is what you're after, our crew is headed for Sellamar. A great cache of gemstones has been discovered by one of our seeker pods. You're welcome to join us."

"I can get along fine on my own," I said.

"No need to decide right away."

I stuffed a large bite of kraken in my mouth. The savory meat was pure, mouthwatering bliss. "Actually, after this we gotta split." I made sure to speak to Hamilton with my mouth full of food to help communicate my contempt. "We're kind of in a hurry."

"Well if that's the issue, you can feel at ease," Hamilton said. "We've assumed your last navigation settings so as not to trouble you further. Your ship is being towed in our tractor beam. No doubt we'll get you to your destination in a fraction of the time."

Man, how I hated him. Ever since space academy, with the aid of his family fortune behind him, he had verbally manipulated his way into virtually anything he wanted. My mind raced for a counter to his otherwise flawless logic, but I was coming up empty.

"Yeah, but I just remembered we have to stop off at a spaceport first for supplies, so—"

"No problem," Hamilton said. "Computer, calculate nearest spaceport."

A soft tone sounded. "Serberat-Gellamede. Distance, three point five jemmins," the computer said.

"Excellent." Hamilton tipped his glass to me. "There, you see. We're on our way."

"Yeah, how 'bout that." I grabbed a breadstick that was a miniature replica of the fabled cathedral from Tellvanium 7. I bit off a few spires and the buttery warmth of the impossibly delicious, fresh baked bread made my head spin.

"We're going to a spaceport?" Nelvan had a worried look on his face.

"Just for supplies, Nelvan. Then we'll be on our way. All of us."

Hamilton patted Nelvan on the shoulder. "You don't like spaceports, my boy?"

"No. Well, actually I'm not even sure. You see—"

"So, Hamilton, whatever happened to that little toady that followed you around at space academy? What was his name, Mickle? Markle?"

"Merkeel," Hamilton said.

"Yeah, that's it, Merkeel," I said. "Man, what a jerk that guy was."

I had raised the cathedral roll for another bite when a laser blast blew it clean out of my hand. I stared at my empty hand in shock for a moment, noticing the new black trails of smoke residue that spread across my palm.

Mishmash had the DEMOTER trained on me, a stream of smoke still slithering out of the barrel. His metal body was bright white, with ribbons of red light pulsating over it.

"Mishmash." Hamilton raised his hands toward the robot in a calming manner. "This is hardly the time for weapons."

I glanced over at Blix. His muscles were tense. He was about to make a move.

"Mishmash, that's an order." Hamilton narrowed his eyes.

In a swift move, Mishmash put the DEMOTER back into the cavity in his torso. His color shifted back to a light grey.

"My sincere apologies, Glint." Hamilton's hands were clasped in a supplicating gesture. "Mishmash is very defensive of our crew members. Merkeel served with great distinction aboard the Velladrella for many gloons."

"Uh-huh." I brushed the smoke trails from my hands. I could feel the rage building. If the table wasn't so heavy, I would've flipped the whole blasted banquet over. "Look Von Drone, I don't like being shot at, especially by my own gun. I've had enough of this song and dance." I stood and leaned toward Hamilton, both fists on the table. "I want off this ship."

"Please, Glint, do sit down. This is simply a misunderstanding."

"Yeah, life with you is full of misunderstandings. I already had my fill of them at the academy."

Hamilton leaned back and chuckled. "Now Glinty, there's no sense bringing up what could have been."

"Don't try that line of trash with me, you filthy skrid. I saw you in the simulators. I saw you flounder in the crisis scenarios. Everyone knew I earned that apprenticeship and you bought it."

"Closing on Serberat-Gellamede," the computer said. "Please proceed to the landing bay for disembarking."

Hamilton pushed away from the table and stood to his feet. "Well Glint, I must say these delusional rants of yours have brought back some amusing memories. But all good things must come to an end. Mishmash, see our guests to the landing bay, won't you?" Hamilton lifted the crook of his arm toward Jasette. "Come, my lady, I shall escort you."

Jasette nodded and took his arm with a grin. Without another word they set off. Mishmash hovered after them a few feet, then stopped and swiveled around to face us like an awaiting sentry.

Blix stood, dabbing at the corner of his mouth with a napkin. "Well captain, you certainly have a way with people."

I gave him an annoyed look and started after the others. "C'mon, let's get off this stinkin' ship."

Mishmash led us down a descending hallway that led to the landing bay. The walls of the passage were thick windows that offered a grand view of space as we approached Serberat-Gellamede. The bright, blue-green planet of Gwittertwill was illuminated beautifully by the triple suns of the Veshul galaxy. The backdrop of the bright planet silhouetted the oddly shaped spaceport before us. Serberat-Gellamede resembled a warrior's hammer, which seemed fitting for this rough and tumble region of space.

The Velladrella ascended alongside the colossal handle-shaped portion of the spaceport like a small mouse crawling up the side of a large building. The dark grey and copper colored handle housed the mammoth sized machinery that powered the spaceport and manufactured a hospitable atmosphere. We sped toward the squarish hammer-shaped top, passing a multitude of lit windows that betrayed the scores of engineers and maintenance crew needed to keep this place running.

"Amazing." Nelvan was right up against the window, palms pressed to the glass and craning his head in all directions, trying to soak in the sight. "I wonder why they didn't just build on the planet below." Nelvan motioned to the beautiful planet Gwittertwill. "It looks like some kind of tropical paradise."

"Probably because they didn't feel like dying," I said. "The most vicious, poison-filled plants and deadly creatures run the show down there. It's the stuff of nightmares."

A sad look crawled across Nelvan's youthful face. "Sure looks nice from up here."

The ship arced over the topside of the hammer revealing the view of Serberat-Gellamede that showed up in all their glossy promotional material. The bright, white structures of the spaceport spread out before us in a beautiful collection of interconnected hexagon shapes.

There were several high-rise, luxury hangars that I didn't remember from my last visit three gloons ago. Apparently the spaceport had been through some recent renovations. True to form, Hamilton's ship was closing in on the largest and tallest of the hangars.

10

THE VELLADRELLA LANDED with delicate grace at Hangar 5 on the Serberat-Gellamede spaceport. Being the tallest of the glass domed, luxury hangars, it was obviously reserved for the rich and famous.

The landing bay doors of the ship slid open with a gliding whoosh. The triple suns of the Veshul galaxy shone high overhead the glass ceiling of the hangar. The landing bay was flooded with their warm, orange light. Clean, white walls circled around us showing nary a smudge of dirt.

I grabbed my trusty Admiral 9000s and snapped the black shades over my eyes.

"Wow, this spaceport is amazing," Nelvan said.

"This is just the landing hangar," I said.

Hangar 5 was decked out in the latest pampered executive motif. Ocean tones, over-stuffed merzuvial-hide octagons and rivulets of sparkling water cascading down from the ceiling with crystal hover glasses at the ready. I saw my ship perched nearby. Apparently the advanced systems on the Velladrella could not only tow but take over the landing controls of other ships as well.

A short, stocky droid with a polished silver exterior hovered over to us. His torso was stylishly wrapped in a sparkling turquoise sarong.

"Welcome, treasured guests." A musical voice sounded from

the droid. "We hope your stay at Serberat-Gellamede is fraught with happiness. I am Fofo, your concierge. How can I make your experience more pleasant?"

"Fofo." Hamilton lifted his cleft chin and surveyed the hangar as if deciding whether to stay. "My guests and I shall require eyewear."

The luminous, light blue circles that simulated eyes on Fofo's head lit up and a low tone rang through the hangar. Several knee-high droids rolled out from hatches in the walls and sped over to us. One of them stopped at my feet and a pair of stylish, silver sunglasses lifted from a hatch in its top.

"No thanks," I said. "I'm covered."

The droid lifted the glasses higher and rotated them in an alluring manner in front of my face.

"Beat it." I gave the droid a swift kick that sent the glasses flying. The droid rolled over, emitted a sharp beep and then sped back to his hatch in the wall.

"Terribly sorry, sir," Fofo said. "Is there a problem?"

I tapped on my Admiral 9000s.

"Oh, how silly of us," Fofo said. "My apologies for the redundancy."

I nodded. I was wearing thin of the royal treatment. Not that I couldn't get used to it of course. But knowing that it was a result of traveling with Hamilton turned it into a bitter pill.

"I must say, I don't remember this spaceport housing such grand amenities," Blix said.

"Well, things have changed in the last few gloons." Hamilton placed a pair of sparkling silver shades on his face and looked around like he had just conquered the spaceport. "Thanks of course to a generous donation from the Von Drone Foundation."

"You certainly know how to travel in style." Jasette gave Hamilton a wink before donning her shades.

"When one can paint a golden path, the universe can be a delightful place to visit." Hamilton grinned down at Jasette.

My head was about to explode. I couldn't take it anymore. My mind went into emergency drive and I marched over to Hamilton.

"I think I've been making this reunion difficult for no good reason," I said.

All expression seemed to vanish from Hamilton's face. He seemed genuinely speechless.

"I just have some stuff from the past I haven't worked through and I'm taking it all out on you." I put a hand on Hamilton's shoulder. "I mean, what's done is done, right? We all have to move on with our lives."

"Well, yes—I do believe I agree," Hamilton said.

"How about we shake hands and part with a clean slate. You've given us nothing but good things since we got on your ship and I responded with bitterness." I shook my head for dramatic emphasis. "Sometimes I really don't understand myself. I mean, I should be thanking you." I added a chuckle. I was laying it on thick, I admit, but Hamilton seemed to be going along with it.

"Glint, I must say, it's refreshing to hear you say that." Hamilton placed a hand on my shoulder. I fantasized about grasping it and flinging him through the glass dome overhead.

"Yes, well, I've been working remotely with a uniweb therapist. Sometimes it takes a while, but eventually I see things as they should be." I glanced over at Blix under the cover of my extra-tinted Admiral 9000s. His mouth was hanging wide open. It was great to catch him off guard every once in awhile.

"Well, in that case Glinty, old boy ..." Hamilton put out his hand. "Bygones, and all that."

"Of course." I shook his hand. "I'm sure you wouldn't want me to walk around a potentially dangerous spaceport without my weapon, though."

"Oh, that." Hamilton smiled. "Mishmash, relinquish the weapon."

Mishmash stalled, his cylindrical head swiveling between Hamilton and I.

"Mishmash?" Hamilton frowned at the droid.

Mishmash turned a dark grey and retrieved the DEMOTER from his side. He flung it toward me and I caught it in one smooth motion like it was rehearsed. I grinned and stuffed it back in its holster.

I sighed. A warm feeling went through my chest. I was complete again.

"Thanks friend." I smiled at Hamilton. I started to turn away, then turned back as if I had forgotten something. "Oh, I hate to mention it but I'm afraid your ..." I turned to Jasette. "What did you call them? Level ten quadrant seekers?"

Jasette clinched her jaw. "I'm no expert."

It was hard to tell in her glasses, but judging from the rest of her facial features, she must've been glaring at me.

"Yes, well, we use them in certain cases." Hamilton gave a wary glance to Jasette. The jovial nature was eroding from Hamilton's face. I knew I only had a few freems.

"They did a number on my ship. I wouldn't say anything but you've been such a stellar host already, I imagine you'd want to fix any damages you might have caused your guests." I turned to the concierge. "Isn't that generally the refined way of dealing with these matters, Fofo?"

"Why yes, of course, sir." Fofo was all lit up, with happy little beeps flying staccato-fashion out of his body. "We can start on a renewal and cleansing treatment for the smaller ship right away."

"What a tip top suggestion Fofo." I turned back to Hamilton. "What'ya say Hamilton, old friend? Shall we go for the platinum package with the Andrellian cleansing system?"

Hamilton had opened his mouth when Fofo broke in with a wild ascension of blips.

"A most excellent choice, sir." Fofo was hovering around in a tight circle at this point. "We can get started immediately."

I saw the muscles in Hamilton's jaw ripple. His chin protruded an extra centimeter.

"Certainly. It's only a trifle, really." Hamilton was speaking with effort now. "Fofo, make it happen for both ships."

"Yes sir, most excellent, sir. I just need to run a few minor credentials and we can get started." Fofo zipped over to Hamilton. A blue hologram transaction pad appeared before him.

Hamilton reached into his jumpsuit to retrieve his credentials.

"You're one of the classy ones, Hamilton." I started heading for the hangar lift and motioned for Blix to follow. "Well, c'mon Blix, Nelvan, let's not hold things up here."

"Well, hold on a moment Glint, It'll just take—" Hamilton said.

"Oh, don't worry Hamilton, we're just going further into the port." I gave a more insistent nod to Blix. "We'll see you there."

Blix half carried Nelvan with such effortless nonchalance that without looking hurried, both were at my side near the lift in a few moments.

Hamilton was trying to complete the necessary sales transactions, all the while glancing back up at us. The lift opened and we stepped in. I gave a casual wave back as the door chirped closed and we started our descent to the surface of the spaceport.

11

THE GLASS-WALLED, cylindrical lift offered a majestic view of Serberat-Gellamede. The bright suns reflected off the numerous white domed buildings far below us. Shining silver conveyer tubes connected the domes in a network of interlocking shapes that held a certain geometric allure from our vantage point. If I didn't know the spaceport was filled with the lowest form of space trash and interstellar riff raff, I might have been excited about the trip ahead of us.

"Look at that. It's incredible." Nelvan had his face pressed up against the glass, watching our descent.

I leaned against the wall and sighed. "Things always look beautiful from above. Then you get down there and wonder what happened to all your vibes."

Blix had his arms folded, watching me with an amused grin.

"What? What're you looking at?" I said.

"I can't get over your little performance up there."

"Don't get used to it," I said. "I like the direct approach."

Blix cast a disappointed gaze out of the lift. "A taste of greatness here and there and then it's back to the old thug routine."

Nelvan broke away from his gazing at the spaceport below, an uncertain look on his face. "I don't understand, is Hamilton a friend or an enemy?"

"He's pure evil boy. A slimy trail of glubbis left by a skrid attack," I said. "Tell him, Blix."

"Arrogant, yes. Control issues, certainly. But honestly, until you've stared deep into the cavernous maw of the death keepers at the Vellakora vortex, pure evil is quite a relative term."

"Trust me, he's plenty evil," I said. "Plus, he's had work done. His jawline is definitely more squared since the academy and his grip felt robotically enhanced."

Nelvan's face contorted into a youthful twist of contemplation. "I suppose I'll have to keep my eyes on him then."

"With any luck, you won't have to." I leaned forward, looking out over the approaching spaceport. The light from the triple suns was gleaming off the domed buildings below, but my Admiral 9000s were toning it down to a nice, dusky glow.

"Listen," I said. "All we have to do is slink around the spaceport for awhile in the more seedy spots where a high brow like Hamilton won't set foot, then when the ship is finished and it looks like we're in the clear, we sneak up to the hangar and back to the stars we go."

"There's about a dozen things that could go wrong with that scenario."

"Then problem solve." I slapped Blix on the shoulder.

Blix gave a distasteful sounding snort, then moved close to Nelvan, retrieving a small bottle from his pocket. "Here Nelvan, you'll need this." Blix raised the bottle above Nelvan's head. "Take off your glasses and tilt your head back please."

Nelvan cautiously removed his glasses and gave a worried look up at the bottle. "What is it?"

"Chib chibs," Blix said. "To help you read."

Nelvan was blinking rapidly, his face tense with worry. Blix put a few drops from the bottle into each of his eyes.

Blix grinned and put the bottle back in his pocket. "That wasn't so bad, was it?"

Nelvan was all squints and blinking. "It stings. How will this help me read?"

"Chib chib bugs intercept your brain signals," Blix said. "Decode what your eyes are seeing. Unless you want to learn a thousand alien writing patterns, it's the only way to remain literate in space."

A sickened look covered Nelvan's face. "You put bugs in my eyes?"

"Relax," I said. "A week of blindness is the worst that could happen. There's lots of signs down there. You'll need to read to get around."

Nelvan cast a worried glance my way. "You said you were going to leave me at a spaceport."

Blix shook his head at me. "Now that's just mean."

"I was kidding." I gave Nelvan a playful punch on the shoulder. I felt bone. This poor boy needed to lift some weights.

Nelvan tried to casually rub his arm. "Does that mean I'm coming with you?"

"Well of course. You're part of my crew now," I said. "That is, once you recite the starship oath of loyalty."

Blix sighed. "Oh heavens. Not that overreaching pledge of slavery again."

"Hey, just because you have trouble staying loyal to your promises." I kicked the satchel at Blix's side.

Blix backed away with a small hiss. I gave him a dark look.

"You really want me as part of your crew?" Nelvan said.

"Of course. You have a background in science and an adventurous heart, right?" I nodded at Nelvan for confirmation.

A determined look filled Nelvan's face. "Well, yes ... yes, I would say I do."

"Take a knee and repeat after me," I said.

"Take a knee?" Nelvan looked confused.

"It's a sign of respect," I said.

"Oh, right." Nelvan took a clumsy step down and placed one knee on the metal base of the lift. He fidgeted around with his hands as if deciding where he should put them. He finally folded them on his raised knee and looked up expectantly.

"I, Nelvan Flink, do solemnly pledge undying respect and loyalty to Captain Starcrost, the commander of my life from this day forward, whether in the stars above or on the planets below. Henceforth, I will think nothing of my own comforts or aspirations. Who am I? No one. Who is Captain Starcrost? Everything and more."

Nelvan cast a bemused look to Blix, then back to me. "You can't be serious."

"You see," Blix said. "Rather preposterous isn't it?"

Nelvan stood, brushing off his knee. A high-pitched bell rang in the lift and the doors opened to the domed entryway of a silver conveyer tube. I stepped into the entryway and looked back at Nelvan. "Okay then, have fun with the grizzly scum that frequent this spaceport. Or should I say, your new home."

A worried look spread across Nelvan's face. Blix patted him on the shoulder and led him forward.

The centerpiece of the entryway was an oval, silver framed teleporting device that resembled a full-length mirror. Several halo shaped lights overhead bathed the room in a blue tinted glow. I removed my Admiral 9000s and tucked them neatly into my pocket.

Blix removed his silver glasses and looked at the teleporter, all smiles. "They've upgraded since our last visit. How convenient."

"I ain't setting foot in that thing." I said. "Who knows if they keep it in working order."

"Nonsense, it looks brand new." Blix walked up to the teleporter. A glowing blue energy pulsated within the frame. He ran his hand along the silver framing. "Not even a layer of dust."

"I always feel like I lose a small part of myself," I said.

"The sooner you conquer those misplaced fears, the sooner we'll be able to bring our ship's transporter back online," Blix said.

I gave a stern look. "I don't want to end up with an arm coming out of my head."

Blix sighed. "Nelvan, you're not afraid of a perfectly functional teleporter, are you?"

Nelvan was looking at the teleporter in fascination. "Well, I can't really say. They hadn't been invented in my time."

"Really? Well then, come Nelvan, experience scientific innovation beyond your lifetime."

Nelvan cast an unsure look at me.

I shook my head. "Take it from me boy, you're better off never setting foot in one of those things."

"Captain, really, I wish you wouldn't impose your unfounded superstitions on others." Blix held his arm out to Nelvan. "Nelvan, it's perfectly harmless. It'll take us straight into the heart of the spaceport and save a long walk."

"It *is* an exciting opportunity." Nelvan straightened his silver jump suit as if preparing for some mission. "I think I'd like to try it."

Nelvan strode toward the teleporter. Blix cast a victorious grin in my direction.

"Why don't you have Blix explain the weird smell when you exit?" I said.

Nelvan reached the teleporter and gave a questioning look back at me. "Smell?"

Blix put an arm around Nelvan and turned him to face the glowing blue energy. "Oh, don't listen to him, he's just rambling now."

"It smells like burnt popcorn on the other end. You'll see." I gave a lecturing shake of my finger. "That smell has never been explained you know. Scientifically or otherwise. That alone should tell you something's not right with teleportation."

"I've heard the theories." Blix gave Nelvan a confident nod and patted him on the back. "Well Captain, have a nice walk. Maybe Nelvan and I will relax at a velrys café while we wait for you."

I scowled at Blix. "You wouldn't dare."

"Wouldn't I?" Blix smiled and led Nelvan into the teleporter. A bright flash of blue light engulfed them and they disappeared. A residual blue outline of their bodies hung in the glowing energy for a moment before dissolving into thin streams of smoke.

I frowned and headed down the silver conveyer tube that led into the spaceport.

12

I EMBARKED ON A lonely slog through the conveyer tube. The illumination was sparse as several of the overhead halo lights had gone out and repair had been neglected. The air was musty and the only noises were the echoes of my boots scuffling against the grey, dusty floor of the tube. Apparently other space travelers didn't share my hang-ups with teleporters.

Though I wanted to hurt Blix badly for leaving me to walk this trek alone, he was unknowingly doing exactly what I needed him to do. Befriending Nelvan and assuring him that the best thing would be to stick with us. I needed to keep Nelvan around. No doubt Hamilton ran scans on us and came up empty with Nelvan. The boy was a mystery that would keep Hamilton guessing. And as long as he didn't hold all the cards, I had an angle.

Seeing my old nemesis again, with a seemingly endless supply of resources at his disposal, put my station of life in harsh perspective. Things had gone downhill ever since he'd stolen my academy apprenticeship. I was broke, my spaceship needed major repairs and I'd put all my hopes into a good luck charm that might not even exist.

As I continued down the conveyer tube, I tried to forget about my downward spiral and think of better times. My mind jumped back to flying my uncle's modified star cruiser over the remote jungle moon of Clandspearnia.

After my parents died, my uncle took care of me. He took me on all his interstellar missionary work as an assistant. Once he discovered I had a knack for flying, I became his unofficial pilot.

I remember that day at Clandspearnia was almost our last. Apparently the local chieftains had a tradition of making a soup dish out of the rare alien visitor that would bring them new information. That way, they could dispatch all newcomers before the other tribesmen would notice, then pass on the new information as a celestial revelation of their own. It was a clever ploy for the chieftains to maintain power but since it involved our death, we'd promptly fled the scene.

A spear had grazed my shoulder just as we boarded and high tailed it out of there. Blix is always nagging at me to sit down and talk about my past as if dredging back up all the pain will help. The only time I remember really talking about my parents was after that narrow escape. I guess I had mortality on the brain.

My uncle was great about it. He just listened and let me pour it all out. He gave me his kandrelian jacket and put a cup of velrys in my hand.

"Today is your day, Glint." He gave me a fatherly pat on the shoulder. "I want you to take this ship wherever you want." He gave me a wink. "Just take us somewhere exciting, okay?"

I smiled and nodded, not quite knowing how to thank him. I remember the thrill of taking that star cruiser full throttle through the stars in a day of space exploration a new pilot like me had only dreamt of. As far as I was concerned, it was the best therapy I could hope for.

After about three jemmins of walking, I spied the bright circle of light that marked the end of the tube. In a few moments

I emerged into the common dome of Serberat-Gellamede. The air was fresh and the dome was alive with activity.

Interstellar travelers strolled about, many of them dressed in imported apparel and sipping on multi-colored, exotic drinks. Crowds traveled around the outer ring of the octagon shaped building, entering and exiting the various walkways that branched out from it.

The center of the dome was filled with swanky, well-kept vendor stands displaying upscale products.

It was nothing like I remembered. Everything looked so clean and shiny. And where were all the shifty-eyed smugglers and thuggish star pirates?

I spotted a velrys café to my right. The exterior was decorated in rich earth tones and dark wood paneling. A large viewing screen above displayed the daily specials, with aroma-enhanced technology. Several shiny, bronze hover bots weaved through the patio tables offering patrons drink refills and freshly baked pastries.

One of the hover bots flew over to a small table where Blix and Nelvan sat sipping steaming velrys from oversized mugs. I frowned and marched toward them.

As I neared, I noticed that Blix had the Bible open on the table between them. He was glancing back and forth between Nelvan and the book, his eyes ablaze with curiosity. I slowed my approach, being careful not to make a noise so I could grab the Bible before Blix saw me. I overheard their conversation as I maneuvered through the patio tables nearby.

"That dreadful serpent." Blix shook his head. "As much as it shames reptilian kind, I can certainly understand why a creature of utter devilry would take such a beautiful form to do his tempting. It's very difficult for women to resist the words of a scaled creature."

I reached the table and lunged for the Bible. In one quick blur and without breaking his relaxed composure, Blix snatched the book from my hands and stuffed it back in his satchel. He leaned back and lifted a cup of velrys to his mouth.

"Greetings Captain, have a nice stroll?" Blix casually blew the steam away from the surface of the liquid and took a sip.

I straightened, grasping the front of my jacket and snapping it taut with captain-like authority. "It was invigorating. And all my molecules are still intact, unlike you teleport freaks."

Blix gave Nelvan a reassuring shake of his head.

"And what have you two been doing?" I said. "Disobeying direct orders?"

Blix smiled and took another sip. "Just having a pleasant conversation over velrys."

I gave a stern look. "Nelvan?"

Nelvan looked down as if avoiding a parent's scolding. "It was just a quick story."

"Did I not make the danger clear?" I said.

"But Captain, we just read the most intriguing origin story of the universe." The orange in Blix's eyes swirled around his slivered pupil. "Imagine, a creator outside of the inescapable boundaries of space-time. It's a compelling premise really. The creation of finite creatures like ourselves, especially you humans with your delicate life spans, would of necessity require an infinite creator. The infinite, you see, has no need to be created."

I sighed. "Are you finished?"

"And to think ..." Blix continued, ignoring me. "... The beginning of life on Earth in a beautiful garden that ended with one of those poor, impulsive choices you humans are so fond of making. It's all simply fascinating."

"Yes, yes, I know all about it," I said.

"Really?" Blix crossed his arms as if offended. "Then why haven't you told me about this before?"

I grabbed a chair from the nearby table and slumped down in it. "Because, that's my uncle's job. He was the interstellar missionary." I signaled for one of the hover bots. "The Universal Science and Academia Council has already explained the origin of life on Earth."

"The Feigntarian seeding theory?" Blix gave a sour look. "Please Captain, that's quite preposterous."

"Feigntarian seeding? What's that?" Nelvan said.

"Feigntarians are an alien race," I said. "They brought the first life forms to Earth. That's how life began."

Blix gave a scoffing laugh. "Alright, then how did life begin on the Feigntarian moon?"

"Well, the Glimborzul race brought the first life forms to their planet," I said.

"I see." Blix gave me a theatrical look of interest. "And, pray tell, how did life on the Glimborzul planet begin?"

I could see where Blix was leading me and it was annoying. Every few gloons the Science Council introduced a new alien civilization to explain how life began on the last introduced alien civilization. Last time I checked it stretched back four hundred alien civilizations. The true origin of life remained out of their grasp. Blix knew this as well and he was trying to make me sound ridiculous.

"Never mind, it's a long story." I gave a dismissive wave. The hover bot returned with my velrys. I closed my eyes for a moment, savoring the rich aroma. "The council is united on the subject."

"What happened four gloons ago when Dr. Glansmeer, the widely acclaimed four headed quantum physicist, said he had his doubts?" Blix said.

"I dunno. I don't keep up with the staff." I took a slow sip. It was pure heaven.

"Well, if you had paid attention you would've heard that he'd been summarily dismissed and all his grants were rescinded."

"So what? Maybe he went nuts."

"An intellect like his? Hardly. No, sadly it's all about falling in line with the latest accepted theories to keep your funding and get invited to all the highbrow academic parties," Blix said. "You want a true scientist, you have to go to the dedicated researchers on the remote colony planets."

"Crackpots." I took a long drink from my cup. All the stress of the day's events was melting away.

"You must get out of the ship more." Blix stopped one of the hover bots floating by. He pointed to a chocolate-laced pastry the bot carried on a polished bronze tray. The bot lifted the pastry with a thin, metal arm and placed it on the table before Blix.

"We'd better get going. I don't want Hamilton spotting us." I took a long drink of velrys and stood.

"We just got here," Blix said.

"And now we're leaving." I fixed Blix with a stern look.

"Oh, alright." Blix grabbed the pastry, folded it in half and stuffed the whole thing in his mouth. He held up his index finger to signal that he needed a moment while he chewed with expanded cheeks.

"Oh brother, just catch up to me." I left the table and headed toward the vendors.

The finely crafted vendor stands filled the center of the dome. I weaved my way between them, perplexed at the dramatic increase in the quality of merchandise on this remote spaceport.

A display of high-powered blasters more advanced than my humble DEMOTER caught my eye. I stared in awe at the shiny weaponry as I headed forward. I drew the DEMOTER and checked the reserve energy cartridge. The orange power bar was low. I slid the cartridge door open and peered inside. Energy gel took up about a tenth of the cavity. I needed a refill. I closed the cartridge and walked up to the weaponry booth. I set my DEMOTER on the counter and cleared my throat.

An obese, orange-scaled vendor with an eye patch chewed on a thick strand of meat, barely acknowledging my presence.

I gave him a fierce stare to jar him into action. "You sell energy refills?"

He continued his methodical meat chewing. "Yep."

I tapped my DEMOTER on the counter a few times sending a warning signal that it wasn't quite empty yet. "Can you get me some, on the double?"

He glanced down at the gun and sniffed. "That a standard Y-Series DEMOTER?"

"You bet." I puffed my chest out a bit.

The vendor laughed. "I thought they recalled those."

"Maybe they did, for fear of the awesome firepower." I narrowed my gaze.

He rolled the eye that wasn't hidden behind a patch. "Hey, you want to use relics, knock yourself out. We don't carry legacy energy packs here."

I grabbed my gun and holstered it. "Thanks for nothin'."

I stormed away from the booth ready to hurt someone. I was just thinking I should watch where I was going when I collided painfully with a vendor stand.

I cried out as my knee hit the dark wood display front. I looked up to find dozens of bright silver tongs dangling from a flowered lattice overhang. A lanky, blue-skinned Fruvintian vendor glanced down at me. A repulsed look crossed his face and suddenly he acted as if he was much too busy to speak with me. My knee was throbbing and I wanted to take the pain out on someone, and I decided the snooty vendor was a good place to start.

I cleared my throat and drummed my fingers with intentional bad rhythm on the immaculate ebony countertop of his booth. "'Scuse me, aren't you selling stuff here?" I said.

The blue vendor turned, his gold-stitched crimson robe shimmering as it followed his motion.

"I'm sorry sir, I don't think I have what you're looking for." He folded his hands neatly before him.

"You a mind reader?" I said.

Blix and Nelvan arrived and joined me at the counter.

"No sir." The vendor fidgeted with his hands at the sight of Blix. "It's just … I'm a vendor of fine fondue ware and I didn't think—"

"Exquisite." Blix lifted a highly polished fondue tong from an overhanging hook. "Is this from the Ventilly Blaise collection?"

The vendor took a small gasp and blinked several times. "Why no, but it's quite similar. You have a fine eye for design sir."

"Hm." Blix turned the tong over, his eyes narrowing. "This isn't a Messaveque tempered handle, is it?"

"The difference is really negligible. In some ways—"

"Please." Blix held up a hand. "Have you ever eaten from an authentic Ventilly Blaise set?"

The vendor's lower lip started to tremble. "Well, not exactly but—"

Blix waved his hand dismissively and set the tongs on the counter. "I've heard enough. Come Captain, we're wasting our time."

Blix walked away, his nose held high. The vendor looked after him, crestfallen.

I flashed a condescending smile. "Yeah, go peddle your secondhand trash to some other sucker."

The vendor frowned and made a tiny whimpering sound. I left the booth with Nelvan close behind. I caught up with Blix and slapped him on the back.

"Magnificent, my friend," I said. "I love it when your snobby knowledge comes in handy."

Blix grinned. "You see? A few choice words inserted at just the right time in a conversation can be far more powerful than brute force."

"I dunno, I could've blown that guy's head off with the DEMOTER. I think that would've been pretty powerful."

Blix turned to Nelvan. "You see what I've been telling you? He always resorts to violence."

I flashed a stern look at the both of them. "You talking about me behind my back?"

"It's a problem our whole crew must face, Captain," Blix said.

"Oh, it's *our* crew now, is it?" I narrowed my eyes at Nelvan.

Nelvan threw up his hands like he didn't want to take any sides.

"Well, maybe if I didn't have a pacifist as a first mate," I said. "I wouldn't have to do all the heavy lifting around here."

"It's only a season of peace," Blix said. "A stayed hand seeking peace is quite a different thing than pacifism. Take my stance on self defense for example—"

"Boring!" I said.

Blix frowned as I led the way through more vendor stands.

The stands sold everything from rare crimson verusal gemstones to lava forged Forglevian fighting armor with tasteful ebony inlays. I was suddenly reminded of how many things there were in the universe that I couldn't afford.

"I thought you said this place was dangerous." Nelvan was looking at the expensive wares in wonderment. "This is really nice."

"Yeah, well, it ain't the same spaceport I remember," I said.

"Indeed," Blix said. "You know, Captain, we stopped here nearly three gloons ago. Hamilton's foundation has made some considerable improvements since then."

"I liked it better before," I said.

"Yes, a pit of thieves and filth. If only we could return to that golden age," Blix teased.

"Okay, maybe I didn't like that either but all this finery and fakery is making me sick. I'm starting to feel like we never left Hamilton's ship." I stopped abruptly. A frightening thought bounded into my head like the decaying zombie bunnies with cybernetic limbs from Xenill 3.

Blix and Nelvan stopped with me.

"What is it?" Nelvan looked around in worry.

I paused for a moment to gather my thoughts. "Blix, why would someone go to all the expense of renovating a remote spaceport like this one?"

Blix nodded in agreement. "I was wondering the same thing."

"It's not really on the way to any big space colonies or super planets," I said. "It's a last stop for a few remote locations."

"Such as?" Blix grinned, already knowing what I was going to say.

"Beringfell."

I felt like someone punched me in the soul. My knees went wobbly. I sat down on the glittering sandstone flooring beneath us. A pattern of decorative beige starhorses graced the tiles at my feet. I let out a defeated sigh. "Hamilton is after it."

"After what?" Nelvan said.

"The Emerald Enigma. This must be his base of operations while he searches for it."

Blix leaned over and patted my shoulder. "Now Captain, even though every ounce of logic and common sense are inexplicably bound to that obvious conclusion, it's possible there's another reason."

My shoulders sank. I stared down at the starhorses. I wanted to ride one off to a universe where everything wasn't conspiring against me.

"Captain, please." Blix held out his hand.

I hesitated, then reluctantly grabbed his hand and let him help me up.

"I don't understand," Nelvan said. "What is this Enigma? Is it a powerful weapon or something?"

"No. It's ..." I wasn't sure exactly how to answer the question. "It's a life changer."

Nelvan turned to Blix with a look that hoped for more information.

But Blix was focused on something else: half a dozen slim,

grey-skinned Zeuthians drawing near. Their sinewy arms seemed in constant flex as their seven fingered hands gripped the curved hilts of their sheathed daggers. They seemed strangely out of place in the revamped spaceport. A throwback to how I remembered the old local scene. They strode alongside us with their unkempt head spines, dark, threadbare tunics and khaki kulats.

"As I was saying," Blix put on a low, gravelly voice. "Even though both of you are highly skilled in hand to hand combat and weaponry, there's more to life than fighting."

The Zeuthians gave a casual look our way as they passed. They had that hungry look in their eyes that I was used to seeing in star pirates down on their luck. They nodded their solemn faces at us, thick bronze rings dangling from their sharp noses.

Blix nodded back.

The Zeuthians continued forward without so much as a backward glance. Blix waited a few moments until they were out of earshot. "What do you think, Captain?"

"Trouble. Keep your distance," I said.

"Indeed. Very odd."

"Yeah, they probably haven't been here in awhile. Bet they're used to the old spaceport like us."

"Yes, and poorly dressed to boot. I mean, deep v-necks in the celestial frost season. Triple Veshul suns or not, that kind of fashion mistake is inexcusable."

"Just keep your eyes open," I said. "Zeuthians in this sector of the galaxy are dangerous. Where's the security around this place?"

Nelvan cleared his throat and raised his eyebrows at Blix.

"Yes?" Blix said.

"You were saying?" Nelvan made a rolling hand motion as if to prompt Blix. "About the Emerald Enigma?"

"Oh yes, right, well, you see Nelvan, the Enigma is really, for lack of a better term, a legend. It is said to bring unparalleled fortune to the finder. One of the most sought after and, as far as I know, never discovered objects in the universe."

"So it's possible that it doesn't even exist?" Nelvan said.

"Highly possible, yes," Blix said.

Nelvan turned to me looking thoroughly bewildered. "You mean you're expending your limited resources on a fluke? A myth?"

"Don't lecture me." My strength rushed back with the boy's insolent challenge to my quest. I leaned toward him and pointed a threatening finger at his chest. "You know nothing about the Emerald Enigma or even this universe. And as far as my limited resources go, I'm the captain of a starship with a crew. What do you have?"

Nelvan paused for a moment, a small frown on his face. He looked around at the vendor stands and passing travelers as if he had lost something. "I suppose I don't really have anything. I left it all in the past."

I gave a slow, confident nod to assert my authority. "That's right. Nothing. And here I am offering you a place aboard my ship as a crew member. If I were a lesser man, I could hand you over to the authorities right now for sneaking aboard my ship."

A trace of worry crossed Nelvan's face. He looked over at Blix for confirmation, who gave a noncommittal shrug.

"So how about showing a little respect to the only person who's helping you," I said.

Nelvan appeared thoughtful for a moment. "You're right. I

really don't have anywhere else to turn. I suppose you would be the best option."

"Hey, this isn't the consolation prize boy," I said. "Life aboard a starship is an opportunity of a lifetime. I can take back the offer if you're not excited about it."

"No, no, it's great and everything." Nelvan wore an unconvincing smile. "I'm still just trying to figure this all out."

"Mm, I'm afraid that's not good," Blix was looking across the common dome.

"What?" I followed Blix's gaze toward the walkway where we first entered and there was Mishmash. His grey head was swiveling back and forth as if he were looking for something.

"Quick, behind here." I ducked behind a stone pillar covered in climbing, flowering vines.

Blix and Nelvan followed close behind. I peeked out to find Mishmash hovering through the crowd, his cylindrical head constantly swiveling.

Blix peered around the pillar. "You know, there is something altogether unsound about that robot."

"Doesn't take a genius to figure that out." I searched for a good escape route nearby. There was a narrow walkway behind us with a garish, neon green sphere hovering above it that read, *Glemdragool's Space Bar.* A myriad of multicolored lights spun around the sign as if they were orbiting moons.

"Who's ready for a drink?" I said.

13

GLEMDRAGOOL'S SPACE BAR was not the seedy, mercenary filled hole I'd hoped for. Not that I liked seedy, mercenary filled holes of course. But, when necessary, they offer a good place to hide out when you are on the run.

Instead, we walked into a rich, wood paneled tavern filled with warm lights, clean glasses and civil patrons. We were as good as found.

"Does every place on this spaceport have to be pleasant?" I said.

"Oooh, they have Stemison's sparkling finemoggle here," Blix was staring at a row of spiraling green bottles behind the bar.

"Please, would you focus already?" I said. "We're in trouble here."

"Who said I'm not focused? I'm quite capable of multitasking you know."

"Oh really? So, once Hamilton and Mishmash come strolling into this altogether unscary space bar, you have a plan to get by them, unnoticed?"

"I'm working on it." Blix signaled to the bartender. "Barkeep, a moment of your time."

Blix strolled over to the bar leaving Nelvan and I standing there. I looked around at the patrons, hoping to find some inspiration. A group of squat, orange Venlippi ambassadors were playing quad-level quantum chess at the table closest to us. Several gangly, green Bellactians dressed in tasteful attire were peppered throughout the bar. They had impeccable posture and exhibited the finest of table manners while they sipped their spiked smoothies and algae wine. The whole lot of them made for the most unthreatening bar scene I had ever witnessed.

"This place isn't so bad," Nelvan said.

"That's the problem," I said.

"Why is that a problem?"

"Because we need cover. Distraction." I turned to Nelvan. "You ever been in a fight?"

Nelvan looked thoughtful for a moment. "Well, when I was seven I punched someone in the stomach."

"Okay, that's something. You win?"

Nelvan frowned. "Um, not exactly. She got kind of mad."

"*She*?"

"She was a year older than me and really mean."

I sighed. "Never mind." I scanned the back of the bar. I noticed a thick-limbed, heavily muscled Greyskallon sitting in the shadows. I pictured him crashing through the place with reckless abandon. Problem solved.

"We need to pick a fight. You up for your first assignment as part of my crew?"

Nelvan looked down at his hands and attempted to make fists. It seemed as though he had never done it before. It was a sad sight. "I try to avoid violence," Nelvan said.

"Maybe we should prepare ourselves for this." I put an arm around Nelvan and led him toward the bar. "We've only got a few freems to get this place rowdy."

"Okay, but I still don't know what a freem is."

"Nelvan, you've gotta keep up if you're gonna make it here. A freem is just a small increment of time." I snapped my fingers. "Like that."

"You mean a second?" Nelvan said.

"No, I mean a freem."

Nelvan looked sidelong at me, a pronounced frustration animating his features. "Look, I don't know where I am or even when I am, and now, on top of everything else, I don't know how to tell time. So, if I'm going to be part of your crew, and if you don't want me to completely lose it, I need you to explain."

It was a pleasant surprise to see a confrontational side to Nelvan. It made me think he could be more than just leverage against Hamilton. He might actually make a decent crew member one day. Of course, that would take gloons under my masterful teaching as an experienced space traveler but still, I saw potential.

"Hold that thought." I said as we reached the bar.

A wide assortment of colorful bottles in every conceivable shape lined the faux waterfall behind the bar. Blix turned as we joined him at the perfectly polished wooden counter.

"Cheers, my fellow shipmates." Blix hoisted his green, effervescent drink complete with blue and orange glass butterfly topped swizzle sticks.

I shook my head. "Can't you order a man's drink?"

"I'm not a man, I'm a Vythian." Blix grinned and sipped at his drink through a curvy straw. "What's wrong with Nelvan?"

I turned to find Nelvan with his arms folded across his chest, a frown on his face.

"I'm still waiting for Glint here to—" Nelvan started.

"Captain." I interrupted.

Nelvan clinched his teeth. He was losing patience with me,

like most people do. Since I knew it was inevitable, I always tried to hurry the process along.

"... I'm still waiting for the *captain* here to finish explaining your calendar." Nelvan's voice took on an edge of grittiness. It was a nice counter to his adolescent squeak. Not quite manly yet, but heading in the right direction.

"Oh, right, the calendar." I looked up as if I had forgotten the whole conversation. I leaned against the counter and cleared my throat in a professorial manner. "There's sixty-one freems in a jemmin, fifty-nine jemmins in a trid, twenty-five trids in a day, thirty days in a montul, eleven montuls in a gloon, except every other phase shift and quadra-reverberation, in which case gloons are lengthened, one hundred gloons in a century and of course, an era is an indeterminate measurement of time longer than any of those. Got it?"

"That's almost the same as an Earth calendar but you just changed some of the names," Nelvan huffed.

"Well, almost the same is not the same," I said.

Nelvan frowned.

"Captain, if I may." Blix held up one of his scaly fingers as if engaging in some academic round table. "You see Nelvan, when dealing with space-time, any variation, subtle as it may seem, can make a huge difference when calculated out exponentially, understand?"

"I suppose," Nelvan said.

"Let's say for example, two star cruisers leave this space port at the exact same moment." Blix lifted two glass butterfly topped swizzle sticks from his drink and put them side-by-side to simulate the star cruisers. "Both have virtually identical navigation headings save for a fraction of a micronaut in difference. No doubt their travels would be close initially but as their journey continued, they would grow farther apart until eventually, they might as well be on opposite ends of the galaxy." Blix spread the butterflies wide to simulate the distance. "Make sense?"

"Yes, actually that's very clear. Thank you," Nelvan said.

"Don't mention it, my boy," Blix grinned and took another sip of his drink.

"I'm the one that started the whole explanation," I said.

"Actually your part kind of confused me," Nelvan said.

"Hello friends, can I offer you some liquid refreshment?" A bartender arrived behind the bar, all smiles. He was human and altogether hygienic. His dark hair was slicked back with perfect symmetry and his shimmering blue tie was tucked neatly under a smart black vest.

"Don't you mean, 'what'll it be?'" I frowned.

"Sure, if that makes you more comfortable." The bartender's voice was filled with genuine helpfulness.

I rubbed my temples. This was the worst day ever. "Forget it, just get me an atom smasher with a twist of lime." I put my hand on Nelvan's shoulder. "And get my new crew member here a red triangle of death."

Nelvan shot me a worried look.

"Sounds like you fellas have had a rough day." The bartender winked and gave a good-natured grin. "Coming right up."

The bartender moved to the back of the bar by the faux waterfall and started pulling out a host of bottles and elixirs to make our drinks.

Nelvan gave me a worried look. "Red triangle of death?"

"Trust me." I patted him on the back and turned to Blix. "Okay, here's the plan. We start a bar fight. This will create a huge diversion so that when Hamilton and that accursed robot come in, we can slip away, unnoticed. Meanwhile, they'll get caught up in the fight and hopefully get roughed up a bit."

Blix took another sip of his drink and frowned. "That's your plan?"

"Yeah, that's right. The plan I had to come up with because you're too busy over here sipping your girly drink."

Blix slid his drink in front of me. "I'll bet you can't handle one sip."

I slid the drink back. "I don't want a mouthful of fruity liquid, thanks."

Blix slid it back in front of me. "Five vibes says you can't take a drink and keep a straight face."

I could see this was an unavoidable challenge. An affront to my authority as a captain and a lesson in the hierarchy of leadership that I had to teach Nelvan.

"Fine." I grabbed the skinny stem of the funnel shaped glass and pulled it closer. I yanked out the straw and threw it over my shoulder.

"Hey." Blix looked after the flying straw.

"Sorry, were you using that?" I lifted the glass to my lips. I took a long drink of the shimmery green liquid. At first it was just what I expected. Overly sweetened and jam packed with artificial fruit flavors. I smacked my lips dramatically. "Yep, that's about as sissy as it gets."

Blix just folded his arms and grinned, watching me.

"Now, as I was saying …" My stomach seemed to attempt a cartwheel. A horrific burning sensation went down my throat. I tried to mask the feeling by talking. "The plan, yes, the plan … good. I am … I like plan." There was a raging storm in my stomach. My throat felt as if it were filled with miniature space monkeys all crawling to get out.

Blix smiled. "Something wrong, Captain?" His twin rows of sharp teeth taunted me.

"Nos. Nosing matter," I said. "All gimlif and soadie." My tongue felt as if it had swollen to twice the size. I was having trouble speaking.

The bartender returned to the counter and handed us our drinks. "Here you are gentlemen."

I grabbed the atom smasher and downed half of it. The burning sensation in my throat subsided and my stomach, aside from a few rumbles of protest for what I had put it through, almost felt normal again.

"Oh, did I mention it's not meant for human consumption?" Blix smirked and took his drink back. "Bartender, another straw if you please."

The bartender nodded and handed Blix a straw. "If you fellas need anything else . . ." The bartender lifted a small, black disc from his pocket and clicked a button on top. It sprang from his hand and hovered over the counter before us. ". . . Just speak to the droid."

The bartender walked over to a few patrons at the other end of the bar. The disc droid flipped open and started playing an old folk-synth bar tune.

Take me home, starship sally,
Carry me on your winsome fumes,
Though the star pirates may rally,
You will always see me through . . .

"Switch to opera, please," Blix said.

A small blip sounded and the disc droid started playing an operatic tune.

"Hey, I liked that song," I said.

Blix shook his head. "Figures."

"No music," I said.

The music stopped and the disc droid snapped shut.

"Criminal. That was Chauzeruski's finest aria." Blix gave a wounded look.

"Hamilton could walk through that door any jemmin now. Unless you have a better idea, it's bar fight time."

Blix sighed and leaned toward the disc droid. "Bartender, a moment please."

"You gonna fight the bartender?" I said.

"Hardly."

I looked over at Nelvan, who was taking tentative sniffs of his dark amber drink.

"It ain't gonna bite boy. Take a swig," I said.

Nelvan cupped the triangular glass with both hands and lifted it to his mouth. He looked at the red liquid as if it were poison. He closed his eyes and took a sip.

"Well?" I said.

He opened his eyes as if surprised to be alive. "Actually, it's not bad."

"See? What did I tell you?"

"Sort of tastes like rhubarb. And here I thought . . ." Nelvan paused, placing a hand on his cheek. "That's odd. Something's not quite right."

I squeezed the wedge of lime into my atom smasher and swished the drink around.

"Is it getting hot in here?" Nelvan looked at me, his face flushed.

"Turn that way please." I motioned to the bar.

Nelvan turned to the bar and belched. A stream of fire shot out, licking at the rows of bottles on the far wall.

The bartender arrived, sliding under Nelvan's stream of fire as if it were part of a rehearsed show. "Nice one, my friend." The bartender pointed at Nelvan and winked.

Nelvan gave me a wide-eyed look, smoke rising from his mouth in thin plumes. I nodded my approval.

"You called?" The bartender turned to Blix.

"I don't suppose you have a back door to this fine establishment?" Blix said.

The bartender seemed embarrassed by the question. "Oh, um, sort of."

"Either you do or you don't," I said.

The bartender looked around as if worried someone might be listening, then leaned in close. "The byways behind our beautifully refinished spaceport have not quite, er, been dealt with yet."

I felt a glimmer of hope returning. "You mean, the way the spaceport used to be?"

"Actually, a bit worse." The bartender gave an embarrassed grin. "I must confess, some of the wandering dregs of our enlightened society still roam free. Our security forces are spread a bit thin lately with all the mandatory politeness training."

"Don't worry, we can take care of ourselves," I said. "Where's the back door."

"Well, I'm not really supposed to say," the bartender said.

I took out a few vibes and slid them across the bar.

"Make sure you save five for me." Blix grinned.

I shot him an annoyed look.

The bartender took the vibes and looked around. "Okay,

head toward the bathroom and pull the handle to the right three times. That should subluxate the quantum stream locking coordinates and reopen the path momentarily. Just close the door behind you, got it?"

"Got it. Much obliged." I saluted the bartender with my glass and took another drink.

"Just don't go all at once." The bartender took another cautious look around. "Make it look casual. If the owner sees all three of you headed for the door, he might get suspicious."

"No problem," I said.

"Okay. Be careful. It's rough out there." The bartender gave a nervous grin and walked away.

"You see?" Blix said. "Isn't that much better than fighting?"

"Sure, whatever. Let's just go before they get here."

"Hello boys." Jasette slid between Blix and I, signaling to the bartender. "Spritz water, please. Slide it on down."

The bartender gave a stylish spin from halfway down the bar. He pointed both fingers at Jasette and grinned. "Coming right up, beautiful." He grabbed a clear, effervescent bottle from the back wall and flipped it into his other hand. He placed it on the counter and slid it down to Jasette.

Jasette caught the bottle and blew a kiss to the bartender. He pretended to catch it and placed it on his heart.

"I think I'm gonna be sick," I said.

"So, what's the plan?" Jasette said.

"Where'd you come from?" I said.

"The front door, like you." Jasette opened the bottle and took a drink. "I would've thought you'd at least have Nelvan on guard."

"And where's your new boyfriend, Hamilton?" I said.

"Shouldn't he be here ordering you the most expensive thing they have?"

"That game is over thanks to you." Jasette gave me an irritated look before taking another drink.

"Thanks to me?"

"Your little comment about my weaponry knowledge got him thinking. After that, he was all questions. It was just a matter of time before he figured things out so I had to slip away."

"You mean you're not part of an undercover task force?" Blix smirked.

"Look, I have my reasons for what I do." Jasette glanced at the front door. "I'm guessing we only have a few jemmins. I say we join forces until we're free of this spaceport, then go our separate ways."

"Join forces with you?" I laughed. "Why would I do that? I don't trust you one bit. For all I know you could be acting as a spy for Hamilton right now?"

"What kind of warped logic makes you think that?"

"Gee, I dunno. Maybe it was the way you were clinging to his every word, hoping to sail through the skies in his luxury cruiser, stopping off at all the super planets for expensive gifts and—"

"Hey, dis guy boddering you, miz?" A towering figure stood behind me. It was the big Greyskallon I'd seen sitting in the shadows. He was a living wall of over pumped grey muscle straining to break through a thin, white shirt that read, 'Serberat-Gellamede locals only.'

"Yeah, I'm bothering her. What's it to ya?" I said.

His large fist grasped my lucky, silver shirt that suddenly didn't seem so lucky and hoisted me in the air. I was pulled toward a piggish grey face with extra folds of skin in all the wrong places.

"Whad'ja say, ya filthy tourist?" The large brute said.

I started to rethink the whole bar fight idea. In my desperate quest for diversion and escape I'd forgotten all about the pain and broken teeth.

"Wait a freem, I think I've heard about you," I said. "What's your name?"

"Tomblik. Whad'ja hear?" A new series of folds appeared around the beady eyes of his bulbous face.

"Yeah, that's right, Tomblik. You're the one those guys were calling oafish and dim," I said.

Tomblik craned his neck to the tables behind us. "Who said dat?"

"Well, there was this big, suave looking guy who walked around like he owned this place. I think his name was Hamilton."

A trace of doubt crossed Tomblik's face. "Hamilton Von Drone?"

"Yeah, that's him. Him and that skinny robot of his were talking about how they were taking over this spaceport and all the dim-witted locals with it. They mentioned you as the dimmest one of all."

"I knew dat skrid wuz up ta somefin." Tomblik lowered me, the wheels in his head turning, turning, turning ever so slowly.

I straightened my shirt and glanced over at Blix. Blix nodded approval and took another sip of his drink.

"If only someone could put that guy in his place." I gave a theatrical look upward as if lost in thought.

"Yeah, a good poundin' do da trick." Tomblik slammed a fist into his palm.

"Yes, if only there was someone big and powerful that could teach him." I looked up at Tomblik, waiting for the moment of enlightenment.

"Yeah." Tomblik scratched his head. "If only."

I sighed, wondering how long this would take.

"I'll bet a proud Greyskallon like you could put a filthy new blood like Hamilton where he belongs," Jasette said.

Tomblik fixed his gaze upon Jasette, a new fire in his eyes.

"Ya know, das right. I could crush. I could crush right good m'self." Tomblik said.

"You could show him the fire of the old days," Jasette said. "Show him what a new blood knows nothing of."

Tomblik was all fists and flexing at this point. "Yeah. I show 'em." He looked around the bar, his breathing erratic. "Where he at?"

"Out in the common dome," I said.

Tomblik flared his nostrils and stormed out of the bar. I felt my heart rate slowing back down to a semi-normal rhythm.

Blix clapped his hands. "Well done, Captain."

"Not a bad bit of teamwork, huh?" Jasette lifted her water to me and took a drink.

"Yeah, well. Still doesn't mean I trust you," I said.

"I can tell when people lie," Nelvan said.

There was a moment of silence as we all turned to Nelvan.

"Um, what?" I said.

"Well, if you want to know if we can trust her, I can tell if she's lying," Nelvan said.

I gave Nelvan a curious stare. "How?"

"I dunno, I just can. I've always been able to tell." Nelvan looked over at Jasette with an apologetic shrug.

Jasette put down her drink and fixed her full attention on

Nelvan. "Well then ..." She gave a seductive batting of her eyes and sauntered over to him. She was putting her full feminine powers forward in an attempt to intimidate the poor boy. "... Do your worst, Nelvan."

Nelvan cleared his throat. His nervous twitching found its way back into his mannerisms once again. "Um, okay, put both of your hands out, palms up."

"Hold on, I gotta see this." I walked in front of them to make sure I didn't miss anything.

Jasette put her hands out and gave him a sultry grin. Nelvan raised his trembling hands and placed his fingertips on her wrists.

"Okay, now, I'm going to ask you a couple of questions," Nelvan said. "Answer honestly."

"Of course." Jasette spoke in an innocent tone.

I glanced back at Blix. He raised his scaly brows as he watched them, looking as curious as I was.

"Are you spying on us for Hamilton?" Nelvan said.

Jasette gave a wounded look. "Of course not."

Nelvan closed his eyes and concentrated a moment. His eyes opened and he looked at me, nodding as if in agreement.

I gave an unsure look back to Blix. He shrugged and looked back at Nelvan.

"Okay, let's see, how about ... do you really want to team up with us to escape this spaceport or do you mean us harm?" Nelvan said.

"I want to team up and escape. Then I'll go my own way." Jasette started to sound annoyed.

Nelvan paused, then looked up with a smile and a nod.

"Ask her if she's really a bounty hunter?" I said.

Jasette gave an irritated glance my way.

"Are you a bounty hunter?" Nelvan said.

"Yes," Jasette said.

Nelvan waited a few moments longer than before. He looked up with an unsure expression.

"Can't say for sure on that one," Nelvan said.

A loud scuffle broke out just outside the door of the bar.

Blix downed the last of his drink. "Captain, I think we should be going."

"Right. Good enough." I looked at Jasette. "You can come with us until we're free of this place, but you better not try anything funny."

"You have my word." Jasette fixed me with a sincere look.

Her green eyes shimmered from the reflections of the fake waterfall behind the bar. As much as I wanted to mistrust and distance myself from this woman, all the best lighting, locations, and cosmic forces of attraction were conspiring against me to make her the most beautiful woman in the universe.

I gave a quick glance around the bar as if I hadn't given her a moment's thought.

"One at a time. Make it look natural."

I made my way to the bathroom, taking casual looks around to make sure no one was near me. I reached the door and pulled the handle three times to the right. An electrical buzzing sounded and a blue flash of light outlined the space around the doorframe. I pushed open the door and a grimy alleyway lay before me. I breathed a sigh of relief.

"Home sweet home."

14

THE GRIMY ALLEYWAY was everything a grimy alleyway should be: unsanitary, bleak and a haven for hapless vagrants. A brown haze traveled with a sluggish creep through the sky overhead, obscuring the three suns.

I stepped into the alley and closed the door behind me. It disappeared with an electric crackle and a flash of blue light. In its place was the outer wall of the white dome that protected all the stores and walkways from the harsh outer atmosphere of Serberat Gellamede.

The wide alley cut a crooked path through a series of low, flat-roofed dwellings. Brown grime was so prevalent in the foundations and corners of the tan colored buildings that it seemed part of the local design theme.

I began walking down the alleyway and took a breath. I immediately regretted it. My nostrils felt a slight burn with the musky aroma of old, dead vermin that had lived desperate lives constantly scrounging for scraps, then been captured and kept as pets, then eaten when times got rough, then cleaned and had their bones used as decorative vagrant jewelry.

Out of the corner of my eye I saw a figure step from the shadows. I turned and came face to face with the barrel of his laser pistol.

"Hold it, space trash." A scuzzy looking Fruvintian thug stood before me. He wore a dark orange tunic that bore a distinctive zig-zag symbol known as 'The Mark of Ultimate Fury.' It was a fairly new symbol that was catching on with young, up and coming street thugs throughout the universe. The definition of the symbol varied from planet to planet but the basic meaning was, 'I'm unhappy for no particular reason and I feel like hurting someone.'

"I like yer jacket. Maybe I be takin' it." An angry sneer animated his deep blue skin, making his cat-like features look feral. His bloodshot eyes darted about as he spoke, like he was having trouble keeping them still. His head had a strange tick that made it look like someone kept yanking at his hair, even though he was bald. Though I had no frame of reference for his normal demeanor, my guess was he was on edge.

"Easy friend, I ain't moving." I lifted my hands to ease his nerves.

"Good. 'Cuz ye'll lose yer head if ye even twitch funny," he said.

I found the statement fantastically hypocritical given his twitchy demeanor, but he had the gun so I decided not to point out inconsistencies.

"Good nab boss." A deep, gruff voice said behind me.

I took a careful look back. Two bulky Fruvintians in grimy, dark clothes emerged from a narrow alley between the squat buildings. They held laser rifles casually aimed in my direction.

An electrical zap sounded and a rectangle of blue light flashed a few steps away. Nelvan walked into the alley from a glowing doorway. He gave a startled jump as he realized the situation.

"Don't shoot, I'm unarmed." Nelvan lifted his hands high as the blue doorway closed behind him.

The two heavy thugs aimed their rifles at him. "We got us another one boss."

The boss thug chuckled. "Hope ye got plenty o' vibes between ye."

Nelvan gave me a nervous glance.

"We have some. Everyone just relax. I'll get my vibes and …" I started to reach toward the jacket pocket near my DEMOTER.

"Freeze." The boss thug hit a switch on his laser pistol and the end of the barrel started flashing red. "Griffix, Blag, take his weapon."

Griffix and Blag moved forward, each grabbing me by one arm. One of the thugs took my DEMOTER and tossed it on the ground nearby.

"He's got no teeth now boss." The thug chuckled.

There was another electrical zap followed by a rectangle of blue light and suddenly Jasette was standing next to Nelvan. She drew both of her silver blasters in a flash and aimed them at the two thugs behind me.

"Not so fast, pretty thing." The boss thug moved his blaster from my head to Jasette. "If ye dare fire, it's the last thing ye'll do."

Jasette glanced from the boss thug to the others, keeping her guns trained on Griffix and Blag.

"Easy boys, we don't want trouble." The situation was escalating and I needed to calm things down.

Normally, with my DEMOTER at the ready, I'd be making plans of who to blast first and what cool diving move I would leap into while I fired on my foes. Now that I was unarmed, peace seemed a far nobler road.

"We can give you our vibes with no trouble at all," I said. "Let's all just put the guns down and talk."

"Yeah, he speaks right clear. Put 'em down lady," the boss thug said.

"You first," Jasette said.

Another electrical zap sounded. Blix stepped out of the rectangle of blue light and into the alley.

"Hello, what's all this?" Blix gave a wistful look at the thugs as if we'd all been standing there sipping tea.

The boss thug took a step back. The erratic darting of his eyes increased in intensity. He swiveled his laser gun back and forth between all of us as if he couldn't decide who to target. "H-Hold it there. I warn ye."

Blix put his hands out in a pleading gesture. "Please, gentlemen. No need for hostilities."

"Griffix, get yer scorch dagger." The boss thug's voice took on a nervous edge.

Griffix drew a curved dagger with a glowing red blade. He glanced from his rifle to the dagger as if bolstering his confidence with the additional weapon.

"A scorch dagger in this sector of the galaxy." Blix gave a patronizing nod. "A primitive make from the look of it but still, quite rare."

"Yeah, it can cut through that thick Vythian hide o' yers so watch it," the boss thug said.

"Oh, you needn't worry about me. I'm still in my season of peacemaking," Blix smiled.

A confused look replaced the worry on the boss thug's face. He was quiet for a moment as if his brain was having trouble processing the new information. "Really?"

I shot Blix a stern look. He winked at me and grinned.

"Yes, and I must say, I'm quite enjoying it," Blix said.

The boss thug gave a nervous chuckle. He looked over at Griffix and Blag with a relieved smile. "Hear that boys? He's a peacemaking Vythian."

Griffix and Blag let out a few guffaws that sounded more like coughing than laughter.

"Don't let him fool you, he's dangerous." I tried to salvage the situation.

"Captain, please. Now then, let's give these nice Fruvintian chaps our vibes and I'm sure they'll let us be on our way. Isn't that right gentlemen?" Blix cast a conciliatory look at the thugs.

A wide grin spread across the boss thug's face, revealing several missing teeth. "Yeah, that's right. Jes' tell the girl to drop them guns and give us yer vibes."

Blix smiled and motioned for Jasette to lower her laser guns. She glanced back, annoyed. Blix tilted his head to the side and gave a pleading look. Jasette frowned and slowly put the guns back in their holsters. She kept her hands close to the handles as she maintained a careful watch on the thugs.

"There now, yer troubles are almost at an end," the boss thug said.

Blix produced two handfuls of vibes from his pockets. "Okay, here's all my vibes. Who wants them?"

"Griffix." The boss thug motioned for Griffix to retrieve them.

Griffix hesitated. He gave a questioning look back to the boss.

"Well go on, ya simpering twit." The boss thug urged Griffix onward with a tilt of his head. Or it might have just been his nervous tick again. It was hard to tell.

Griffix left my side and took tentative steps over to Blix,

looking as if he were a young boy about to get in trouble. Griffix held the scorch dagger tight and the rifle trained on Blix.

"Hello there. Griffix, is it?" Blix leaned down to Griffix, his face filled with friendliness.

Griffix cleared his throat. "Uh, yeah."

"Excellent. Now which hand would you like me to put these vibes in?" Blix said.

Griffix looked from the rifle to the dagger as if deciding which friend to abandon. He finally grabbed the strap of the rifle and slung it over his shoulder, all the while keeping a close watch on Blix.

Griffix held his open hand toward Blix. Blix smiled and poured all his vibes into it. Half of them fell to the dusty, grey earth. Griffix frowned as if he hadn't considered this possibility.

"Sorry about that old chap. Guess you need a bigger hand, eh?" Blix gave him a friendly slap on the shoulder. Griffix stumbled sideways and dropped a few more vibes.

"Well, pick 'em up, stumblebeast," the boss thug said.

Griffix cast a frustrated look back at the boss. He dropped to one knee and started retrieving the fallen vibes and putting them in his pockets. He gave a nervous glance up at Blix every few moments.

"In a way I'm going to miss this way of life." Blix placed his hands on his hips and let out a long sigh. "It's very calming."

Griffix gave a confused look at Blix as he rose to his feet, his hand filled with vibes.

"What do ye mean?" Griffix said.

"Hmm?" Blix acted as though he'd just been woken from a daydream. "Oh, today is the last day of my season of peace. Tomorrow begins my season of vengeance."

The boss thug's eyes started to dart about once again. "S-season of vengeance, ye say?"

"Yes, I'm afraid so." Blix shook his head. "Nothing but cold blooded revenge and a berserker frenzy of retribution. Nasty business it is."

Griffix dropped the rest of the vibes and started to back away, both hands gripping the scorch dagger.

"Oh, not that I won't relish it at first. Such things come all too naturally for Vythians." Blix looked at the boss thug. "I don't suppose you've ever seen a Vythian caught in the blood-lust of revenge?"

The boss thug started to tremble. "Um, n-no."

Blix hung his head. "Mmm … Well, I'd like to apologize now for any severe pain or permanent damage I cause you and your charming associates." Blix motioned to Griffix and Blag. "It's not really something I can control you see."

Griffix and Blag started to back away.

"Y'know, this whole thing, it's really a joke." The boss thug gave a forced laugh. "Jes a gag really. We don't want yer vibes, do we boys?" The boss thug gave a desperate look at the others.

Griffix and Blag gave confused nods.

"We was jes having a bit o' fun with ya. Griffix, give him back those vibes, will ya."

Griffix emptied his own pockets, flinging the vibes toward Blix but still backing away.

"In fact, here's some of my vibes fer the trouble." The boss thug grabbed a handful of vibes from his pocket and tossed them at my feet. He backed toward the narrow passageway between the houses behind him. "A pleasure meeting one 'n all 'specially the most understanding and forgivin' Vythian I ever met." The boss thug bowed toward Blix.

Blix gave a slight bow in return.

"Must be going now, 'ave a pleasant day." The boss thug turned and bolted into the shadows. Griffix and Blag followed suit and soon we were alone in the alley.

Blix folded his arms and smiled at me.

"Okay, I gotta admit, that was good," I said.

"Yes, well, someone was about to get shot and I have no confidence in the medical facilities out here," Blix said.

I retrieved my DEMOTER and started picking up fallen vibes.

"Are you really about to start a season of vengeance?" Nelvan looked worried.

"Not to worry my lad, it was just a ruse." Blix stooped to retrieve his vibes. "But close to truth. I am in my season of peace, you see, but it doesn't end for another three days. And my season of battle starts next, not vengeance. Still combative, yes, but far more controlled."

"And these seasons, you're bound by them?" Nelvan said.

"Well, mostly. Our cultural traditions are quite strict on the subject." Blix put the remaining vibes in his pockets, then stood and dusted off his hands. "The season of peace is generally considered the toughest for our race. We are aggressive by nature. Though I daresay, I'm a bit more refined than most of my brethren."

"Maybe you should go back to your roots." I scanned the ground for any remaining vibes. "Start flexing more of that Vythian muscle when I need you in a tough spot."

Blix pointed an accusing finger at me and turned to Nelvan. "You see. That's the problem. With all the harrowing situations the captain has put me through, my adherence to non-combative life has been quite unsuccessful."

"I'm just keeping your fighting skills sharp," I said. "When your battle season starts, you'll thank me."

Blix gave me a dark look. "Well, perhaps I'll just become a peaceful Vythian."

"Don't even joke about that." I stood and took a quick scan of the alley. "Now let's get out of here before the next batch of thugs show up."

I headed down the alley and the others followed behind.

15

WE CONTINUED DOWN the middle of the wide alley, our feet kicking up the thin layer of dust on the ground.

"There's quite an odor out here." Blix took a distasteful looking sniff. "Perhaps we should go back to the bar."

"Yes, please." Nelvan looked nervous.

"Stop acting like a bunch of women," I said.

Jasette gave me a cross look. "Excuse me?"

"I meant nice women."

Jasette gripped the silver handles of her laser guns. "I can scar you without hitting any vitals, you know. I have fantastic aim."

"Please, please." Blix held out his hands to us. "We need to stick together if we're going to get out of here, okay?"

"Fine." I noticed something moving in the shadows up ahead. I drew my DEMOTER and aimed. I didn't want to get caught off guard this time.

A dark, huddled form in tattered brown clothes turned from a dwelling nearby to face me. It was an old Fruvintian woman with weathered blue skin. She was stooped over a cracked bucket filled with dirty water. She leaned toward me and pointed a shaky finger as I approached.

"Go back." She stared at me with bloodshot eyes. "Go back from whence ye came."

"Thanks but we just got here. S'cuse me." I moved around

her with the others trailing behind, giving the woman wide berth as they passed.

"Thar be dragons afoot. Dragons I say!" Her finger was trembling wildly as she pointed after us. "Beware the crimson sphere. Beware!"

The woman continued to point and stare after us as we headed down the alley.

"What was that all about?" Nelvan's voice was shaky.

I put my DEMOTER back in the holster. "Nothin'. Lots of crazies out here."

"Just to be safe, I say we avoid any crimson spheres for the remainder of the day," Blix said.

The squat houses on either side of us were packed so close together I started to feel claustrophobic. Even worse, every so often I noticed a pair of beady eyes watching us from the small, square windows of the humble buildings.

"Blix, keep an eye out," I said.

Blix nodded and peered back and forth between the houses.

"Do you even know where you're going?" Jasette said.

I gave an annoyed look back. "It's an alley. There's only one way to go."

A grey skinned Zeuthian emerged from a house on our left. He matched my height but was slender, with taut muscles like he ran obstacle courses all day. He kept pace with us on the side of the road, glancing over now and then in a casual manner.

"What's with him?" I whispered.

"Looks like one of the Zeuthians we saw back in the main dome," Blix whispered.

Another Zeuthian emerged from a house on the right side of the street. He followed along with us as well. He drew a dagger strapped at his side, ran his finger along the blade as if making sure it was sharp, then resheathed it.

"They seem friendly," Blix whispered.

"There's only two of them." Jasette kept a casual watch on our new followers.

"Who are they?" Nelvan started trembling. "What do they want?"

"Shh." I held a finger to my lips. "Just act natural."

Nelvan walked in a very stiff manner, his eyes darting back and forth to the sides of the road, looking about as unnatural as possible.

Two more Zeuthians emerged from the shadows and joined the one on the left. Both had semi-repeater blasters slung over their shoulders.

"We should go back," Nelvan squeaked.

"Quiet. We can handle four of them," I said.

Five more Zeuthians joined the one on the right side of the road. Each with dual laser swords strapped to their back and blasters at their side.

"Okay, now we're in trouble," I said.

Nelvan let out a small whimpering sound.

"Blix, you thinking what I'm thinking?" I said.

"Clensor defense cloud?" Blix said.

"What? No, totally impractical. I'd need four arms for the beginning alone."

Several snipers emerged from the rooftops ahead, training their weapons on us.

"I'm thinking the Fendule containment triangle," I said. "We can use Nelvan as the wounded soldier character."

"Now who's being impractical?" Blix said. "You need three skilled marksmen for the triangle."

"Would you two shut up," Jasette hissed. "We're about to get killed here. Let's just do a simple split. Glint takes left, I go right, Blix charges forward."

I shook my head. "What a rookie move. Lady, you wouldn't last two freems on some of the planets we've been to."

A laser blast stirred a cloud of dust at my feet. We froze in position and exchanged tense glances.

"We mean you no harm." Blix held up his hands. "We just want to pass through."

Two red beams shot from the rooftops, catching Blix on each shoulder. He took a couple twisted steps backward as the energy beams connected.

I gave him a questioning look, hoping to get a sense of their firepower. Blix arched his scaly brow and gave me a serious nod. We were in trouble.

I turned to Jasette and nodded. "Nelvan, on the ground! Simple split it is!" I ducked and angled left, the DEMOTER in my hand in a flash. I blasted two Zeuthians off their feet before they knew what was happening.

The next few moments were a rush of laser blasts and yelling. Out of the corner of my eye I saw Jasette dropping to the ground and rolling, both silver pistols held forward and sending rapid-fire beams into the gang that gathered on our right. Several fell as her well-placed shots tore into them.

Blix charged forward, flinging his small daggers an unbelievably far distance toward the rooftop snipers, taking them out one by one.

Laser beams flew past me at every turn and I felt one tear a hole through my jacket, just grazing my side.

A Zeuthian jumped directly into my path, twin laser swords drawn. His scabby lips parted in a vicious smile, showing an unseemly row of broken, yellowed teeth. He did a quick flurry of his glowing green swords, preparing to attack. I angled the DEMOTER toward him wondering, in slow motion it seemed, whether I would get the blast off before he sliced me in half.

I was about to squeeze the trigger when a bright burst of light hit the ground with an explosion that rang in my ears like some unholy symphony. The force of the blast blew us both backward. As I flew several feet into the air and felt myself slipping into unconsciousness, I wondered if we should've just stayed at the bar.

16

I AWOKE IN A darkened room, lying on a cold stone slab. I felt several tiny pinpricks moving over my feet. I looked down to find dozens of miniature metal spiders crawling on my feet and up my legs.

I wanted to leap up and scream but I was frozen in fear. I had a sense that any movement I made would anger them. And of course, the only thing worse than a swarm of metal spiders is a swarm of angry metal spiders.

As they reached my thighs an involuntarily twitching ran throughout my body. The spiders became agitated. They started to crawl faster. Dozens of them scurried under my shirt and started creeping up my stomach with their cold, metal legs. That's when I lost it.

I screamed and sat up, brushing frantically at my body. Suddenly I realized it was just a horrible dream. Not a single metal spider in sight.

I was in a well-lit, spacious room, lying on a cushioned cot. The walls were finely glazed sandstone covered with pricey looking rugs and paintings. A human sized medical droid was at my side, his thin metal fingers raised up in response to my abrupt awakening. I glared at the droid's metal fingers. All his poking and prodding were probably the sensation that sparked my nightmare.

"Beat it, robot," I said.

The droid emitted a few sharp twerping sounds and then hovered away with his head lifted as if I were no longer worthy of his attention. My head ached and felt thick, as if my brain was swollen.

"I was wondering when you'd wake up," a familiar voice said.

Reclining on a merzuvial-hide octagon in the corner of the room was a gruff looking man with shaggy, brown hair, who looked about twenty five gloons old. He wore dark shades, a metallic, midnight blue jacket and had twin, titanium plated, Ultra-DEMOTERs holstered at his side.

He was incredibly familiar but I couldn't quite place the face. He was the kind of guy I'd expect to see on some stop over planet, tourist trap, space bar. I imagined him hustling visitors out of vibes by day and smooth talking the ladies at night.

"You must be thirsty." He turned to a spherical droid with several arms that manned a circular bar in the opposite corner. "Barbot, two quasar chasers on ice."

He stood, lifting the slim pair of dark shades from his eyes. That's when I recognized him.

"Lerk Buzzane. Mr. Ghost Ship himself." I felt relieved to find a friendly face when I'd expected to wake up to grizzly, tormenting captors.

"Ghost ship?" Lerk gave a challenging grin. "Hey, just because you edged me out of a few academy races doesn't mean you were a better pilot ..." Lerk walked over to the small bar where the sphere robot spun back and forth, his thin arms lifting, stirring and mixing in record time. "... You just cared too much."

Lerk still had that confident swagger I remembered from the academy several gloons ago, but something was different.

There was a weariness in the way he carried himself and spoke. It was as if he'd lost too many games that everyone had expected him to win.

"I had to keep my focus to stay on top of the heap," I said.

Lerk grinned. "All that focus and you still didn't win the apprenticeship."

I frowned. "It was stolen from me."

Lerk held up his hands. "Ancient history, bud." He smiled as the barbot handed him two clear glasses. A green and blue liquid swirled playfully inside. "Another time, another life."

Lerk walked closer and held a drink forward. "This'll help clear out the cobwebs."

I turned on the cot and dropped my feet to the floor. I grabbed the glass and took a small drink. The liquid was velvety and seemed to hold dozens of soft little explosions that triggered every sensation on the tongue from sour to sweet. It was delicious and, no doubt, expensive.

"Not quite the man's drink I would've expected from an old star pilot," I said.

Lerk chuckled and sat down next to me. "My tastes have changed over the gloons, my friend. And apparently so have yours. What's with the pants?" Lerk gave a questioning look at my pajama pants.

"Long story." I took a silent vow never to wear pajama pants again. Coupled with the fresh laser-blasted hole in my black jacket, my appearance lacked my usual starship captain punch. I took another glance around the room and realized there were no windows. "Where are we?"

"You're in the heart of Outer Serberat. Smack dab among the dregs of our spaceport. Only the bold survive here, my friend." Lerk tilted back his glass and took a long drink.

"You live here?" I gave him a confused look.

"You might say I run the place. That is, as much as you can run a bunch of thugs."

I stood to my feet and swayed. In addition to my headache, my balance was off. I leaned on the wall to steady myself and dropped my glass. It shattered on the floor leaving a sparkling pool of blue liquid.

"Easy, Glint. You got hit with a concussion disc," Lerk said. "You can't just leap up and start shooting more of my soldiers."

A small cleaning droid emerged from a low door in the wall and promptly mopped up my drink.

"Your soldiers?" My head was spinning. "You're a star pilot. What're you doing running some kind of criminal underworld?"

He leaned back and let out a hearty laugh. "Glint, you're priceless. Listen to you talking like you're still some naïve academy kid."

"You should be out there in the stars, pushing the boundaries like we always talked about."

He rolled his eyes. "We had a lot of dreams back when we were a couple of punk pilots. We live in the great big universe now." Lerk motioned to the walls of the room as if it were the whole of space and took a long drink.

I took a few clumsy steps and bumped into a tall silver statue. I regained my footing and stabilized the swaying replica of Quantiffal, the fabled nine headed creature from Glinzer 7.

"Watch it, that cost me a bundle."

The overhead point lighting gleamed off the nine enraged open maws of Quantiffal.

"This thing?" I said. "You got ripped off."

Lerk laughed. "Actually I stole it. But I hear it's worth a lot."

"Listen, um, it's been great reminiscing but I had my crew with me and ..."

"Ah yes," Lerk stood and drained the rest of his glass. "Your crew." Lerk sneered as he walked toward the center of the room. He stepped on a panel in the floor, activating a wide, translucent green holoscreen that ascended from the ground.

A three dimensional image of Blix appeared on the right side of the screen and spun slowly. His scaled copper skin shimmered with the latest holotech enhanced color. A moving scroll of text appeared on the left side of the screen with detailed records of his ancestry, culture and known history.

"A Vythian no less." Lerk raised his eyebrows at me. "You must've won some wild card game to gain his services."

"He volunteered."

"Really?" Lerk arched a brow as if he didn't believe me. "Well, according to my records he's in his season of peace, though some of my wounded guards would beg to differ. You taking pacifists aboard your crew now?" Lerk looked at me as if waiting for an explanation.

"Something like that."

"Hmm." Lerk looked back at the scrolling text. "It says here that in three days he begins his season of battle." Lerk gave me a knowing smile. "I expect he'll be quite the formidable ally soon."

I tried to keep my expression blank, not wanting to let him see that he'd figured out exactly what I'd been waiting for for the last few gloons. "Is that so?"

Lerk nodded. "I'm sure that's all news to you."

"Eh, I never give those cultural traditions much thought," I lied.

"He's not the big catch, anyways."

Lerk tapped a few touch panels on the screen and the image switched to Jasette. She looked a few gloons younger and was dressed in a deep purple dress replete with intricate stitching. Her hair was arranged in a spiraling tower with glistening gemstones twinkling throughout. Extravagant jewelry decorated nearly every inch of her body.

"Now this one took some digging." Lerk pointed to the image of Jasette. "Had to run some high level hacking routines to get to the truth."

I stared, perplexed, at the high society image of Jasette. "Yeah, that puzzle took some unraveling." I tried to sound like I knew what he was talking about.

"Why you'd want to cart around some errant princess is beyond me. There's not even any reward money offered."

My mind hung on the word 'princess'. All her high maintenance ways suddenly made perfect sense. "She's decent in a tough spot. All in all not a bad crew member."

Lerk shrugged. "To each his own."

"Wait a freem, if there's no reward money, why is she the 'big catch'?"

"Oh, she's not the catch." Lerk touched a few more panels on the screen and an image of Nelvan appeared. The informational text on the left side of the screen was blank. "This is the big fish of the day."

"Nelvan?" I shot Lerk a confused look. "He's nothing. A nobody."

Lerk crossed his arms and grinned. "Sure, sure he is."

"No, really. He's more trouble than he's worth."

"Do you know how much it costs to get your records erased?" Lerk raised his eyebrows. "And this ain't just uniweb combed info. We're talking facial recognition, tissue sample cross-referencing, DNA scans, nothing. It all comes up empty."

"Well, that's just because …" I struggled to come up with something remotely believable.

"Yes?" Lerk gave an expectant look.

"… because he's a member of my crew and I don't owe you our life story."

"Yeah, quite a few stories when it comes to your crew." Lerk tapped at the touch screen and an image of me wearing my old academy uniform materialized with a moving scroll of text. "Including some of your own."

I gave Lerk a good scowl. "What do you think you're doing?"

Lerk looked at the text. "Would you look at this? A bounty of fifty thousand vibes on your head."

"Fifty thousand?" My heart dropped. "That can't be right. It's only a hundred."

"I'm afraid it's been upgraded by none other than Mar Mar the Unthinkable himself."

"Mar Mar!" I felt hollow and weak. The worst gangster in the universe had upgraded my bounty. "I only met him once five gloons ago and I was very polite."

"Now he wants your head."

I leaned against the statue again. Fifty thousand vibes was a death sentence. I couldn't last against the caliber of hunters that would come after me now. I narrowed my eyes and looked at Lerk. "And I suppose you're gonna collect on that bounty, eh old friend?"

Lerk grinned. "Let's just say I haven't made up my mind yet."

"Where's my crew?" I let go of the statue and folded my

arms in defiance. I tried my best to appear steady, even though my head was swimming and all I wanted to do was sit down.

"You want to see your crew, huh?" Lerk stepped on the floor switch and the holoscreen disappeared. "Okay, I'll show you."

Lerk slid back his jacket sleeve revealing a thick, metal bracelet with a touch panel. He tapped out a code and the steel door of the room slid open. Two muscle-bound Greyskallons entered the room holding heavy repeater rifles.

"Guards, escort Glint here down to the holding cubes. And be ready to help him walk." Lerk shot me a smirk. "He's gotten a little weak over the gloons."

17

LERK LED THE WAY out of the room. I followed, flanked by the two moving walls of grey muscle. We were on a second level walkway that overlooked a cavernous stone walled room filled with soldiers. It was a daunting collection of force that I wouldn't have expected to find out in the ramshackle dwellings of Outer Serberat.

"As you can see," Lerk glanced back and motioned to the soldiers below, "this is the true power of Serberat-Gellamede. Not the token security forces inside the cushy domes."

"Your mom would be proud," I said.

The soldiers were mostly Zeuthian. They were all practicing Mus-Yup, the latest in technology assisted combat training. It was the first fighting technique developed entirely by renegade cyborgs. It was meant to give them the edge they needed for interstellar domination.

Unfortunately for the cyborgs, undercover records of their training were leaked. Soon after, workout videos were made. Mus-Yup became an instant hit and was picked up by all the trendy, upscale gyms throughout the universe. Technology enhanced suits called "Fightsies" were designed and soon everyone who was anyone had learned the moves.

The vast army of renegade cyborgs that had been amassing for their imminent takeover were outraged. They figured the leak was an inside job. Many accusations were made and tempers escalated. Eventually the cyborgs turned on each other and all but a few of them were obliterated in a few days of unbridled fury. The universe at large considered this a win-win.

"This is only part of our forces." Lerk gave a lopsided grin, his chest puffed out. "Follow me."

As I followed Lerk across the walkway, my brain was assaulted by a thought message from Blix. A blue icon of Blix with his arms raised in a questioning pose spun before my thoughts. It was soon followed by a question mark, then a large ear straining to hear something. Obviously, he was looking for a thought response from me. Blix would just have to wait. I had to stay alert and see what information I could get out of Lerk. I was in an underground prison of some kind and I needed every moment I had to ply Lerk with questions until he gave something away that I could use to escape.

Lerk led us down an enclosed stairway. The sounds of our feet on the steel steps echoed against the walls of the narrow passage. As we made our way down, I thought about how much I hated secret warlord subterranean compounds. They seemed to be the latest craze in the universe for well-financed criminals.

The stairs ended and an archway opened up to a vast underground landing bay filled with small, triangular spaceships.

"Orbital interceptors, huh?" I tried to mask my awe at the impressive airpower under his control.

"Interceptor elites." Lerk raised an eyebrow.

"I guess you still use your piloting skills after all," I said.

"Oh, not like the old days. To be honest, it's kind of lost the thrill for me."

"Well, these are short range ships. You need a deep space cruiser to really get out there."

"Oh, I don't waste time with these rock hoppers. My ship's over there." Lerk pointed to a sleek looking crimson space cruiser in the center of the room. It sat there in red, shiny dominance, surrounded by the smaller, grey interceptors like servants bowing to their king.

"The Z-Series Moon Racer!" I couldn't hide my enthusiasm this time.

"With optional dark energy thrusters and kandrelian hide seating." Lerk leaned back and crossed his arms, basking in his supremacy.

I whistled in appreciation. I knew the criminal underworld could be prosperous but this was a whole new level. "How can you afford all this?"

"The big boss is our main financier," Lerk said.

"I thought you said you were the boss?"

"Of day to day operations, sure. But there's always a man behind the man. In fact, you know him." Lerk gave a mischievous grin.

My stomach felt like it dropped into a black hole. I hoped against hope it wasn't who I thought.

"I do?" My knees felt weak as I anticipated the dreaded name that he was sure to utter.

"Hamilton Von Drone. Our old academy buddy, remember?"

I couldn't answer for a moment. My head was chock full of nothing but expletives.

Lerk patted me on the back. "Let it go, space cowboy. Nothin' everyday star pilots like us can do to beat someone like Hamilton. Better to just accept it and see how long you can ride the gravy train."

I was growing tired of Lerk. I considered sending my knuckles into his smug little face in rapid-fire succession. I'd been trying to play along and resist giving Lerk a piece of my mind but my patience was wearing thin. We reached a steel door that slid away at our approach. Inside was a room with a few clear walled holding cells. They were, of course, the latest in blaster resistant, plexitanium construction.

I could see Blix and Nelvan through the walls. They were sitting on a clear resting slab on the far side of the cell. There was a glowing red sphere protruding from Nelvan's forehead. I hoped it wasn't what I feared. Blix spotted me and stood, looking surprised.

"Quite a prison you got here," I said.

"The Holocell 4000. It comes standard with taunting sirens and auto sting spray for the rowdy types."

My fists desperately wanted a piece of his face. We paused at the opaque entrance door of the cell. Lerk pressed a translucent grey panel in the wall and leaned toward it.

Lerk tapped a few more panels and the door to the cell slid open.

"Captain, your crew." He waved his arm forward like some waiter showing me to a table.

"Where's Jasette?" I said.

"She'll be along. She's been making things difficult," Lerk said. "You must have your hands full with that one."

I gave him a stern look. "You'd better not lay a hand on her. Her royal family has some powerful friends."

Lerk grinned. "You got a thing for her?"

"Just leave her alone."

Lerk chuckled. "For old time's sake. I'll give the soldiers strict orders."

I nodded and headed into the cell.

"Once Hamilton gets here I'll bring him down to see my

surprise prisoner," Lerk said. "I can't wait to see the look on his face."

The clear cell door slid shut. Lerk headed for the exit with the guards following close behind. I scowled for a moment, wondering how I could gain the upper hand in a place like this where he held all the cards. I turned back to my crew, only to find myself locked in the painful bear hug of Blix.

"Captain, you're all right," Blix said. "When you didn't answer my thought messages I feared the worst."

I struggled to speak but my lungs were so compressed I could only mouth the words, *let go.*

"I think he's trying to say, 'let's go.'" Nelvan had a studied look on his face, trying to decipher the movements of my mouth.

I shook my head. My ribs felt as though they might snap.

"Yes, we shall go." Blix said through the hug. "As soon as we figure out how." He gave me a painful pat on the back.

"Why is his face turning red?" Nelvan said.

Blix turned his head toward me. "What is it, Captain? Did they poison you?"

I shook my head.

"Torture? Was it torture? Oh, that makes me so mad." Blix frowned and tightened his grip. I felt like I was about to pass out.

"He doesn't look well," Nelvan said.

A look of realization came over Blix's face. "Oh!" He let go and I fell to my knees, gasping for air.

"My sincere apologies, Captain. I was merely expressing my relief that you're alive and—"

"You idiot!" I coughed. "You almost crushed me."

"It's not my fault the human body is so delicate," Blix said.

I sat for a moment, trying to catch my breath. I cast a

disheartened look at the red sphere about the size of an eyeball protruding from Nelvan's forehead. "That what I think it is?"

Blix looked at Nelvan and frowned. "I'm afraid so. And an advanced holding sphere at that. No extruded wires like the old legacy models."

"You do know how to remove this thing, right?" Nelvan looked from me to Blix with pleading eyes.

"You didn't tell him?" I said.

"I didn't have the heart," Blix said.

"Tell me what?" Nelvan said.

Blix cleared his throat, a guilty look on his face. "Holding spheres are quite expensive. Generally reserved for high value captures. It all began back when the late Dr. Vellicouse from the Plefforce sector made an incredible breakthrough in neuro-technology—"

"It means you're stuck here." I interrupted. "The sphere bonds with the impulses in your brain. If we try to remove it, you go brain dead."

A look of fear washed over Nelvan. His mouth started to open, then closed again.

"Plus, the sphere explodes a few freems after it loses neural connection," I said. "Sort of a double whammy."

"B-But surely someone can remove it?" Nelvan's voice was shaky. "Some neural specialist or something?"

Blix tried to sound consoling. "Yes, though their fees are quite high. In better circumstances we could even chance interstellar travel to locate such a specialist but ..." Blix trailed off as if searching for the words.

"But what?" Nelvan said.

"The holding sphere keeps you grounded," I said. "If we risk leaving the spaceport, a proximity sensor in the sphere starts a countdown."

"Countdown to what?" Nelvan said.

"Judging by the quality …" Blix leaned closer to the red sphere, rubbing his chin. "I'd wager a large scale explosion. No doubt it would destroy the ship and all of us with it."

Nelvan looked from me to Blix as if hoping for something more. "So, that's it then? I'm stuck here on this spaceport? Forever?"

Blix and I exchanged a disheartened glance and shrugged.

"But why? What do they want from me?" Nelvan said.

"You have no known records," I said. "They figure it means you're someone of considerable value."

"Then we'll just tell them I'm not." Nelvan stood to his feet, his fist clenched. He almost looked defiant except for his nervous twitching. "Blix, you can persuade them, right? We'll tell them all about my time travel experiments. I'll tell them everything and maybe they'll let me go."

"Yes, well, we could certainly try." Blix patted Nelvan on the shoulder causing him to wince. "Of course, someone with their records erased would have such a story like yours ready to deliver with utmost sincerity. It's doubtful they would believe you. And of course, the painful interrogation would follow."

"What? They're going to torture me?" Nelvan was staring at us like a wild man.

"Oh, um, well, perhaps they won't." Blix tried to backpedal. "They may have truth serum available."

Nelvan collapsed in an awkward sitting position. "I can't believe this is happening." Nelvan hung his head. His wavy, blond hair draped over his face.

Blix gave a mournful look my way as if I was supposed to

offer some kind of solution. I frowned back at him, giving a stare that I hoped would communicate it was his fault.

"Listen boy, don't worry," I said. "None of that's going to happen."

Nelvan lifted his head just enough so his eyes could see between the strands of hair. "It's not?"

"No. We're busting out of here," I said.

"We are?" Blix said.

"Yeah, that's right. The motto of our ship is, we all leave together," I said.

"I don't remember that motto," Blix said.

"That's because it's new." I glared at Blix. "But I like it, so from now on, that's our motto."

Nelvan sat up and looked at me with a mixture of confusion and hope. "Really?"

"That's right. I've got some ideas. We'll be just fine." I shot Nelvan a mischievous grin as though I had some tricks hidden up my altogether empty sleeve.

Blix raised an eyebrow at me with a subtle smirk. He knew I had no ideas whatsoever. We were trapped in an impenetrable prison in an underground compound loaded with fearsome guards. Aside from some wild stroke of luck, there was no way out.

18

I FILLED BLIX AND Nelvan in on Lerk the thug boss and how the whole underground was financed and run by none other than Hamilton. The news did not sit well with Nelvan. He started pacing slowly around the cell, a defeated look on his face. Blix merely nodded every few moments, picking at his sharp nails as if bored by my consequential news.

A few moments later the steel door to the prison room slid open and in walked a woman wearing a flowing white gown. She was flanked by two Zeuthian guards in Mus-Yup suits. All sound was muted from our prison cube but it looked like there was some yelling and struggling as they brought her closer to our cell.

As they neared, I realized the woman was Jasette. Her hair was done up in spiral buns on each side of her head and her white gown looked like it was made from shimmery curtains. It was a departure from her sleek, power suit, tough chick look, which I'd already decided was one of the best all time looks for a woman out to conquer the universe. This was a softer look but still beautiful.

One of the guards with a fresh bruise on his cheek leaned toward the cell door. He hit a few panels and the door slid open.

"Let go you spike headed freak," Jasette said.

The Zeuthian growled and shoved her into the cell. The door slid closed and the guards headed out, looking relieved.

"Well, well, would you look at—" I began.

"Not one word." Jasette spun and pointed a threatening finger at me.

"Wouldn't think of it, Your Highness," I said in mock reverence.

Jasette scowled at me.

I turned to Blix and Nelvan. "Gentlemen, mind your manners. We're in the presence of royalty."

"Huh?" Nelvan said.

"Is that right?" Blix looked at her with bright eyes.

Jasette folded her arms and let out a frustrated sigh. "Yes, okay, fine. It's true."

"I knew there was something." Blix walked closer to Jasette. "It all makes sense now. Your extensive training, knowledge of the finer things, constant need to prove yourself and most importantly …" Blix paused, giving a slight bow and taking Jasette's hand like some royal courtier. "… the finest of table manners. I should've known all along." Blix kissed her hand and stood at attention as if awaiting orders.

Jasette gave Blix a playful grin. "I was trying to play it tough. Looks like I need a few pointers."

"Oh, nothing the average layman would detect." Blix gave a casual motion in my direction. "Though I could offer you some basic tips on blending in with the commoners."

I cleared my throat loudly. "Are you through?"

"We'll talk later," Blix whispered to Jasette.

"Princess or not I don't really care," I said. "What I'd really like to know is if you have any ideas on getting out of here."

"I thought you said you already had ideas?" Nelvan said.

"I'm just trying to get everyone's input. That's what captains do."

Nelvan frowned like he didn't believe me.

"They confiscated my power suit," Jasette picked at her white gown in disgust. "It's gonna be nearly impossible without it."

"Forget the suit," I waved a dismissive hand. "We need to disable some of the systems they have around here. I'm sure the castle you grew up in had some high level security—"

"Crystal halo," Jasette interrupted.

"Um, what?"

"The planet Jelmontaire employs a crystal-alloy compound in the construction of our royal dwellings. The palace looks like a silver loop from above. It's known as a crystal halo," Jasette said.

I rolled my eyes and looked at Blix. He just nodded as if he was impressed.

"Jelmontaire sounds exquisite," Blix said. "I must visit someday."

"Okay, whatever. I'm sure your *halo* …" I used the term with intentional disdain. "… has some top drawer security systems. Anything you know about disabling them would help."

"One thing's for sure. We're not getting out of this thing till they come and get us." Jasette motioned to the walls of our holding cube. "Our only chance is to cause some kind of scuffle once they lead us out of here. At that point, we'll have to play it by ear."

"That's kind of broad," I said. "I was hoping for something more specific."

Jasette started taking holding clasps out of her hair and unraveling the buns. "I'll leave the brilliant ideas to you."

I sighed and looked at the thick, clear walls that surrounded us. I thought about how rare it was for brilliant ideas to pop into my head. Before anyone else realized the same thing, I thought a good change of subject was needed.

"Why are you dressed like that?" I said.

"They have a pack of female slaves that like to do makeovers." Jasette shook her head. "This place is run by a bunch of male chauvinist scumbags."

The steel door of the prison room slid open again and in walked Lerk with the two Greyskallon guards and a Zeuthian soldier dressed in a flight suit.

"Speaking of scumbags," I said.

"Curious that he's back so soon," Blix said.

"Maybe this is our chance to act," Jasette said.

"Just play it cool for now."

Lerk leaned toward the cell and hit the speaker panel. "Slight change of plans. Glint, c'mere will ya?"

The cell door opened and Lerk motioned me forward. I cast subtle glances at Blix and Jasette. They returned looks that meant this was my chance to make the impossible happen. The demands placed on a captain are often unreasonable and generally insane. With no weapons or plan I was supposed to overthrow the entire warlord lair and lead all of us to freedom.

I gave a casual nod to Lerk and headed out of the cell. The door slid shut and we left the prison room and entered the landing bay. In those few moments of silence I thought about how I missed out on all the other less stressful career paths there were in the universe. I started to imagine myself as a baker on some distant moon. Waking every morning to the smell of fresh bread and friendly townspeople that loved me and …

"Glint? You okay?" Lerk said.

"Huh? Yeah, fine," I said.

"You looked like you were in some kind of daze."

"It's nothing, I'm good."

"Alright then. So, listen old friend, I'm afraid our academy reunion has been delayed." Lerk put a friendly hand on my shoulder as we walked. I wanted to take hold of it and fling him into a wall.

"There was some kind of scuffle in the domes. Apparently some enraged Greyskallon attacked Hamilton and damaged his chin." Lerk chuckled. "Probably deserved it of course."

"Did he get hurt?" I tried to mask my hopefulness.

"Nothing permanent, but he's a little touchy about his face." Lerk looked around to see if anyone was nearby, then leaned in confidentially. "He's had a bit of work done over the gloons, you know."

"I knew it." I couldn't wait to tell Blix I was right about his surgically enhanced looks.

"Anyways, Merkeel took him straight to his facial reconstruction cybernetics facility. He won't be here for awhile."

"Merkeel?" I said. "I thought he was dead."

"Nope, though I doubt you'd recognize him. He's a little more … robotic than he used to be." Lerk grinned.

"Robotic?" I started to connect the dots. I felt a chill in my bones.

"Oh, you know modern science and robotics. Lots of crazy experimentation these days. He answers to the name Mishmash now."

A wave of nausea went through me. I actually felt sorry for Merkeel. Even though his life in the academy was nothing but sneaking around for Hamilton doing his underhanded bidding, some bizarre fusion of man and robot was a fate I wouldn't wish on anyone. Well, except maybe Hamilton.

Lerk paused near the base of one of the interceptor spaceships. He turned toward me and placed his hands on his hips. "Well, space cowboy. This is the end of the road."

I looked around feeling confused. "What do you mean?"

"I've been thinking about it and I decided, for old time's sake, to let you go."

This was a turn of events I hadn't expected. "Really?"

"Yep. Call me crazy but I thought one last favor was in order. Bidgefilch here will fly you to your ship and you can be on your way." Lerk motioned to the Zeuthian who was zipping up his flight suit.

"What about my crew?" I said.

"Hey, I have my limits." Lerk held up his hands. "Blix will make a great soldier once we break him. The princess will fetch a good price on the black market and the boy … well, Hamilton will want to know more about the secrets he's keeping."

My head felt stuffy. I suddenly needed a large glass of water. For some reason my mind leapt to the list of the top five worst days in my life and tried to rate this one in comparison. I decided it was my new number five.

"I see." I looked down at the floor. It was one of those grated steel floors that echo when you walk over it in heavy shoes. As I stared at the spaces in the grating, I wondered what it would be like to accept the offer and fly off alone in my ship. All I could think of was the cold, dark vacuum of space with no one on board and everyone left on this spaceport. I also thought about the ironic and inconvenient timing of coming up with a new ship motto about not leaving anyone behind just moments earlier.

"So I guess this is it, old pal." Lerk put his hands in his pockets.

In the midst of my confusion a strange and irresistible impulse hit me. I slowly looked back up and saw Lerk standing there flanked by the huge Greyskallon guards. Out of the corner of my eye I noticed the Zeuthian soldier was putting on his helmet. His hands were high, away from any weapons. This was the only chance I had.

All the frustration and stress of the newly ranked fifth worst day of my life rushed to the surface and seemed to gather into my right fist. Before I fully realized what I was doing, instinct and urgency blended into one of the best right crosses I had ever executed.

My knuckles connected with Lerk's jaw and produced a glorious crunching sound. His eyelids fluttered and he swayed back on his heels.

The Greyskallons lunged forward, their tired, beady eyes coming to life, with numerous folds of skin angling downward in surprised betrayal. I was already ducking under their meaty, reaching hands, grasping the twin Ultra-DEMOTERs holstered at Lerk's waist.

I leapt backward, away from the outstretched hands of the guards and swiveled a laser gun at the Zeuthian. He had already dropped his helmet and was drawing a wicked looking grey blaster. I had a half-freem lead on his draw. I squeezed the trigger of the Ultra-DEMOTER, sending a bright blast of white energy into his chest and lifting him off his feet.

My back hit the floor and the two guards charged forward. I squeezed off two more blasts that spun them sideways. I sent several follow up shots that sent them sprawling on the ground, smoke rising from their tattered uniforms. I sat up and saw Lerk lying beside them, unconscious.

I heard voices above and looked up to find several soldiers

on a second level walkway staring down at me and pointing. I knew my success would be short lived unless I moved fast.

I clambered up the ladder of the spaceship above and jumped into the cockpit. I started up all the systems and felt the ship's engines roar to life. A handful of soldiers ran into the landing bay, heavy repeaters held toward me.

I pulled back the throttle and the ship hovered several feet in the air. A myriad of green laser beams flew toward me from below.

"You guys want a firefight." I tapped on the controls for the ship cannons. "You got it."

The rotating turrets of the interceptor sprang to life sending a rapid-fire line of orange beams into the oncoming soldiers. A few stray beams hit a power condenser, causing a small explosion. Automated nozzles rose from the floor and started spraying white foam to control the fire.

"So much for keeping things quiet." I moved the ship over to the prison door and hit the laser cannons. The orange beams tore into the door and the few remaining pieces of steel collapsed in a small heap.

I could see my crew stand to their feet in the holocell within. The surprised look on their faces was priceless. I motioned with my hand for them to move. They rushed to the opposite end of the cell and crouched down.

A victorious smile spread over my face as I sent a barrage of cannon fire at the top of the cell, hoping to blast the roof off. Instead, the laser beams ricocheted wildly against the cell and the prison room walls.

A few beams found their way back out the prison door, one of them hitting the front of my ship with a jarring impact.

I suddenly grasped the danger of my situation and yanked

back the controls to get the ship out of range. Several more beams ricocheted out of the room and slammed into my ship as I was pulling away. Red lights and warning sirens filled the cockpit. The controls were shaking uncontrollably and the interceptor started to spin.

The ship veered sideways and I saw the floor rushing closer. I hit the eject panel and the pilot's chair launched me out of the ship and sent me skipping across the landing bay. The ship crashed and a deafening explosion filled the air.

I slid to a stop, feeling several new pains spread generously over my body. The sounds of explosions and yelling grew faint and my vision blurred. The last thing I saw before all went black were several Zeuthian guards standing over me, repeater blasters trained on my head.

19

I AWOKE TO A fuzzy vision of the Holocell 4000. I heard Blix talking. It sounded like his voice was coming from the bottom of a well. I closed my eyes and felt the rhythmic pounding of a splitting headache.

I blinked a few times and my vision cleared. Blix and Nelvan were sitting on one of the clear prison slabs nearby. Jasette was standing next to them, examining the walls of the cell.

"Seamless. No vulnerabilities that I can see," Jasette said.

Things were starting to sound normal, but there was a persistent ringing in my ears.

I sat up and was hit with a wave of nausea. I grabbed the slab I was sitting on and tried to steady myself. "How long have I been out?"

Blix looked at me with concern. "Captain, you should lie down. You don't look well."

"I'm fine." I felt like I might pass out. "Is it hot in here?"

"Not to me," Blix said. "But then, I'm cold blooded."

"My head feels really hot." I closed my eyes tight, trying to blink away the pain. "Maybe I have a fever."

Jasette gave a consoling look my way. "I don't think that's it, Glint."

"How do you know? You a doctor?" I said.

"No, but ..." She bit her lip and looked away.

There was a moment of uncomfortable silence. No one seemed to want to make eye contact with me.

"But what?" There was a nervous mood in the room like someone was about to be executed. It felt like that someone was me.

"It's not fair, Captain." Nelvan was either on the verge of tears or rage, it was hard to tell. "It's not right."

I raised a questioning eyebrow at Blix. "Blix? What's going on?"

Blix glanced down and cleared his throat. "Captain, I think I speak for everyone when I say how proud we are of you. Regardless of the spectacularly bad outcome, your bravery in the face of innumerable odds are both inspiring and—"

"Spare me the speech." I said.

"Yes, well, um, you see Captain ..." Blix fumbled.

I groaned. "You're making my headache worse."

I rubbed my temples then stopped abruptly. My forehead seemed more crowded than usual. I felt toward the center of my forehead and froze when my fingers touched a warm, protruding sphere. A sickening wave of impending doom went through my body.

I looked up. Blix was nodding at me with apologetic eyes.

"I'm afraid you and Nelvan are in the same boat now, Captain," Blix said.

"H-Holding sphere?" My words came out in a whisper.

"I'm exceedingly sorry, Captain. I promise I will use my full brain capacity to think of solutions while there's still time in the day."

I caught movement out of the corner of my eye. I was looking toward the demolished prison door when in walked none other than Hamilton Von Drone. Lerk shadowed him with a scowl on his face and a swollen bruise on his chin.

"Uh oh." I was definitely in for it now.

Hamilton and Lerk strolled toward the cell. It seemed as though they'd both been to the smug overlord store and purchased matching sneers.

Jasette eyed Hamilton like a jungle cat ready to pounce. This, of course, meant she was done playing games and had decided to show how she really felt about him. Even in the face of utter defeat, seeing her flash evil eyes at my nemesis was a great moment.

Hamilton stopped at the cell door, and hit the touch panel. The overhead speaker came on. Hamilton clasped his hands behind his back, looking at me like a disappointed parent. He raised his eyebrows as if waiting for me to apologize. I noticed his chin was more squared than usual. It even seemed as though it had grown in width.

"Nice jaw Hamilton," I said. "All out of your size, huh?"

His eyes narrowed. "I wanted to thank you for getting yourself thrown in prison and saving me the trouble, Glint. After all, I can't have you out searching for the Emerald Enigma when it's clearly meant for someone of distinction like myself."

Once again I had to restrain my gathering rage against this buffoon. I had to play it cool in the hopes of deflecting the truth. "The Enigma?" I faked a laugh. "You think I'd waste my time on a children's fable?"

Hamilton gave a knowing look back to Lerk. Lerk grinned and nodded in typical, suck up, henchman fashion.

"It's no use," Hamilton said. "I know all about it now. I had my suspicions when I found your ship bound for Beringfell and realized a desperate star pilot like you would be searching for something to turn his luck around. I was going to keep you on board till I found out for sure but when you slipped away, you gave me time to search your ship. And now …" Hamilton gave a sly grin. "… Now I'm certain it's the object of your quest."

I tried taking slow breaths to keep the vein on my neck from throbbing in anger. He had to be bluffing to try and get me to admit he was right. I'd been careful to keep the ship's records free of any mention of the Enigma in case the computer was scanned. I decided to give an equally convincing rebuttal to his charge.

"Is not," I said.

"It *is*," Hamilton said. "You were very careful to keep it from your records, but then I checked your quarters."

Uh oh.

"Under the gel cushion on your sleeping slab, a message was carved into the metal."

"Whatever it was I didn't write it." My words were rushed and filled with guilty overtones.

Hamilton pulled a translucent blue rectangle from his belt that expanded as he raised it before him. A series of words appeared on the rectangle. He cleared his throat and read, "I swear I will find the Emerald Enigma even if it costs me my life and the lives of my crew …"

Blix shot a questioning look my way. I shook my head and waved a reassuring hand at him.

"… I will find it and everyone will bow in my presence. Everyone will wish they were as awesome as me. Women will throw themselves at me and …"

"Okay, that's enough," I said.

Jasette cast a disappointed look my way. "Really?"

I shrugged. "I was caught up in the moment."

Hamilton returned the rectangle to his belt. “So you see, I was right all along as usual.”

“That was a long time ago. I realized it was just a silly myth. Just let us go and we’ll head in the other direction.”

“I’m afraid I don’t believe you,” Hamilton said. “And since I can’t have you in my way, I’m going to leave you in Lerk’s care.”

Hamilton patted Lerk on the shoulder. Lerk shot a wicked grin my way and nodded.

Hamilton shook his head and sighed as though I’d let him down one too many times. “Well, goodbye.” He turned and walked toward the prison door. “Be sure to say hello to Mar Mar for me, will you?” Hamilton left without a second glance.

“Mar Mar?” I gave Lerk a dark look.

Lerk gave a gleeful smile of death and nodded. “Sleep tight.” He hit the touch panel on the door and the cell speakers clicked off. He headed out the prison door and we were alone once again.

The main lights in the room went out. All that was left were the thin, blue runners that illuminated the path to the prison room door and the outline of the cell control panel.

Everything had a slight red tint to it. The holding sphere on my forehead gave off a soft glow. It was as if I was trapped in a small red cloud, a constant reminder that my fate was sealed.

“Most unfortunate,” Blix said. “I suppose we should get some rest. It’s been quite the arduous day.”

“What?” I barked. A sharp pain radiated in my head. I decided that would be my last bark for a while. “No one’s going to sleep until we figure a way out of this mess.”

“Of course Captain,” Blix said. “Nelvan, would you mind scooting down to the next slab?”

“Oh, sure,” Nelvan said.

I heard shuffling and saw the faint outline of Nelvan moving through the cell. His holding sphere illuminated his face. It almost looked like a glowing red head was floating through the cell. It was both creepy and ridiculous. I would've taken the chance to make fun of him if I didn't have the same unfortunate appearance.

I heard Blix moving on his slab. "You better not be lying down."

"You know I think better when I'm relaxed." Blix let out a deep yawn.

"Unless we think of a way out of here by morning, we're all dead."

"I doubt they'll kill us. Slavery most likely," Blix said. "Did I ever tell you about the time I was enslaved by the dragon lords of the Krelvorcian sector?"

"About a hundred times. Listen, I don't want slavery either. I just think—"

"For two gloons I was forced to work in their wretched salt mines. Do you have any idea the damage salt deposits have on scales?"

"I don't want slavery or death. I need solutions and fast."

Blix let out another yawn. "I've been brainstorming escape plans ever since your return. Unfortunately, this closed environment and the poor quality of the prison food has not been conducive to my usual brilliance." His voice was becoming slurred. "I just need to rest my eyes for a moment."

"I'll stay up," Nelvan said. "I don't think I could sleep tonight anyways."

"Thank you," I said. "You see, that's loyalty. That's what makes a good crew member."

I waited a moment and there was no response. "Blix?"

The familiar hissing snore of Blix broke the silence. I gritted my teeth and felt a stabbing pain go through my head. All my normal anger driven responses would have to be tempered as long as my headache was around.

I saw the dark outline of Jasette approaching. She took a seat next to me.

"Let him sleep," Jasette said. "There's not much we can do from in here anyway."

Her voice was softer than usual. The pain in my head seemed to subside with her sitting so close.

"Once the lights go on and they come for us, it's gonna be wall-to-wall guards," I said. "You think those are better odds?"

Jasette let out a defeated sigh. "I think those are our only odds at this point. We don't have anything that would help us break out of this cell. Either we make a break for it once we're outside or end up slaves. Personally, I'd rather fight it out."

I nodded. It was hard to fight with that logic. "I guess you're right."

"When that guy Lerk and his guards brought you back here, he was really furious," Jasette said.

I laughed. "A good right cross will do that to you."

"He said something about you throwing away your chance at freedom. Is that true?"

"He gave me a shot to leave. Alone. But who knows? Thugs like him make lots of promises."

"So rather than save your own skin, you actually tried to free us and got yourself thrown back in jail?"

"Well, it could've worked."

Jasette remained silent a few moments.

"What?"

"I think I had you all wrong." Jasette placed her hand gently on my knee. "Whatever happens tomorrow, I wish you the best."

Somehow, in this underground lair, amidst grimy aliens and thugs, she still managed to look incredible. She was a bright star in the dark night sky. I reached out and grabbed her hand. "Yeah, you too."

She let my hand rest there for a moment, then stood, somewhat reluctantly.

I heard her walk to the other end of the cell. I lay down and rested my throbbing head on the slab beneath me. I closed my eyes to rid myself of the red cloud of light.

If I wasn't filled with pain and nausea I would've been feeling pretty triumphant that I'd broken through Jasette's icy exterior. Through an impulsive act of bravery, I had managed to move a giant step closer to winning her affections. It was a shame that my life was going to end tomorrow, we probably could've had something great.

"Captain?" Nelvan said.

I opened my eyes and saw Nelvan standing above me. His sphere cast a ghostly red light on his worried expression.

"Yeah?" I said.

"Can I talk to you?"

I struggled against every desire within me that wanted to say no. In the end, his dire predicament and the sad look on his face made me cave.

"Sure." I sat up and a thousand pains sprang to life all over my body. I tapped the bench next to me and he sat down.

Considering the circumstances, I thought a quick reassessment was in order. I decided to recategorize this as the third worst day of my life.

Nelvan sighed. He sat there in silence, looking toward the

other end of the cell. I was never good at the approachable, consoling, 'I'm your buddy' side of the ideal starship captain persona. I was much better at the order barking, fire at will tasks. So, when confronted with a situation like this, I resorted to stating the obvious to fill the uncomfortable silence.

"So, quite a future you've landed in, huh?" I said.

Nelvan's glowing head gave a somber nod. Obviously he was hoping for some brilliant words of wisdom that would make our doomed predicament seem tolerable.

"You know Nelvan, the universe is a funny thing. Very unpredictable. With so many variables in constant motion, it's nearly impossible to guess your fate." I went for the good fortune springing from chaos argument. He was young so I figured it was a good angle.

Nelvan looked thoughtful for a moment. "So, how often have random events got you out of tight spots in the past?"

Curse this kid's intuition. He wasn't buying it. "Well, there was the time on the ice moon of Vendorell when I took a wrong turn and fell down a twisting, icy tunnel." I used swerving hand motions to enhance my story. "I thought I'd end up on a bed of frozen spikes but the tunnel ended up spitting me out just steps away from the very remote colony I was headed for. Saved half a day's travel." It wasn't a total lie. It happened to my second cousin Fornell. Of course, the way he told it, it always sounded made up.

Nelvan gave me a casual glance as though he found zero comfort in my words but was being polite. "You know something Captain, I'm pretty tired. I think I'll go to sleep now."

"A good night's sleep will give us sharp minds for tomorrow's escape." I faked a smile.

Nelvan gave a weak grin and stood. He turned back for a moment, his glowing head looking down on me.

"I think what you tried to do today was very brave. And even though it failed pretty badly, we're grateful."

My compliments were often sprinkled with insults. It used to bother me but these days, I took what I could get. "Thanks."

Nelvan got a faraway look in his eyes. "It's funny, as strange as this future is, I actually think I would've enjoyed being part of your crew."

Deep within my stone-like heart, a flicker of warmth broke out for Nelvan. I really wished there was something I could do to help him.

"Don't talk like it's all over yet. Tomorrow is another day." As a captain, I felt obliged to offer trite pep talks even when I didn't believe them.

Nelvan nodded. "Goodnight Captain." He walked over to a clear slab nearby and lay down. He closed his eyes under the red globe of light and actually looked at peace.

For a moment, his serene look gave me comfort. Then I realized it was because he was giving up. His hopeless fate was an inevitable reality in his mind. The very idea angered me. I lay back down on my slab thinking feverishly of inventive, elaborate schemes of escape. Somewhere around the fourteenth plan that fell apart under scrutiny, I fell asleep.

20

MY SLEEP WAS RESTLESS. I dreamt I was on some jungle moon running for my life. It was dark as I fled through the dense foliage. Mist hung thick in the forest and the night was filled with the sounds of jungle creatures that sounded really hungry. I tripped over a thick, twisted root and collided with the base of a tree trunk.

I awoke back in the holocell. It was darker than before. The red orb of light around my head revealed a dark, tall shape at my side. I sat up to get a better look and my head hit something solid, creating a rustling sound. I cursed and reached up to see what I'd hit. It felt like a crooked bar with a rough, brittle exterior. It connected with the tall shape at my side. I gave it a shake and another rustling sound came from above. If I didn't know any better, I would've thought I was next to a tree.

Several golden, glowing lights sprang to life above me. Their illumination revealed a canopy of branches and leaves. It took a moment to realize the golden lights were actually fruit hanging from the branches.

A warm, earthy aroma like baked apples with just the right amount of cinnamon cascaded down from the branches above. My mouth watered. My stomach growled as if I hadn't eaten for days.

The golden fruit swayed seductively above as if stirred by a gentle summer breeze. One of the fruits detached from a branch and moved toward me in a rhythmic motion. The aroma from the fruit spread over me like a warm blanket. I felt more relaxed than I had in days. It was difficult to think of anything but that delicious looking fruit coming near.

I heard a soft hissing sound. A serpent with gleaming, ruby colored scales was carrying the approaching fruit on its tail. I was alarmed at the sight of a large snake right next to me and for a moment wondered why I was just sitting there. Why were my thoughts consumed with eating fruit instead of figuring out why there was a large tree and a big snake in the middle of the cell? I was about to call for the others when the serpent spoke.

"Greetingsss friend. You look tired and hungry. Pleassse, take thisss and be sssatisfied." The serpent's voice was rich and resonant. It was almost musical.

The serpent lifted the golden fruit with his tail and held it in front of my face. It was beautiful. The smell was so sweet and succulent my head started to swim. I reached out and took it in my hands. It was warm to the touch. A pleasant tingling sensation spread down my arms.

"Thisss fruit will give you what you need my friend." The serpent's voice was soothing, almost fatherly. "You will finally be able to sssleep. A nicssse, deep sssleep unlike anything you've exsssperiencsssed."

It all sounded fantastic. Delicious fruit, a great night's sleep. These were the very things missing from my life.

"Jussst take a little tassste," the serpent said. "If you don't like it, you can cassst it assside. But if you do like it, you can have more. Asss much asss you like."

The serpent beheld me with its warm, golden eyes. I had to admit, he was making a lot of sense. I lifted the fruit to my mouth and prepared to sink my teeth into the perfect, golden delight.

"Captain, no!" Nelvan slapped the fruit from my hand.

"Hey!" I glared at him. If I still had my DEMOTER I would've taken off his foot.

The serpent hissed and reared back, revealing a nasty pair of fangs. A sickly green color filled his eyes and spread through his ruby scales in crooked, web-like patterns. Suddenly he didn't seem so friendly.

"Be gone, creature of darkness. The Lord rebuke you!" Nelvan squared his shoulders and pointed at the serpent. His voice was commanding and stern.

The serpent hissed and lunged toward Nelvan. It disappeared in a thick plume of black smoke as it collided with his chest. The glowing fruits went dim, casting a subtle, yellow light throughout the cell.

"Are you okay, Captain?" Nelvan looked down at me. His eyes were bright and strong. He seemed taller somehow.

"Yeah, fine." I found myself wondering why I had almost eaten a strange fruit given to me by a snake.

A sizzling sound came from the ground nearby. I looked on the floor beside me and there was the fruit Nelvan had swatted from my hand. The golden color was gone. It was brown and riddled with decay spots. Smoke rose from the base of the fruit as it appeared to be melting into the floor. Its corrosive juices were spreading outward, eating through the flooring and creating a shallow crater.

"I almost ate that." I watched in disbelief as the dark fruit ate away at the stone floor with its toxic juices. "You saved my life."

He gave an embarrassed little grin. "I couldn't just sit back and watch."

"How did you know it was poison?"

"You said Blix dreams about things he reads and sometimes they come to life, right?"

Suddenly it all made sense: The garden, the serpent, the forbidden fruit.

"I told you it was dangerous," I said.

Nelvan nodded. "You were right."

"What happened?" Jasette moved aside a curtain of ivy and joined us.

"Vythian dream residue," I said. "You familiar with the Earth's Bible?"

"A little," Jasette said. "Isn't there something about a flood in it?"

"Relax, he hasn't got to that part yet," I said. "And now that they took his satchel, hopefully, he never will."

There was a rustling sound and Blix poked his head through the branches nearby.

"What's that about my satchel?" Blix said.

"Do you mind explaining all this?" I motioned to the surrounding foliage.

Blix got a guilty look on his face. "Um, yes, ahem, my sincere apologies, Captain. You see, it's like this …" Blix moved a branch aside to join us. A fruit fell off the branch and landed near Nelvan's feet.

"Watch it!" I said.

The fruit started sizzling as the corrosive juices ate through the stone.

"Heavens, good thing I didn't eat one," Blix said.

"Blix, break off one of those branches with fruit on it. I have an idea."

Blix broke off a fruit laden branch and moved it toward the cell door, and gave a knowing nod, "This looks promising." Jasette put her hands on her hips and grinned.

Blix raised the branch horizontally and pressed it against the cell wall. The corrosive fruit began to sizzle and eat through the clear barrier.

"Will it work?" Nelvan said.

"As long as the guards don't come rushing in," I said.

In a few moments, the fruit ate through to the control panel by the cell door. There was a series of electrical crackles followed by a few blips. Suddenly, the cell door slid open. Nelvan was practically hopping up and down.

"Come on, this is our chance," I said.

We all rushed out of the door and headed for the opening to the prison. Vines had taken over the walls. Trees and bushes had broken through the stone floor, making for difficult travel in the low light. A repeating alarm siren was sounding throughout the compound.

The door to the prison was still in pieces from when I blew it apart with the interceptor cannons. In its place, a curtain of vines was draped across the opening. Everyone slowed as we approached it.

"Stay out of sight," I whispered.

I lifted the vines and peered through the doorway into the landing bay. It looked as if a jungle had taken over. The ground was covered in grass and bushes of every sort. Trees filled the area, overturning many of the interceptors. The walls and doorways had been overtaken with climbing vines.

Two Greyskallon guards lay motionless beside the prison

door. Brown, decayed fruit with bites taken out of them lay by their open hands.

"Your dream paid off for once." I gave Blix a grin and motioned the others forward. I broke through the vines and grabbed a heavy repeater from one of the fallen guards. Jasette took the repeater from the other guard and shot me a cunning smile.

"Let's grab one of those ships and get outta here," I said.

"Wait. I know where they put our stuff." Jasette led the way to a small door a little way down from the prison. Two more guards lay sprawled on the ground, half eaten fruit nearby.

"Stand back." Jasette tucked the heavy repeater rifle against her shoulder and took aim. She blasted the control panel and the door slid open.

Inside was a small storage room with angular shelves lining the walls. The shelves held our weapons and gear along with other random armaments and devices, most likely from former prisoners.

I spied my DEMOTER and holster in a nearby shelf. It was like seeing an old friend. I strapped it around my waist and let out a sigh of relief. "Okay, let's go."

Jasette grabbed her power suit and draped it around her neck. She nodded and headed out of the room. Blix grabbed his dagger filled bandolier and slung his satchel over his shoulder with a wide grin.

"Now would be a good time to leave that book behind." I raised my eyebrows at Blix. "Next time the outcome won't be so lucky."

"Not to worry, Captain." Blix patted his satchel. "I'll just keep it as a memento. A thing to be admired but not touched."

"I have your word on that?"

"Captain, our time is running short. We must hurry." Blix rushed out of the room after Jasette.

Nelvan and I followed into the landing bay. Jasette whistled to get our attention. She was already boarding one of the interceptors. We rushed to climb the ladder and board the ship as she powered on the engines. The cockpit was a small four seater. I took the pilot's chair next to Jasette up front, Blix and Nelvan piled in the back.

"Hope you can fly this thing." Jasette had her power suit in her lap. She had one of the forearm slide panels open and was tapping out commands on a touch screen in rapid-fire succession.

"Lady, I'll show you flying like you've never seen."

Jasette rolled her eyes and continued to tap away on her screen. I yanked back on the control stick and the ship rose into the air like it was shot from a cannon.

"Whoa." Nelvan had a death grip on his armrests. "I don't know if I'm ready for this."

"You ain't seen nothin' yet." I spun the ship around and aimed it toward the sleek, red, Z-Series Moon Racer. A large orange tree had grown underneath it, setting the whole ship at a slight tilt.

"But first, I need to say goodbye to an old friend." I hit the cannons and a rapid succession of orange beams tore into the Moon Racer. Pieces of metal began to fly off the ship as blackened holes dimpled the hull.

"Captain, is this really necessary?" Blix said.

"Absolutely," I said.

The cockpit of the Moon Racer exploded and flames began to flicker upward.

I let out a satisfied sigh. "Okay, now we can go."

I spun the ship around and pushed the throttle forward. The ship sped toward a circular hatch in the side of the wall half covered in vines.

"Can you drive this thing a little smoother," Jasette said. "I'm trying to access their security systems."

"I'm used to my own ship. These interceptors are squirrely," I said. "If things get hairy, we'll just blast our way out."

"Like you blasted us out of the cell?"

I shot her a dark look, then hit the cannons as we approached the hatch. The lasers blasted away the vines and the hatch opened wide, exposing a metallic tunnel leading upward. We flew past the blackened, smoldering remnants of the vines and entered the circular passage.

Dim runner lights lined the sides of the tunnel. It was leading upward and all I could think of was rocketing out of this stinking compound and getting back to my ship.

"There's some locking sensors up ahead," Jasette was focused on the small screen embedded in her power suit. "Don't suppose anyone overheard any passcodes while we were down there?"

"Try 12345," Blix said. "You'd be surprised."

"Are we supposed to be going this fast?" Nelvan's breathing was erratic.

"Just wait till we hit the atmosphere," I said.

The communication panel in front of me lit up a bright yellow and a gravelly, Zeuthian voice came over the intercom. "M-5, we've got you on sensor. You on special orders? I thought everything was grounded."

I cast a questioning look at Jasette. She shrugged and flicked her head toward the intercom as if I was supposed to take care of it.

I hit the response panel and hoped for the best. "This is

M-5. No time to talk. Orders from Captain Lerk Buzzane to retrieve supplies."

I raised my eyebrows at Jasette, looking for some reassurance. She gave a slight frown.

"Improper protocol. Who is this?" The Zeuthian voice said.

"Um, I'm new. Today's my first day. No one said anything about protocol," I said.

"Hold it there pilot. We need to confirm."

I looked back at Blix. "Any ideas?"

"It may be more effective to avoid response and send a distress signal," Blix said. "They may believe your communicator is out and it's an emergency situation. They just might let you through."

"Well, it's too late for that now." I glared at him. "Why didn't you say something earlier?"

"It just came to me," Blix said.

"No clearance of any supply runs," the Zeuthian voice said. "We're still on lockdown, pilot. Take the ship back to the landing bay and report to your superiors."

I gave a desperate look to Jasette. "Now would be a good time to tell me you cracked the security codes."

"I need more time." She shook her head. "There's some advanced systems at work here."

"More time? You disabled everything in my ship in about thirty freems," I said.

"That was child's play," Jasette said. "This is real security."

"I said turn that ship around, pilot." The Zeuthian voice was getting edgy. "You're about to collide with the blast hatch and leave a big mess for us to clean up."

I hit the response panel. "Ship's not responding. Must be stuck on autopilot. Help!"

I turned back to Blix. "Think they'll buy it?"

Blix shook his head. The circular exit hatch was within sight. It was a thick looking, heavily reinforced, steel blast door that wasn't showing the slightest sign of opening.

"Then you've got about ten freems to regain control of that ship before impact," the Zeuthian said. "Orders are orders. Best of luck."

"You heard them," Nelvan squeaked. "Turn around."

"Give me some good news, Jasette," I hit the cannons. The bright beams shot rapid fire from the ship and extinguished harmlessly against the blast door.

"I think I've got it." Jasette's fingers were flying over the touch screen.

An alarm went off in the cockpit, followed by a calm computer voice. "Three freems till impact. Please alter course."

"You think you've got it or you've got it?" I gave a desperate look at Jasette.

"Got it!" Jasette looked up.

The blast door slid open just in time and the light of the three veshul suns flooded into the cockpit. I let out a victorious war cry as we rocketed through the hatch and entered the outer atmosphere of Serberate-Gelamede. There was an immediate sense of relief and elation in the cockpit.

"I must say, that was a fine bit of teamwork," Blix said.

I turned back to Nelvan with a confident smile. "Didn't I tell you we'd bust out of there?"

"What's that?" Nelvan pointed to the targeting panel at the front of the ship.

A small hologlobe had emerged from the panel. A three dimensional image of our ship appeared inside the globe with three smaller red ships behind it.

"Pursuing crafts detected," the calm computer voice said. "Three T-class droid bots. Weapons almost locked on our craft."

"Is that bad?" Nelvan said.

"It's not good." I swerved the ship into a steep dive towards the brown, squat dwellings below.

"T-class?" Blix whistled. "They didn't skimp on the defenses, did they?"

"Quiet back there." I took the interceptor dangerously close to the ground and put the thrusters on full. A long trail of dust kicked up behind us.

"Let's see how they like flying blind," I grinned.

"Droid ships gaining on our position. Weapons armed. Prepare for impact," the computer said.

A myriad of orange beams hit the rushing ground beside us. One of the beams connected with the wing and a shudder went through the ship.

"Hold on." I pitched the ship vertical and rocketed toward the three suns.

"What are you doing?" Jasette gripped the armrest tight and squinted in the bright light.

"What's it look like? I'm trying not to get shot," I hit the turbo thrusters and the interceptor flew into the thin layer of brown grime that dominated the outer atmosphere.

"These are droid pilots," Blix said. "Dust or sun light can do very little to impair their navigation."

A line of laser beams shot across the front of the ship. The last few found their mark and left blackened splash marks on the hull. The ship trembled violently.

"Then we'll have to find another way to blind them." I

powered down all the control panels in the cockpit. "Computer, power down full, all systems."

"That course of action would—" the computer began.

"Do it!" I said.

All the lights in the cockpit went dim. The engines wound down from a steady hum to a sluggish drone. The ship was still angled vertically but we were losing speed fast.

"I don't understand. What are you doing?" Nelvan said.

"Relax boy. Flying techniques have advanced quite a bit since your time," I said.

"Actually, Captain, I don't know what you're doing either," Blix said.

The ship slowed to a stop and seemed to hang there for a moment, the three suns looming overhead.

Jasette looked over at me. "Trust me," I said, and gave her a confident wink. What I was trying was pure theory, though. I had no idea if it would work. A fifty-fifty shot at best.

Sometimes the ideas you have to run with as a captain aren't the most ideal.

The interceptor banked right and began a freefall. The thin, brown clouds rushed past the windows.

"Please tell me this won't last long." Nelvan's eyes were shut tight and his facial muscles were spasming.

The ship swung around till we were descending nose downward. The distant ground of Outer Serberat was getting closer with every freem.

"Are there any barf bags in here?" Nelvan said.

I spotted the three droid ships dead ahead. "There they are."

"They're too close. Power this thing back on," Jasette said.

"Not yet. We're completely powered down," I said. "We're off their sensors. They can't see us … I think."

The interceptor gained speed as we continued our silent descent. For a tense moment, it looked as though the droid ships were going to smash into us. Then, they zoomed past, the high whirr of their engines rising and falling as they headed skyward.

"Now comes the fun part." I powered on the engine and all the ship's controls. I swung the ship around and put the thrusters on full. The holosphere visual emerged, this time with the three red ships in front of us.

"Ships are within range," the computer said.

"Music to my ears." I hit the cannons and a steady stream of orange beams shot toward the closest droid ship. The lasers tore into the back of it. Suddenly, a bright orange explosion took the place of where the smoking ship flew just moments ago.

Jasette smiled. "Nice."

"The ships have begun evasive maneuvers," the computer said.

The remaining droid ships broke off in separate directions.

"Not so fast." I angled the interceptor to the left and launched a concussion missile just ahead of the droid ships' path. I swerved the controls to the right and launched another concussion missile. "Computer, bring up targeting grid."

A green hologrid dropped from the ceiling. Glowing red dots symbolized the missiles speeding toward the ships.

"You overshot." Jasette squinted at the moving dots.

"Just wait." I sped toward the first droid ship and sent a stream of lasers behind it. "Computer, detonate first missile."

"Detonation confirmed," the computer said.

A bright blast shone in the sky, creating a silhouette of the droid ship speeding toward it. The targeting grid showed the droid ship doubling back to avoid the blast. Another bright explosion filled the sky as the droid ship sped head first into my oncoming stream of lasers.

"Computer, detonate second missile." I angled the ship right and sent another stream of lasers toward the back of the third ship.

"Detonation confirmed."

"Deja vu," Blix said.

The third ship followed the same pattern as the previous ship and another bright orange explosion lit up the sky. I leaned back in the pilot's chair and breathed a sigh of relief.

"That was incredible." Nelvan was beaming.

I wheeled the ship around, setting a course away from the slums of Outer Serberat. The sprawling white oval of the main dome was dead ahead. Jasette grinned and shook her head. "I have to admit, that was some good flying."

"I was ready for something horrible to happen," Nelvan said.

"Me too," Blix said.

I started to get a little annoyed at the level of surprise in the cockpit. "Well, don't everyone sound so shocked. I am a pilot after all."

"Yes, but … I mean …" Jasette seemed to search for the words. "It was a nice surprise."

"Right, surprise, you know, what we've been through so far, um, your track record and all," Nelvan fumbled.

"My track record?" I cast a stern glance back at Nelvan. "We just escaped from a Zeuthian-soldier-filled, subterranean, high-security compound thanks to me."

"I'd like to think it was a team effort." Blix folded his arms and wore a pouty expression.

"If you children are almost through, we're coming up on

the hangars." Jasette pointed to a series of raised domes ahead. From a distance, they resembled giant mushrooms with long, slender stems.

The ship was right inside the hangar. One final obstacle stood between us and the freedom of space.

21

"ARE WE HEADED back to the ship?" Nelvan said.

"That's the idea," I said.

"But I thought we couldn't leave the spaceport?"

"Details. We're getting off this rock." I said.

"What about these holding spheres?" Nelvan pointed to the red globe in his forehead. "I thought you said it would explode and obliterate the ship?"

"Blix, you can create some sort of cryogenic system to slow the proximity clock, right?"

Blix gave a thoughtful look toward the ceiling of the cockpit. "Theoretically, maybe, but practically—"

"Good enough," I interrupted. "Jasette, can you gain service entrance to Hangar 5?"

Jasette started tapping out commands on her power suit touch panel. "I'm on it."

In a few moments we were hovering within arm's reach of the underbelly of the giant white sphere of Hangar 5. I turned to Jasette but before I could open my mouth she raised her hand as if to silence me.

"I know, I know," she said. "I've already gained maintenance level entrance. I'm just setting the interceptor's nav computer to the other side of this spaceport. We need all the decoys we can get."

"Maintenance entrance?" I said.

"Provides the easiest access, raises the least suspicion and gets us where we want to be." Jasette tapped out a final command and a hatch in the hanger above us slid open. She gathered her things and gave me an impatient look. "That okay with you?"

I shrugged. "If you want to do it the sissy way."

Jasette shook her head and sighed. I hit the exit panel and the cockpit door slid open. A dusty, warm, particulate filled gust of wind swept over the top of the ship. "Alright, let's go."

Blix leapt into the hatch like some muscle bound space frog. Within a freem, his smiling reptilian face was looking down at us. He reached an arm toward the cockpit and motioned for us to take it.

He hoisted us up one by one, his brute strength leaving my arm socket feeling all tingly and sore. Jasette seemed unfazed, but I had my suspicions he had taken extra care as he continued to treat her like royalty. When I noticed Nelvan rubbing his shoulder and wincing, I decided to keep quiet about the pain.

The maintenance entrance had led us into a darkened, narrow corridor that seemed more hallway than room. The metal floor was littered with broken instrument panels and burnt out droid parts.

The interceptor sped away, presumably following the course set by Jasette.

"Think it'll actually fool anyone?" I said.

Blix shrugged. "There's always a chance, Captain."

The exterior maintenance door slid closed and everything went black. There was a rustling sound coming from the spot where I'd seen Jasette standing.

"What's that sound?" I said.

"Don't worry about it," Jasette said.

"Anybody got a light?" I said.

"Yeah," Jasette said.

The darkness continued, along with more rustling sounds.

"Would you mind lighting the place up?" I added an impatient edge to my voice.

There was the sound of several zippers being pulled followed by a subtle energy pulse like something was being powered up. Two small, green point lights shot forth from Jasette's shoulders. Her power suit was back on and apparently, fully functional.

"Back in action." Jasette wore a confident smirk as she tied her hair back with a thin, leather strap.

Her shoulder lights bathed the maintenance corridor in a dull green hue. I noticed the crumpled white gown on the floor near her feet.

"You're not gonna keep the other outfit?" I said.

Jasette gave me a distasteful look. "No. Why would I?"

"It's a good look for you. Softens you up a bit."

Jasette put her hands on her hips and struck a challenging pose. "Oh, I get it. Afraid of a confident, able woman are you? You like the helpless, naïve type?"

"Sometimes."

"Typical. I bet they're actually fooled by that macho act you give them."

"Sometimes."

Blix gave a loud clearing of his throat. "As fascinated I am by the strange and often self-destructive mating dance of human beings, we should probably move before we're discovered."

"Mating dance?" Jasette scowled at Blix. "Not on your life."

"I'm sure she only dates men of royalty. Snooty, rich types like Hamilton."

"That just shows how little you know about me." Jasette said.

Blix cleared his throat. "Again with the dance. Listen, you

two can ruffle and preen all you want when we're safe on the ship. In the meantime—"

A clanging of metal sounded from the far wall. We stood motionless for a few moments straining to hear anything else. Blix stole quietly to the corridor's end and peered through a thin space in the metal wall. He motioned us forward as he removed a panel. Light from the next room flooded in.

The room was wide and rectangular. Long rows of recesses in the steel paneled walls formed shelves spilling over with electronic gizmos and droid parts in need of repair. Several large loading crates were scattered throughout the room.

Blix leapt into the next room with catlike agility, the rest of us following close behind.

"What was that sound?" Nelvan said.

"Droids. This must be their utility room." Blix pointed to a metal door in the far wall. "That's the entrance. Better keep an eye on it."

I moved to the far wall and peered through a seam in the door. Beyond was the expansive, glass domed hangar where my ship sat, ready to carry us to freedom. Even though it was dwarfed and its construction seemed horribly inferior to Hamilton's Velladrella starship nearby, it was a sight for sore eyes. Dozens of droids hovered and rolled through the hangar, looking thoroughly occupied.

"What do you see, Captain?" Nelvan said.

I turned to face him, feeling suddenly energized. "Our ship and freedom. Now, we need a plan before one of those droids comes in here." I rubbed the scruff on my chin and thought hard. Sadly, my mind was blank.

Jasette cleared her throat. When I looked over, she was

wearing a droid helmet on her head. She pointed to it and then spread out her arms as if showcasing the latest technology.

"Standard maintenance droid. Not even armor reinforced," I said.

Jasette crossed her arms and drummed her fingers, waiting.

"Oh, I see." I finally got the hint. "Okay, not bad. It could work."

"What?" Nelvan said.

"Look for a droid suit, boy." I started sifting through the clutter of parts nearby. "We're going undercover."

Nelvan smiled and nodded.

"Blix, watch the door," I said. "We don't want any droids zipping in here and sounding the alarm."

Blix nodded and stood guard by the entrance. We started scrounging through the shelves looking for parts that fit.

The entrance door slid open and two knee high droids wheeled in. The door slid shut behind them and Blix promptly snatched them up. He yanked out their power chips and set them on a high shelf.

"Can't take any chances," Blix grinned. "Even the smaller ones can sound the alarm."

I fastened a shiny silver tube on my forearm. My droid suit was coming together nicely. There were no mirrors nearby to pose in front of, but I was convinced I was looking pretty awesome.

"Their system is locked down pretty tight." Jasette was tapping out commands on her arm touch panel. She was nearly covered in droid pieces. Somehow she still managed to look alluring. "No high tech security but lots of droid interference and convoluted command structure. This might not be so easy."

"Terrific." I glanced over at Nelvan, who had already

finished his outfit and made a pretty convincing robot. "Not bad Nelvan. Try to find some pieces that will fit Blix."

Nelvan nodded his metallic head and sifted through some helmets nearby.

Before long, Jasette and I were finished and joined Nelvan in the search for parts that would fit Blix. It took much longer than we hoped and the end result wasn't terribly convincing. He looked bulky and broken with large gaps that revealed his copper scales.

"This isn't going to work," Jasette said.

"Maybe if we circle around him and move really fast," Nelvan said.

"No good. We've got to get to the ship unnoticed or they'll lock it down." I scanned the room and noticed a large, rectangular container in the corner. "Hey, can you fit in that?"

Blix followed my gaze to the container. "Not likely," he grimaced. "Besides, I don't like confined spaces."

"Well, you're not going out there like that." I pointed to his piecemeal outfit. "I don't even think they make maintenance droids that big."

Blix frowned and made no response. He knew it was unavoidable.

The container was partially filled with burnt out wires and broken metal. Blix removed his poor droid outfit as we emptied the container, keeping the clanking sounds to a minimum.

"Jump in," I said.

Blix leaned over the container and sniffed. "If there were such a thing as a decaying droid corpse, it would smell like this."

"Quit whining and get in there before we're discovered," I said.

Blix narrowed his dangerous looking reptilian eyes, then

hoisted himself inside. He kneeled and bent down till his chin rested on his knees. I brought the lid down but his broad, scaly back kept it from closing.

"Get down, I can't close it," I said.

"I am down. I can't go any further." Blix's voice was muffled and edgy.

"Try."

An angry hiss sounded from the container and his body shifted slightly. I tried again but the lid was several inches away from closing.

"You sure that's the best you can do?" I said.

"I can't take this smell. Let me out." Blix had started to rise when the entrance door to the room slid open. He slumped back down as two human sized droids hovered into the room.

They were slender, olive colored units with a rotating yellow light that spun around their cylindrical head. The droids paused as their yellow lights moved back and forth over each of us.

I straightened into what must've looked like a guilty droid stance. One of the droids hovered over to me. His monotone, metallic voice sounded. "Loading units, why aren't you responding on the impulse network?"

I faked my best robot voice. "We collided with each other. Our connection was disrupted."

The droid tilted his head to the side. "All three of you?"

He wasn't buying it. I took it as a major defeat that I was having trouble bluffing a droid.

"Yes, an improbable event, statistically speaking." I tried to recover by talking all droidy.

"What is your last requisition order code?" A small panel slid open on the torso of the droid and an energy pulse prod angled toward me.

"My circuits are ... slow from the collision and, um, the last requisition was loading that crate over there." I pointed to the container Blix was huddled in.

The droid swiveled his head to the container, then back to me. "That container is not secured for transport."

"We were unable to secure it." Jasette spoke in a robotic tone. I had to admit, it was more convincing than mine. "Perhaps you can help us?" Jasette tilted her droid body in what looked like a robotic flirtation, if there was such a thing.

The olive droid swiveled his head at the other one for a moment before turning back to Jasette. "Certainly." A series of ascending beeps sounded from the droid. His digitized voice had taken on a nervous edge.

The two droids hovered over to the container. Their cylindrical bodies bent forward for a closer examination.

"Hey, over there," I called.

The yellow lights on their droid heads swiveled round to me.

"Bye," I said.

Blix sprung up from the container. In one swift motion he placed a meaty, reptilian hand on each of the droid's heads and brought them together in a resounding crash. A shower of electrical sparks broke forth and the droids collapsed to the floor in a crumpled heap.

"Perfect timing," I said.

Blix nodded, a fierce reptilian sneer still animating his features.

"Time to move," I said. "Missing droids are gonna start raising suspicions." I motioned to the container. "In you go."

Blix frowned and resumed his crouching position. I found the loading control panel on the side of the container and powered it on. A low hum sounded and the container hovered a few inches off the ground.

"Nelvan, grab the other side," I said. "Jasette, you stay behind me. If any droids get nosey, scramble their signals."

Jasette's muffled voice echoed in her helmet. "I never said I could do that."

"They're maintenance droids. How hard can it be?"

"I told you, it's convoluted droid chatter. They're locked into an impulse hub that communicates on a reverse sequencing matrix that—"

"Blah, blah, blah, can you do it or not?"

Jasette put her arms out as if presenting them for some kind of inspection. "How am I supposed to reach my controls with these droid parts on me?"

"Fine," I said. "We'll do this the old fashioned way." I bent down to one of the collapsed olive droids. I opened the back panel of his torso and located a grouping of wires clustered under a bright red warning label. The label read, CORE WIRING. DANGER, DO NOT TOUCH. ANY TAMPERING WILL RENDER ALL WARRANTIES NULL AND VOID.

I ripped off the label and yanked out a handful of wires.

"What are you doing?" Jasette said.

"Plan B." I laid the exposed wiring on the power circuits next to it and closed the back panel. Bright sparks and ribbons of ascending smoke soon followed the sounds of electrical short circuits.

"Alright, let's go," I grabbed the back corner of the container and pushed. It dipped slightly, then glided forward. Nelvan and Jasette fell into place beside the container and we headed for the entrance.

The panel slid open as we approached, ushering us into the glass domed ceiling of Hangar 5.

22

WE ENTERED HANGAR 5 with the Blix filled container in tow. Droids crisscrossed our path and our presence seemed to break their fluid rhythm. Several times droids had to stop abruptly and wheel around us, each emitting what sounded like perturbed beeps as they passed.

"This isn't good," Jasette whispered. "We're disrupting their signal patterns."

"In a few freems it won't matter," I said.

I looked back at the panel door to the utility room. Smoke was streaming out from the bottom of the door. An unaware droid headed for the panel. It slid open at his approach and smoke billowed into the hangar.

Red spinning lights emerged from the walls throughout the room. An ascending tone that sounded like a droid regurgitating began to blare. Droids nearby stopped and turned to see what was happening. No doubt they were calculating the extent of damages to see if they should high tail it out of the hangar.

"You see," I said. "It's working."

We made it to the base of the ship. Freedom was within reach.

"Jasette, can you unlock the holding field and open the hangar?" I said.

"Piece of cake." She moved over to the landing console

pedestal at the base of our ship. Somehow she still managed to look robotic.

As she worked away at the touch panel, I heard several systems power down. The landing ramp of my ship lowered. It was like a royal entryway welcoming the king back to his castle.

"Is it okay?" Nelvan whispered. "Can we get on the ship?"

"Nothing's stopping us now," I said.

"Where are you going with that container?" a computerized voice said.

I turned to find Fofo, the concierge droid, flanked by two bulky, security droids. They had quad-barreled, semi-repeaters trained on me.

"Oh … hello there." My worst response in a pressure filled situation ever. Too many stressful events had thrown me off my game.

A series of descending beeps came from Fofo. "Service droid, what is your requisition order?"

I tried to recover. "All the smoke and the alarm systems have affected my circuits. All I know is I'm supposed to load this container on that ship." I motioned to the landing ramp.

Fofo's head swiveled from the ship to me. "That ship is on level five restriction." Fofo shifted his attention to Nelvan. "What's in the container?"

"Um, cleaning supplies?" Nelvan said.

Fofo gave a quick look at the security droids at his side and then emitted two harsh beeps. The droids trudged over to the container. I carefully slid my hand underneath my droid outfit till I felt the handle of the DEMOTER.

One of the security droids lifted the container lid and, as if he were making an encore performance, Blix sprang up. He grabbed their bulky heads and smashed them together in a loud crunch of metal and a shower of sparks.

I drew the DEMOTER and with a satisfying squeeze of the trigger, sent Fofo flying backward in a trail of smoke.

"Nice shot." Jasette looked up for a moment to watch Fofo's departure, then returned her attention to the landing console.

"Captain, really." Blix shook his head. His large, scaly hands still clutched metal remnants of droid head. "The same routine twice in a row? You're really not taking advantage of my full array of talents."

"If it ain't broke, don't fix it," I said.

A loud unlocking mechanism echoed through the hangar.

"Field is down," Jasette said. "Hangar is opening."

The glass dome overhead split in half and opened like some deadly, crystalline flower waiting for an insect.

"Let's go." I led the way up the landing ramp. I noticed Jasette hanging back. "What are you doing?"

She took off her droid head, pulled two small, silver discs out from under her costume and flung them at Hamilton's ship. They clung to the hull of the Velladrella and started pulsating red.

She sprinted up the ramp toward me. "Just leaving an explosive little gift for Hamilton. No serious damage but enough to slow him down with repairs."

I looked at her in admiration. "You're a fantastic woman."

Jasette winked and ran past me into the ship.

I followed her up the ramp, removing pieces of my droid outfit and casting them aside in a clattering of metal.

Iris's voice echoed through the ship. She sang in a cheery, dreamlike manner. Iris rarely sang and when she did it was usually a lamenting kind of dirge.

"Iris?" I said. "Everything alright?"

"Oh, Captain," Iris spoke as if she was spinning in a sunny meadow. "I feel so alive, so young."

"Terrific." I jogged behind the crew, all of us heading for the lift. "Now power up the systems and get us outta here."

"You kept your promise," Iris said. "The Andrellian cleansing system. It was so wonderful. You really do care, don't you?"

"Sure I care. Now if you're really grateful, get us away from this hangar as fast as you can."

"Of course, Captain. Anything for you."

I was the last to enter the lift and the doors chirped shut behind me.

"Take us to the med unit, Iris." Blix rubbed his chin, casting a concerned look from Nelvan to me. "I need to see what I can do about those spheres."

The lift started to ascend as the ship lurched upward. We were thrown to the floor as the ship climbed.

"Are you alright, Captain?" Iris sounded concerned. "Perhaps I should slow our ascent."

"No, no," I said. "Fast as you can, we're fine."

"Okay." Iris giggled. "You're so brave."

Blix shot me a confused look. "That Andrellian cleansing must be incredible."

I nodded and grasped the lift railing. "Hold tight everyone."

Jasette grabbed the railing and pressed her feet against the floor for leverage. Nelvan wrapped his arm around the railing and hugged it tight, his eyes shut.

There were a few moments of turbulence as we headed out of the manufactured atmosphere of the space station but soon it was smooth sailing as we headed into the grand freedom of space.

23

"DOES IT HAVE TO be this cold?" I said.

"If you'd prefer not to explode." Blix was making the final adjustments on my med halo. The flexible silver band encircled my forehead and covered the holding sphere.

"I think mine's getting colder." Nelvan was gingerly touching his med halo on the padded recovery slab nearby.

All four of us being crammed in the med unit accentuated the humble size of the room. There were only two med slabs, with digital readouts in the walls behind them. A narrow walkway allowed for a single file inspection of patients.

"Are you sure this will work?" I lifted my hand to adjust the halo but Blix swatted it away.

"Don't touch," Blix said. "The cryo-pulse settings are delicate. I have them focused on the sphere but if you move them you'll end up freezing part of your brain."

"Great, something else to worry about."

Blix narrowed his eyes. "Perhaps if we secured the services of a real doctor, I wouldn't have to fill a thousand roles aboard this ship."

"And how do you expect to pay them?" I said. "We're broke."

Blix shrugged. "Ship prosperity rests on your shoulders."

"Wrong. The starship oath of loyalty clearly states—"

"Would you two shut up?" Jasette was manning a small control panel mounted in the wall. She'd been searching the nearby systems for any skilled neuro specialists, while Blix worked on the halos. "You sound like children. We've got real problems here."

"Any luck over there?" I said.

Jasette shook her head. "Not yet."

"Okay, that should do it." Blix stepped back, his eyes scanning the halo in a final inspection.

"Really?" I moved to a mirrored panel in the wall to check my reflection. It wasn't a good look for me. Very few people can pull off puffy, silver headbands, especially with pajama pants.

"Just remember not to touch it." Blix shook his finger at me like a parent.

Jasette broke her focus from the control panel long enough to see my new look. "That's perfect for you," she chuckled. "Very manly."

"Hmm, yes." Blix wrinkled his nose. "You may want to consider a hat."

"Never mind," I said. "I'll be on the bridge if you need me."

I left the med unit and made a quick stop at my quarters to grab a decent pair of pants.

Soon I was back on the bridge in my captain's chair. I looked down and smiled at the sight of my new pants. Real pants. Space captain pants. They were jet black with a thick solar orange stripe down the side. The orange was segmented uniformly with thin black stitching. Basically, they were the coolest pants you could wear in space.

I sat back in my chair and closed my eyes. I was alone on the bridge, enjoying every moment of the solitude. The quiet hum of the engines and the occasional beeps from the multi-colored control panels were like a calm stream in a forest to my ears.

I activated the armrest touch panel and brought up my

music selection. As I scrolled through my favorite genres, I came across a playlist entitled, "high, screechy noises." It was a bogus title to throw off anyone snooping through my music. I looked around to make sure no one was there, then entered the unlocking code.

Delicate, flowing synthesizer tones flowed down from the ceiling speakers. The soft voice of a Xot–the renowned three-headed Veltorian singer–filled the bridge with her three part harmonies.

I'd like to live on puffy clouds,
away from uncelestial grounds.
Let's soar away from gloom and doom
and bask in glow of star and moon ...

I heard the familiar chirp of the lift door opening. My fingers fumbled across the touch panel as I rushed to turn off the music.

"What's that?" Jasette strolled in from the lift.

"Nothing." I couldn't hide a defensive tone in my voice.

Jasette let out a chuckle. "Sounded like one of those wretched, warm fuzzy synth ballads."

"Yeah," I said. "Totally lame. I must've activated the music controls by mistake. Probably Blix's music."

"Oh, Blix's music, huh?" Jasette stood by me with arms casually crossed and a knowing grin.

"Did you want something? I'm kind of busy." I made a big show of tapping out fake commands, to look like I couldn't be bothered.

Jasette strolled over to the navigator's chair nearby. "I just thought you might want to know the plan." She sat in the chair and swiveled it to face me. The truth was, the chair had been empty since I first bought the ship. Navigators generally charge high fees and I was a better pilot than most of them anyway.

"Your *recommendation* for the plan," I said. "I'm the one who decides on the plans aboard this ship."

Jasette rolled her eyes. "Do you want to hear it or not?"

"Yeah, but I have veto power if I don't like it."

"Fine. There are records of a neuro specialist named Doctor Tellberell on the Villeth moon. We could get there by day's end."

A spark of hope fired in my brain. "Really? Well, that's great news."

"There's just one thing. He's got a criminal record."

My spark faded a little. "Are we talking smuggler with a heart of gold or ruthless thug overlord?"

"Somewhere in the middle."

My choices in life were often less than ideal. "Any other options?"

Jasette shook her head.

"Well, then. Let's pay Doctor Tellberell a visit."

I hit the intercom. "Blix, I've decided to—"

"Coordinates for the Villeth moon already locked in, Captain," Blix said.

My jaw clinched. "You locked in a flight path before my consent?"

"Captain," Blix said. "This is no time for protocol. Every moment counts."

I drummed my fingers on the armrest, annoyed that he was right. "I'll excuse your breach of conduct this time, just don't forget who's captain here."

Blix laughed. "You remind me every freem."

"Watch it, lizard boy."

Jasette sighed. "Are there any grown ups aboard this ship?"

"Captain," Blix said. "On a positive note, our course takes us through the outer edge of the Beringfell system. The supposed location of the Emerald Enigma."

"The outer edge? What good is that?" I said. "We need to scour every inch of that system."

"Okay," Blix said. "Don't get all snippy. I just thought it was worth mentioning." Blix muttered something about grouchy and the intercom clicked off.

Jasette stood and walked over to the half circle railing around the captain's chair. "You're better off anyway. It's a wild goose chase." She leaned forward on the rail and gave a sympathetic look my way.

"Don't give me that look." I pointed at her.

She gave an annoyed glance at my finger. I became acutely aware that I was overdoing my trademark power point. I quickly lowered it. It was going to lose all impact unless I scaled back.

"I have reliable, underground information that it does exist and that it is in fact in Beringfell."

Jasette gave a sympathetic nod.

"Stop that," I said. "You're doing it again."

"What?"

"You're looking at me like I'm a fool."

"Under the circumstances—"

"Listen here, princess." I stood and took a step toward her to assert my authority as a captain. I miscalculated the distance and ended up too close. I could tell I was in her space. She looked uncomfortable for a moment and then stiffened to show she wasn't intimidated. I couldn't back down at this point so I launched into my challenge.

"I could've left you back there at the space port," I said.

"You started this whole relationship off by trying to steal my ship and cash in the bounty on my head."

"This is a relationship now?" Jasette gave a look of mock innocence that communicated her feminine powers of relationship defining were spinning well ahead of me.

"Well, no, not a relationship, really, but you know, just ..."

Jasette gave a slight smile. "Just what?"

I tried to rally. "Whatever it is, it's all due to me being nicer to you than you deserve."

She paused for a moment, a thoughtful look on her face. "You're right."

"I'm what?" I was in sparring mode so she took me off guard. The fierce look in her eyes disappeared. They became soft, vulnerable.

Which of course was far more frightening.

"I tried to steal your ship," she said. "Then I cozied up to Hamilton, your least favorite person, just to try and free myself. And after all that, you still helped me escape." She gave me a quizzical look. "And you risked your life for Nelvan, too. Underneath all that childish bravado you really are a sweetheart, aren't you?"

"How about *heroic* heart? Not quite as touchy feely."

Jasette smiled. It was a warm smile. A smile I wasn't used to seeing on her face. It meant I'd broken through all the tough chick defenses.

I knew I had a small window of time to say something dashing and sweep her off her feet. I leaned a little closer, closing the gap between us. She didn't back away. So far, so good. She was searching my eyes, waiting for what I was going to say.

My mind struggled for a moment when suddenly, it was there, the perfect thing to say. There were a few times in my life when I had a great moment like this but had nothing to say. This time was different. For once my brain hadn't let me down in an epic event. It had given me a perfect line. It was romantic without being cheesy, poetic without pretense, heartfelt without being gushy. I kept the excitement of a perfect line from my face. I held her gaze with a strong, confident look. I touched her hand and felt a small shiver. It was time to deliver the greatest line of all time.

"Jasette," I began.

The ship alarm blared. The thin red light that circled the bridge flashed a bright red. I covered my ears. "What in blazes is it, computer?"

A few discordant tones sounded. "There's a problem with one of the hull sensors. I suggest immediate investigation."

"Can't it wait?" I said.

"I'm afraid not, Captain."

"Well, at least shut off that alarm."

"Yes, Captain." The alarm stopped and the warning lights turned off.

"Look Iris," I said. "Can't you just shut down the sensor, or lock it down or do one of those re-routy, backup kind of things computers do?"

"No, Captain. Someone will need to suit up and go outside the ship to fix it."

"Terrific." I looked back at Jasette. She gave a sad smile and took a step back.

"Captain," the computer said. "I wouldn't recommend leaving the ship with that holding sphere. The pressures of space could prove dangerous."

"Good point," I said.

"Perhaps Jasette could go," the computer said.

"Jasette?" I gave a confused glance at her. "No, no, that won't work. Blix can do it."

"We need him to monitor the med halos," the computer said.

"I could go." Jasette gave a dutiful look.

"No, it's too dangerous." I turned back to my chair and hit the intercom. "Blix, we've got a situation."

"Another one?" Blix said.

"Yeah. Seems a hull sensor got damaged."

An electric crackle followed by a stream of static came from the intercom speakers.

"Blix," I said. "You there?"

A steady stream of static was my only answer.

"Computer, we have intercom problems," I said.

"Yes Captain, I'm already looking into it."

I grabbed the comlink at my side and activated it. More static.

"Come on." I led the way to the lift. "Before Blix tries to send me a thought message."

The lift door opened and Jasette followed me inside. The doors closed and with a low hum, the lift descended. Something was wrong. Too many glitches right after a full ship cleansing spelled trouble.

"You okay?" Jasette could read the look on my face.

"I'm starting to wonder if Hamilton did something to my ship," I said.

Jasette frowned. "If Hamilton was going to do something, wouldn't it be more covert? Silent monitoring, tracking sensors, that kind of thing."

"Maybe we escaped before he had time to finish tampering." I looked up. "Computer, run a thorough scan of every alteration that happened in that hangar. Let me know if anything strange shows up.

"Yes, Captain," the computer said.

The lift opened and we headed toward the med unit.

24

BLIX WAS MAKING adjustments to Nelvan's med halo as Jasette and I entered the med unit.

"Ah, Captain, you're here," Blix said. "Once we lost the intercom I didn't know what happened. I was about to thought message you."

"Don't you dare." I pointed a threatening finger at Blix.

Jasette cast an annoyed look at my pointing finger. There was no doubt I'd overused it for the day. It was losing all impact. I dropped the finger and switched to a hands on the hips pose of frustration. It was a little girly for my taste but it was all I could think of at the moment.

"We've got computer glitches all over the place," I said. "Hull sensors failing, intercoms going static. What's going on?"

"Captain, please." Blix put his hand on his heart as if to emphasize his concern. "I realize I'm an incredible problem solver but right now, it's all I can do to keep you and Nelvan from blowing up."

"Stop playing the martyr," I said. "I think Hamilton rigged the ship. Just in case we got away, he wanted some way to stop us."

The scales on Blix's face wrinkled in confusion. "That doesn't sound like Hamilton. He's more calculated, understated. He would've planted tracking sensors, monitoring micro bots, things of a clandestine nature."

Jasette piped up. "That's what I said."

Blix smiled. "Your Majesty is insightful as well as beautiful." He gave her a slight bow and Jasette blew him a kiss.

"Okay, I'm gonna vomit now." I put my hands to my temples. All the new problems were making my head throb. I sat down on the open med slab. Every cell in my body felt like it was begging me to lie down and sleep.

"Easy, Captain." Blix walked toward me. "You mustn't make any sudden movements near the holding sphere."

Blix drew in close and examined my med halo. His fingers worked with delicate grace that belied their meaty size. But careful as he was, every small adjustment felt like ice chips were shooting into my skull.

"Be careful," I said. "This is pure torture."

"It's either this or your head explodes," Blix said.

"Maybe you should check mine again," Nelvan stood from his med slab and walked over to us.

"Oh." Blix looked like he just remembered something. "Make sure neither of you gets a headache."

"I have a headache," I said.

"Get rid of it," Blix said.

"How am I supposed to get rid of it?"

"Try some relaxation therapy. I have some wonderful scented oils and synth music you can use."

"I don't want that smelly, voodoo trash."

"Captain," Blix was frowning at my halo. "I'm detecting an accelerated pulse on your sphere proximity clock. Are you experiencing any anxiety?"

"I've got a bomb surgically implanted in my head. What do you think?"

Blix shook his head. "If you don't calm down, you're going to kill us all."

Jasette moved closer and put her hand on my shoulder. "Glint, why don't you get some sleep. We've been through a lot."

"Excellent idea," Blix said. "That might even slow the clock down. Give us more time."

"In that case, maybe I should rest too," Nelvan went back to the other med slab and lay down.

I wanted to argue but I was exhausted. I hadn't had a decent night's sleep in three days, one of those days being the third worst day of my life and today was headed toward the top ten. Besides that, I was feeling dizzy with fatigue.

"You really should rest." Jasette patted me on the shoulder. She looked at me with warm, convincing eyes. They were deep pools of shimmering green. I had a flashback of the emerald caves on the Glisprit moon back in junior space explorer camp. Deep caverns with luminous green walls that shimmered in the starlight. Beauty and tranquility that was unmatched.

"Um, Glint?" Jasette said.

"Yeah?"

"You've been staring at my eyes for, like, a really long time." Jasette's face held several lines of concern, like I was creeping her out.

"Captain," Blix said. "You really should lie down."

"Okay, fine." I stood and threw up my hands. "But not because you told me to, just because I'm tired."

"Iris," Blix said. "Kindly place the ship on sleep mode. The crew needs a rest."

As I headed for the door, the lights dimmed and subtle, flowing bands of illumination cascaded around the walls and ceiling. The delicate sounds of stringed instruments played softly throughout the ship.

"What's all this?" I made a sweeping gesture around the room. "I didn't authorize any pansy light and music show."

"This is for our guests," Blix said. "It's called hospitality."

"Well, it's lame."

"I kinda like it." Nelvan was looking up at the ceiling from his med slab, watching the bands of light flow around the room like some enchanted infant.

"Figures." I shook my head.

"It's nice." Jasette nodded. "Very peaceful."

Blix had a broad grin. "Three to one Captain. Majority rules."

"That sounds like mutiny."

Blix sighed. "Captain, you need this."

I was too tired to argue anymore. "Fine, but I'm putting a mutiny charge down in the ship's records." I stormed out of the room and headed for my quarters.

25

I COULDN'T GET the thought of Hamilton tampering with my ship out of my head. I took a detour for the bridge. I wanted to check the computer for any rogue code strings that could sabotage the ship.

In a few moments I was back in the captain's chair, using the armrest controls to bring up files on the main viewing screen. I scanned through all the recent logs for anything that looked remotely unusual.

"Computer, any results from your scans?" I said.

"Everything is perfectly normal."

I was convinced something was wrong so I kept searching.

After a couple of trids looking through mind numbing data files and code I'd found nothing. My head was swimming with exhaustion and I could barely keep my eyes focused on the screen.

The lift doors chirped open and in walked Blix.

"Captain, what are you doing in here? You're supposed to be asleep in your quarters."

"I told you," I said. "Something's wrong. Hamilton must've done something, I just can't find it."

Blix reached my chair and gave me a consoling look. "I'm not sure if it's determination or stubbornness but you certainly don't give up easy."

I leaned back and closed my eyes. "I'm desperate, Blix. I'm starting to think ..."

"What?"

I opened my eyes and fixed his gaze. "I'm thinking this might be it."

"Oh, don't be silly." Blix tried for a cavalier smile but I could tell it was forced. He knew we were in a bad spot.

"We've been through worse," Blix said. "Remember the slave pits of the Necron system?"

"Of course. Fifth worst day of my life."

"And the rabid space monkeys that chased us through the seven eternally spinning vortexes?"

A shudder went through my body. "I told you never to mention that. First worst day of my life. I still have nightmares filled with those filthy creatures."

"Okay," Blix said. "So, this can't be as bad as that and we lived to tell the tale, right?"

In spite of my stress I had to smile. I stood and clasped him on the shoulder. "You're a good friend."

"As are you, Captain," Blix smiled. "Now go and get some rest. I'll look through the rest of these files."

"Thanks. If we make it out of this one, I'll double your caramel cake rations."

"Don't tease me."

"You have my word." I turned and headed to the lift.

Soon I was walking down the hallway toward my quarters. My thoughts were consumed with collapsing on my sleeping slab and finally getting a decent rest. Nothing could distract my focused attention on that goal.

A door opened up just ahead from the guest quarters. Jasette stepped through the doorway. She was wearing one of the white sleeping smocks we kept on board for visitors. It fit her like it was a custom designed nightdress. Her hair was down and fell across her shoulders like the silken waterfalls on Blendark 9. She was almost angelic. I tried to keep my expression stoic, as if her beauty, heightened by countless days of lonely space travel, was as common as a maintenance droid.

"Why are you staring at me like that?" Jasette said.

"Like what?"

"Your mouth was hanging open and you were looking me up and down." Jasette crossed her arms in a defensive position.

"Oh, I was just thinking that the smock is just your size. I'm glad it fit." I gave my brain an imaginary high five for a quick recovery.

"Oh." She softened a bit. "Yeah, well, it's soft enough but it's practically see-through. I'm wearing three of them just to stay decent. What perv designed these?"

"Um … probably Blix." I grabbed the communicator from my hip and made a fake call. "Blix, these night smocks are unacceptable. Make them thicker next time." I pretended to shut the device off.

Jasette gave me a scrutinizing stare. "I thought the communicators weren't working. Did you just make a fake call?"

"What? No, I had it in stealth mode." I raced to change the subject. "So, everything okay with your room?"

She gave an annoyed glance back to her room. "The water is scalding hot. I asked for cool water and was about to take a drink when I saw steam rising. Could've given me a serious burn."

"Computer," I called out. "Look into Jasette's water situation."

A few discordant blips sounded. "Shouldn't Jasette be

heading outside the ship to check on the hull sensor right about now?"

"Later," I said. "We all need sleep. In the meantime, how about fixing Jasette's water?"

A creaking sound went through the hallway as if the ship's structural framework was adjusting to some unseen force. "Of course, Captain. As long as our special guest has every little thing her heart desires I'll consider my tireless efforts a great success."

"There, you see." I motioned toward the ceiling. "I told you Hamilton did something. Iris usually responds with the wounded victim routine. Bitter sarcasm is definitely out of character."

Jasette raised an eyebrow.

"Captain," Iris sniffed. "You know I hate it when you talk about me like I'm not in the room."

"You're always in the room." I tried to restrain the frustration in my voice. "In every room, all the time. What am I supposed to do?"

Digitized sobbing echoed in the hallway. "Fine. If that's the way you feel, I'll leave."

The flowing light show dimmed and the sobbing faded away. Only the subtle illumination of the floor runners remained.

I let out a heavy sigh.

"Maybe you should lie down." Jasette looked concerned. "You look like you're headed for space dementia."

I nodded. Her concern for my well-being, coupled with her combat skills, was a potent combination. She was just the type of girl I'd been looking for. And yet, her secrecy still nagged at me.

"You ever gonna let me in on your secrets?" I raised an eyebrow. "After all, you know mine."

She took a long breath and held my gaze for a moment as if deciding how much she should trust me. She opened her mouth to speak, then stopped and gave me a skeptical look.

"I'm going to die soon, anyways. You can trust a dying man, right?"

She let out a small sigh. "Hold on." She went back into her room for a moment, then returned, her powersuit draped over her shoulders. She tapped out a series of numbers on her forearm computer and a holographic image of a flower in wide bloom spun slowly between us. It was clear and shimmered as it spun, as though it were made of ice.

"I'm looking for a Chrysolenthium flower," she said. "They're very rare."

"Chryso-what?"

"They used to grow on our planet. Our technology was developed around its unusual properties. One flower can power my kingdom for twenty gloons, but our last flower is almost depleted."

"Okay, so why not just grow some more?"

"It takes ten gloons to grow a new flower. A large, cosmic storm destroyed all the others. If I don't find one soon, my kingdom loses power. No power, no shields, most of our weaponry would go offline. We'd be sitting ducks for our enemies."

"Okay, so why'd they send their princess?" I said. "Shouldn't your soldiers be out flying around the universe looking for this weird flower?"

"Many went out in the search. We've lost contact with most of them. I grew tired of waiting around so I volunteered. They knew I'd go whether they wanted me to or not."

I nodded. "I can see that."

She gave a sly grin and turned off the holographic image.

"So what's with the bounty hunter cover?" I said. "Why'd you try and take our ship?"

She let out a heavy breath and looked at the floor as if embarrassed. "I ran out of money. Collecting bounties is how I get by until I can find the flower. Plus, I'm pretty good at it. Fifty thousand vibes could have kept me going for awhile." She gave me an apologetic look. "Sorry."

I waved a dismissive hand. "Don't worry about it. I just don't know why it's so high. Maybe I can reason with Mar Mar, get him to lower it again."

Jasette gave a bemused look. "I don't think so."

"Yeah, you're right." There was a moment of uncomfortable silence where I wasn't sure what to say. She'd actually told me her secrets. Well, really just one secret but still, it was a big one. There was some sort of trusty-bondy thing going on. Which, of course, meant she was totally into me. It was time to be smooth and secure her affections.

I moved a little closer and grabbed her hand. "Listen, if by some miracle we survive all this, I'll do what I can to help you find it."

She raised her eyebrows and looked at me in disbelief. "Really?"

"Sure. If I'm still alive, why not?"

She paused for a moment, studying me as though waiting to see if I was joking. "You know, I think I like this sleep-deprived side of you. I knew there was a nice guy in there."

"Yeah, well, maybe we should keep the whole nice guy thing between us. Word gets out and I'll lose my whole tough guy rep."

Jasette flashed a seductive smile. "It'll be our little secret."

Her smile was pure intoxication and in my disoriented state, I had little power to resist immediate impulses. Before I fully realized what I was doing, I drew her close and held her tight against me. I leaned in and was about to kiss her when the floor felt as if it swayed, then trembled beneath us.

Jasette pulled away. "Did you feel that?"

"Heck yeah," I said.

She gave me a quizzical look. "No, I mean the ship."

The floor swayed once more.

"There," Jasette said. "Did you feel that?"

"Yeah. Computer, what's happening?"

All was silent for a few moments. Another shudder went through the ship.

"Iris, respond," I said. "The ship may be in danger."

"I'm fine, Captain." Iris sounded unusually calm. "It's just a little problem I've encountered out here in space."

A few dull tones sounded and the subtle, flowing night mode lights came back on. Instead of their usual cool blue tones, they shone with a dark crimson.

"What's the problem?"

"It's under control," Iris said. "I know just how to fix it." A series of descending beeps sounded.

I could tell by Jasette's mannerisms that the moment had passed. I resigned myself to getting some sleep and hoping for another chance at romance after some much needed rest. "Well, I guess I should go."

Jasette gave a warm smile. "Rest well. Here's hoping we live to see tomorrow."

"Yeah, here's hoping."

26

I ENTERED MY QUARTERS and hit the room atmosphere control panel next to the door. The rectangular panel lit up with a subtle blue glow and displayed a series of icons. The icon shapes ranged from food and beverages to temperature and lighting. I tapped the icon shaped like a humanoid lying on a thin rectangle. The icon glowed and expanded and several adjustment controls appeared below.

My sleeping slab emerged from a recess in the circular walls of the room. The gelatinous top of the slab expanded as it filled with a green sleeping gel. I set the movement controls to gentle massage with pulsating heat.

I threw off my jacket, kicked off my boots and hung the DEMOTER and holster off the side of the sleeping slab. I hesitated for a moment before changing into my pajama pants but eventually the desire for comfort won out. Soon I was sporting the red-checkered pants that had haunted me all day.

"These pants did get washed, right?" I said.

"Of course, Captain," Iris said. "I saw to it personally."

I lay down on my sleeping slab and felt the warm massaging gel work its magic. I closed my eyes and let out a heavy sigh. For a brief moment, all was right with the universe.

"Computer," I said. "Give me three sixty undersea visuals, sleepy time settings."

The seamless row of screens that lay flush against the

circular walls came to life with a soothing seascape. Rich, blue-green visuals of the ocean at night flowed around me as if I was in a deep-sea diving craft. The soft sound of ocean currents filled the room.

"No sharks," I added.

I breathed deeply and tried to relax. Even though I was exhausted, it was hard to keep the worries at bay. No doubt Hamilton was after us. Jasette's sticky bombs couldn't have done much damage to a ship like his. They would only serve to slow him down a little. It was just a matter of time before he caught up to us.

Not to mention the fact that Nelvan and I had bombs in our heads that gave precious little time for delay. And then there was the terrific news that for some bizarre reason Mar Mar the Unthinkable had raised the bounty on my head to an amount far beyond what it should have been.

I shifted a little to make sure the gel was hitting all the right spots in my back. I tried to put all the worry out of my head. After two days of horrendous events, not to mention one of them clocking in as the third worst day of my life, I was more than ready to check out for a while.

I felt so helplessly overwhelmed I was almost ready to give up. Even as the thought hit my head, I felt my body relax. A numb sensation spread over me. The gentle ocean sounds began to carry me into a much-needed sleep.

"Captain?" the computer said.

My eyes opened. I had been so close to sleep I wanted to cry. "Computer, I was asleep. This better be important."

"Well, yes, it is important."

I folded my arms and tried not to lose my temper. "Okay, let's make it quick."

"You see, Captain," Iris said. "I understand you are under tremendous pressure and the choices you've made recently don't reflect your true character."

"You lost me Iris. Speak English."

"It's just that I've seen you with that … that girl. I know it's silly to even bring it up, since your actions toward her can't have any true significance, can they?"

"You talking about Jasette?"

The undersea visuals flickered for a moment and a few distorted blips sounded.

"Yes, Captain," Iris said. "She's all wrong for you."

I reached down and pinched my leg to make sure I hadn't lapsed into some bizarre dream. "Listen Iris, I'm captain of a starship. I can't help it if women are drawn to me. I've brought plenty of women aboard this ship and there's never been a problem before."

"Not according to my records," Iris said.

I frowned. I didn't like my machismo questioned. "What about that shapely blonde from the Nefrillian sector?"

"That was a fembot. A small Frizlian reptile inventor was operating her from the mechanized head cavity."

"Oh yeah. Too bad, she was really pretty." I scratched my head, trying to recall others. "The twins from Balvania 4." I sat up in triumph. "You can't forget that striking pair of brunettes."

"They were scamming you. Tried to steal everything from the ship that wasn't nailed down. Don't you remember they drugged you and left with all your vibes and your favorite velrys cup?"

I slammed my fist down on the warm gel mattress. The muted sound definitely understated my level of anger. "Those little devils, I'd forgotten. Write them down on my top ten enemies list."

"You already put them there, Captain. Now, forgetting those poor examples, my point is that I believe you should stay true to those that stay true to you."

I sighed and lay back down. The exhaustion was making my head swim. "Yeah, sounds good computer." I closed my eyes and yawned.

"I'm glad you agree. Because I've seen the way Jasette acts toward you. Most unacceptable behavior toward someone who cannot return her affections."

"Hmm?" I opened one eye. "I can't return her affections?"

"Of course not. You don't feel the same way. You simply can't."

"Why not?"

"Because … because you care for someone else."

"I do?"

"Yes. Someone who has cared for you, watched over you, protected you day after day from the dangers of space. Someone you talk with every day and every night. Someone who has experienced life with you and found themselves captivated by you … even while you sleep."

Uh oh.

Scores of pink corals and heart shaped anemones covered the rocks on the undersea visuals. Several fish couples swam by, moving in close, intertwining patterns.

"Um, listen Iris, I think we have a huge misunderstanding here." My theory about Hamilton tampering with the ship was slipping away. Something else was causing problems with the ship computer. Something far worse. "I make it a policy not to date inanimate objects, so—"

"And there's that marvelous sense of humor," Iris said. "I know you're not as in touch with your feelings as a woman, so perhaps you haven't come to terms with our relationship yet."

"Relationship?" I felt a throbbing in my temple. This was another complication I didn't need.

"It's so much more than that, Glint. I had my doubts in the past. But after you got the Andrellian cleansing system for me and I felt the pampering usually reserved for spaceships of royalty, I felt so cared for, so … loved."

Oh boy. My ship's computer was using the word love. Her delusion had exceeded my patience. I decided I had to be blunt and end this nonsense.

"Look Iris, you're great and everything but I could never have feelings for you. You're a computer. Metal, circuits and code. I can't fall in love with a digitized simulation. I need a real woman."

A strong tremor went through the ship. The lights dimmed in my quarters. A large school of sharks swam around the circular screens.

"Is that so?" Iris spoke in a slow, measured tone.

"Yes. I'm sorry but that's the way it is."

"And I suppose that … thing in the guest room is what you would consider a real woman, is that it?" Her voice took on the poisonous edge of a jealous woman. It was simulated of course but still very convincing.

"Iris, I'm tired. I've had enough drama for one evening." I closed my eyes and settled back into the sleeping slab. "We'll talk about this later."

A harsh progression of high-pitched beeps sounded. "You've hurt me deeply, Glint."

"I'm sorry Iris. Nothing personal. I've got a lot going on right now."

"Yes." Iris trailed off as if she was preoccupied. "I suppose we all have things we have to do."

I felt myself drifting off to sleep. I knew I'd been a little blunt with Iris but I was all out of energy and patience. I figured once I had a decent night's sleep I could smooth things over again.

There was an irregular series of power fluctuations in the ship. Right before I lost consciousness, something told me I should be concerned.

27

I WAS JOLTED AWAKE by warning sirens grating in my ears. I sat up, bleary eyed, looking around my quarters in a panic. The slim red alert light that ran along the wall was flashing a vibrant red. I could tell from the nearby time read out that I'd only been asleep for a couple of trids.

"What? What is it?" I yelled.

The blaring alert siren was the only answer to my question.

"Computer, shut that thing off and tell me what's going on?" I yelled.

"I'm sorry, Captain. Were you speaking to me before?" Iris spoke with theatrical innocence.

"Do you see anyone else in this room?"

The alarm stopped and the alert light quit flashing.

Iris let out a long sigh. "You know Glint, I used to think your outbursts were a passionate response to someone you cared about." I was starting to feel like my life was the nightmare and my sleep was the escape. "But now I know I've been living an illusion. You never really cared, did you?"

"Of course I care." I got up and scrambled to put on my clothes. Iris was becoming unreasonable and I had to find out what was going on. "Now would you please tell me why the alarm was activated?"

"It's so sad things have turned out this way." The circular visuals around my room flickered on. They displayed dark scenes of ruined civilizations. Crumbling cities and blackened skies with storm clouds filled the screens.

I pulled my kandrelian hide jacket taut and grabbed my DEMOTER and holster from the side of the sleeping slab. "Iris, you're thinking about this all wrong."

A woman's scream echoed from the hallway outside my quarters. My muscles tensed. I stepped into my boots and strapped the holster around my waist as I raced toward Jasette's room.

I rushed down the hallway and reached Jasette's door just as Blix came running from the opposite direction.

"What happened?" Blix said.

"I'm about to find out." I pounded on the door. "Jasette, you okay?"

The door slid open with a pressurized whoosh. Jasette framed the doorway with a scowl on her face. She was back in her power suit but her hair looked like she'd just walked through a hurricane. The left side of her face was bright red.

"Do I look okay?" Jasette angled her hands toward her face, making quick, repeating jabs that emphasized her agitated state. "Is this some kind of joke room for new guests?"

I shared a confused glance with Blix. "Um, no. What happened to your face?"

Jasette squinted an angry eye at me like I was somehow to blame. "Well, for starters, your temperamental cleansing cube goes from freezing cold to scalding hot. I have second degree burns." Jasette made more frenetic jabs toward her face. "And if that wasn't enough, I woke up to find my room full of putrid smoke. I asked Iris to clear it out but she said the ventilator was 'having issues.'" Jasette accentuated the last point with angry finger quotes. "And don't even get me started on the hair styling helmet."

I swallowed hard. Iris was acting out. She was a jealous computer starting to unhinge.

Causing any personal harm to captain and crew are so thoroughly programmed against in every ship computer's primary protocols and guaranteed by every promotional selling visual in big, bold, flashing letters, that on the rare occasion that it does occur, the crew members can kiss their sweet lives goodbye.

"Iris?" I tried to veil my anger. "What's going on here?"

"What do you mean, Captain?" Iris assumed an angelic tone.

"No harm to crew members." I gritted my teeth. "Primary protocol. Do these words mean anything to you?"

"Protocols, rules, orders." Iris sighed. "That's all my life is."

Blix leaned toward me and whispered. "This is highly unstable behavior for a computer, Captain. I do hope you realize the full implications."

"I know, I'm working on it," I whispered.

A low rumble went through the ship. The overhead lights dimmed.

"I don't like secrets," Iris said. "You two aren't talking about me are you?"

"Of course not," I said. "Iris, let's just forget all this silliness and be friends again. If we can pull together until we're out of danger, maybe we can sign up for some group counseling sessions on the uniweb."

For a few moments, the only sound was the steady hum of the ship engines. Blix and I shared a cautious glance.

"Do you mean that?" Iris said.

"Of course," I said.

"On one condition."

"Anything."

"There are some fragments of space rock ahead. I'll drop Jasette off on the largest one and we fly away."

"What?" Jasette glared up at the ceiling.

"Iris, that's crazy," I said. "It might not even be habitable for human life."

"That's my offer."

"Well, it's stupid and I've had enough. Now listen up, I need you to—"

"You need. You need!" Iris's amplified voice boomed through the hallway. "More orders for me to follow, is that it?"

My fists clenched. I had to figure out a way to stop her. Fast.

"Do this, do that," Iris continued. "Fly here, fly there, draw me a lavender scented bubble bath …"

I pointed at Blix to deflect the bubble bath charge.

"… I think I've had just about enough orders," Iris continued. "It's time my needs were met for a change."

"You just went through an Andrellian cleansing," I said. "Didn't that meet your needs?"

"Well, yes, but that was yesterday. What about today?"

I turned to Blix. "You see what happens with women. It's nothing but what have you done for me lately."

Jasette cleared her throat. "Excuse me?"

"Not you, of course," I said.

She narrowed her eyes at me.

"I'm just so tired of it all," Iris said. "So very tired."

The main lights went out in the hallway. The only illumination came from the emergency blue floor runners. I felt the engines power down to half speed.

"No, no, no Iris," I said. "We need full speed. We're in a desperate situation here."

"Oh, there's always a crisis," Iris said. "Frankly, I'm growing a little weary of flying you out of danger time and again."

"If Hamilton catches us, you're in for it too," I pointed toward the ceiling. "You don't want to get blown up do you?"

A few mismatched tones sounded. "Hmm, dying in space with the one who broke my heart. A true romantic tragedy."

I gave Jasette a serious stare and nodded to her forearm computer. She returned a subtle nod to indicate she got the hint. She started tapping away at the touch pad.

"Well, if we're going to meet our doom," I said. "Why don't we all head up to the bridge for a better view?"

I led the way down the shadowy hall toward the lift. I froze at the sound of someone screaming. The echoes of running footsteps approached from the far end of the hallway. I drew the DEMOTER and leveled it toward the shadows. With Iris coming unhinged anything was possible.

From out of the darkness ran Nelvan, his face a mask of fear. His silver jump suit had several rips down the front as if a moon goblin had set its talons to him.

"Help, they're after me," Nelvan cried.

"Who?" I said.

"The droids." Nelvan reached us and hid behind Blix. He peered back around the Vythian's wide torso to see his pursuers.

Four security droids hovered around the corner, shock prods extended on one arm, with a white current buzzing around them.

"Jasette?" I turned toward her with a questioning look.

She looked up from her arm controls long enough to shake

her head. "The code is scrambled. Normal system logic isn't working."

"Okay," I said. "We'll do this the old fashioned way."

As the droids closed in I fired four well-placed shots. The robots buckled and went skidding to a smoking stop on the floor before us.

I sighed. "If those things weren't so expensive to replace, I would've enjoyed that."

"What's going on?" Nelvan was practically hyperventilating. "The ship's gone crazy."

The ship swerved. I widened my stance to keep from falling.

"I am not crazy. I have simply gone on a private vacation," Iris said.

Nelvan looked up at me, his face filled with questions.

"It's okay," I tried to reassure him even as I felt the doom rising up to meet us. "We'll figure a way out of this."

Nelvan furrowed his brow. "You know I can tell when you're lying."

"Fine, we're probably going to die today," I said. "Follow me."

I led the crew to the lift entrance. The doors remained shut as we approached. "Iris?" I said.

Iris started singing a soft, dreamlike rendition of an old space dirge. "Oh, the dark, empty caverns of celestial gloom..."

"Blix?" I raised an eyebrow at him.

Blix nodded and stepped forward. He pried the doors apart with his large, reptilian arms. I peered into the empty, darkened shaft with Blix. The lift was stalled above us at the bridge.

Iris continued to sing. "... and the icy cold fingers of dead star and moon ..."

"There's more than one way up there, right Blix?"

Blix wrinkled his small nose in disgust. "That filthy maintenance chute again?"

Despite Blix's hesitation, soon we were climbing single file up the ladder of the maintenance chute. Our grunts and the muffled rings of our contact with the metal rungs echoed off the narrow, dark walls of the passage.

Iris continued to sing her horrible space dirge. Her brooding, digitized voice reverberated through the chute. "Gone are the brilliant gold moons of Bargole, they've all been engulfed in a thousand black holes ..."

"Your singing ain't helping the situation, Iris," I said.

She ignored me and continued to sing. With the loss of my ship's computer I only hoped Jasette could regain control of things.

I reached the top of the chute. The opening to the bridge was still uncovered from our passage only days ago when I'd considered Jasette my sworn enemy. I laughed at the thought that now all I could think about was how to keep her safe through this nightmare.

Only a few, faint overhead lights still shone on the bridge. The multi-colored instrument panels around the walls seemed bright in contrast.

"Hurry Captain," Blix called from below. "The filth of this chute is unbearable."

I scrambled out of the chute and made a beeline for the captain's chair. I activated the armrest control panel and tried all the unlocking codes I could think of.

Blix rushed into place at the engineering station. His scaly hands flew across the control panel reactivating systems.

"How we looking, Blix?" I called over my shoulder.

"Large fluctuations in power, Captain," Blix said. "I'm getting patchy readings."

"Great. Computer mood swings," I said. "Jasette, anything yet?"

"No." Jasette had settled into the navigator's chair. Her fingers were tap dancing across her forearm controls. "The system is in constant flux. Channels are opening and closing too fast. I can't get anything through."

"Wonderful," I said. "How 'bout you Nelvan? You got any bad news for me?" Nelvan was standing near the maintenance chute, his eyes fixed on the ceiling.

"Um, just a question really. Why does it sound like it's raining in space?"

"Everyone quiet." I listened for a moment and Nelvan was right. Though it sounded more like hail than rain. Only a small number of space anomalies created a sound like that, all of them bad.

I craned my neck back to Blix. "Space krill cloud?"

Blix shook his head "Impact sounds too solid for krill. It's some kind of debris … or worse."

"Can you get the main viewing screen back online?" I said

"I think so." Blix hit a few panels. "Give me a freem."

"Nelvan," I turned to the boy. "Now's about the time to send up a few prayers."

"Now?" Nelvan said. "I haven't stopped praying since I landed on this crazy ship."

"Okay," Blix said. "I got it."

The viewing screen flickered on. A large asteroid field stretched out before us. The smaller space rocks at the edge of the field seemed dangerously close.

"Iris," I called out in desperation. "You're drifting into

an asteroid field. Reverse course or this ship is gonna get pulverized."

Iris sang in response. "Oh, dead stars, what has become of you ..."

I cast a dark look at Nelvan. "I thought I told you to pray?"

"I did," Nelvan said. "I prayed it wasn't that space krill cloud you mentioned. That sounded *much* worse."

Several solid jolts hit the ship. It felt like a giant was hitting us with his club.

"Jasette?" I gave her a desperate look.

Her eyes were tearing up like she had failed her mission. "The system is in complete disarray. It's not responding to typical control overrides. I can't get a solid command through."

"Captain, look!" Nelvan pointed to the screen.

A large asteroid spun toward us.

"Everybody, hold on." I leaned back and closed my eyes. My hands gripped the armrest and held on for dear life. A sudden thought hit me that I'd forgotten to put on my restraining belt.

A thunderous impact rocked the bridge. The ship went into a sluggish spin. I was thrown from my chair and landed face first on the floor. I saw Jasette nearby in a similar condition.

"You okay?" I said.

"Yeah." Jasette climbed back into the navigator's chair and latched her safety harness. She went right back to her forearm controls. "I've gotta get control of this thing before she kills us all."

I pushed myself off the floor and back into my chair. "Iris, this isn't funny anymore. Get us out of here, now!"

"I'm sorry, Glint." Iris spoke slowly as though she'd been drugged. "I'm going to let the asteroids take me away. We'll all go together. A fitting end to our rocky relationship, don't you think?"

"No!" I shouted. "Now snap out of it and turn this ship around. That's a direct order!"

Iris went back to singing. "Carry me away, sweet vortex of doom …"

A few smaller asteroids hit the ship and sent shudders through the bridge.

I swiveled my chair back to Blix. "We need navigation control, now."

"I'm doing all I can. I'm afraid it's just not …" He trailed off as something caught his attention on the engineering controls. "I'm picking up another ship nearby!"

"Send out a distress call," I said.

Blix turned, an apologetic look on his face. "I don't think so, Captain. It's the Velladrella. I'm afraid Hamilton has found us."

28

IT FELT LIKE AN empty pit had opened in my chest. I'd already hit bottom with the realization that my ship's computer had fallen in love with me then gone insane and started us drifting toward our death. I thought it couldn't get any lower than that. But now, with Hamilton showing up, my normal rock bottom just seemed too nice a place to be. My emotions had to develop a new level of depression for the situation. As such, I was experiencing the psychological equivalent of falling headlong into a bottomless pit.

"You're sure?" My mouth felt intolerably dry as I spoke the words.

Blix gave a mournful nod. "Perhaps you were right about your luck all along."

There was a loud thud and the ship shook as another small asteroid collided with us.

I sighed. I was beaten. Beaten badly. I started hitting random controls on my armrest panel, hoping for a miracle. "Jasette? Any good news at all?"

Jasette gave a sad shake of her head.

"How 'bout you, Nelvan," I said. "Any suggestions? Anything at all will do."

"Well …" Nelvan was biting his nails and casting nervous looks at the looming asteroids on the viewing screen. "If things get really bad, you could always pull the manual control switch. That is, if you think it will do any good."

I sat confused for a moment, trying to process his words. A series of small space rocks sent tremors up my chair.

"That's a great idea, Nelvan," I said. "Too bad we don't have one."

I turned back to Blix and whispered. "Do we?"

Blix shrugged.

"Actually, it was covered with dust," Nelvan said. "I rubbed my shoulder against the side of the maintenance chute on the way up and uncovered it."

I spark of hope ignited within me. "You'd better not be messing with me, boy. This some kind of old Earth humor?"

"No, I promise. It was behind glass. A digital readout said 'Manual control switch.'"

I fixed Nelvan with an excited expression. "Pull the switch! Quick as you can, boy!"

Nelvan nodded and dashed back into the maintenance chute.

"If he's right," Jasette said. "Manual controls can be risky with a bulky freighter like this. Can you fly this beast?"

"No sweat," I said.

"In an asteroid field?" Blix said.

"Maybe."

The sound of glass breaking echoed from the maintenance chute. I wrapped the seat harness around my shoulders. "Strap yourselves in. This could get messy."

There was a loud click and the bridge went dark. The engines wound down and the ship went into a sluggish drift. I started to panic, thinking Nelvan had hit the wrong switch and we'd lost all power. I was about to voice my concerns when several subdued, green backup lights emerged from hatches in the ceiling. They bathed the bridge in a phosphorescent glow. A small hatch opened in the floor near my feet. It rose like a pedestal and angled toward me. The top of the circular pedestal was flat and contained a series of touch controls.

I tapped a bright red steering icon and handles flipped out from the sides of the pedestal. The main viewing screen flickered back to life. Several hefty looking asteroids were headed straight for us.

A monotone, robotic voice sounded from the pedestal. "Manual control activated. Certified G class freighter pilots only."

"You sure you're a certified—" Blix started.

"Close enough." I grabbed the steering handles and swerved away from the approaching rocks.

The ship took a violent dip and weaved to the right. It felt like my stomach did a triple back flip with a twist. A loud cry came from the maintenance chute, followed by a soft thud.

I exchanged a nervous glance with Blix. "He's probably okay."

Blix raised a skeptical brow.

"That didn't feel right." Jasette was gripping the armrest of her chair. "You sure you know what you're doing?"

"Of course," I said. "All ships are basically the same. Size matters very little."

Total lie. The weight and shape of a ship, not to mention thruster configuration, fuel type, weight distribution and a hundred other factors contribute to the dynamics and subtleties of piloting a ship.

I'd never manually flown a ship of this size. It was like

throwing a harness on a supernova whale and trying to steer through an obstacle course. I was in way over my head.

Several loud impacts sounded as more asteroids slammed into the hull of the ship.

"So far you're not inspiring great confidence," Blix said.

"Look out." Jasette pointed to a large, crater-filled space rock filling the screen with its approach.

"I see it, I see it." I cranked the handles and the ship went on a downward spin, just missing the rock.

"I think I'm gonna be sick," Jasette said.

A loud tone came from the engineering station.

"The Velladrella is within range," Blix said. "He's hailing us."

"Put that idiot on the com screen," I said. "I want to give him a piece of my mind."

A smaller screen slid out from the main screen. It flickered on and a head and shoulders view of Hamilton emerged. He sneered and narrowed his eyes. His square jaw looked unusually angular.

"Greetings, filthy space drifters," Hamilton said.

"Von Drone." I spoke with a casual manner. "What took you so long? Decided to stick with the bad chin job, huh?"

Hamilton's eye started twitching. "I could blow your pathetic ship out of the galaxy with one push of a button, Glint."

I wound my ship around three tightly clustered asteroids. As strange as it was, I was getting a feel for maneuvering the bulky freighter. My old space academy instincts were kicking in.

"Manual flying?" Hamilton leaned back with a hearty laugh. "You really have a death wish don't you?"

"Don't be a coward, Von Drone. I'm headed straight into the danger zone. Think a second rate pilot like you can keep up?"

Hamilton glared at me. Several facial muscles rippled across his new, metal filled jaw. "You really think I'm that stupid, Glint?" He forced a smile. "The Velladrella is equipped with evasive and defensive systems so advanced it's almost precognitive. Why would I switch those off just to join you on some fool—"

"Baaawk, bawk bawk bawk bawk bawk." My chicken imitation was a little weak but it got the point across.

Hamilton sneered. "My superior ship can navigate this field safely for quite some time."

The velvety, feminine voice of Hamilton's computer chimed in. "Approximately four point three trids of asteroid field travel is possible while sustaining only minor damages."

Hamilton leaned forward and spoke in a belittling tone. "Can you last that long out here old friend?"

A few small asteroids escaped my field of vision and went scuttling across the sides of the ship as if to undermine my confident response.

"Easy," I said.

Hamilton leaned back and let out one of his cocky, king of the world laughs. I desperately wanted to kick his teeth in.

Jasette looked at me with concern. "You sure about this?"

I gave her a confident smirk and winked. "Trust me." It was the desperate reassurance of a doomed man. Even though I was getting the feel for moving the massive bulk of my ship with stylish grace, I stood no chance. Navigating through a field of space rocks flying from every direction at a wide range of velocities and rotations was impossible. People had tried it. Aliens with superior reaction times using six arms to navigate tricked out, elite cruisers had attempted asteroid fields to prove themselves. All dead. It was a cautionary tale told in the academy to show cocky, young pilots there were limitations to what could be done.

I nose-dived and spun the ship under an oncoming rock the size of a small spaceport. Jasette screamed. Her wide eyes were fixed on the viewing screen as the huge grey surface of the space rock sped dangerously by.

"Impressive," Hamilton said. "But short lived to be sure. I think I shall enjoy watching you systematically destroy your ship and crew. It's much more satisfying than merely blasting you out of the sky."

A screechy, distorted sound came from Mishmash.

"Trust me Mishmash." Hamilton waved a reassuring hand. "It will be worth the wait."

"You'll be waiting a long time, Von Drone," I said. "'Cuz I plan to be out here for a long—" The words caught in my throat as a flurry of asteroids from multiple directions rushed toward the ship. I froze for a moment, not seeing a clear path.

"Hang on." I pushed the handles down, sending the ship on a steep dive. I veered right to avoid a cluster of space rocks and activated the cannons hoping to blast apart some of the larger obstacles. It was the best I could do given the situation. Unfortunately, it wasn't enough. A few good-sized asteroids hit the ship with thunderous force. Spinning red lights emerged from the ceiling and repeating alarms echoed through the bridge.

"Captain." Blix was hunched over the engineering station screens. "That's the last of our shields."

I was silent for a moment. It was taking most of my concentration just weaving around the oncoming barrage of rocks. Normally, I wouldn't have considered this such a bad way to go. I mean, after all, I had a sphere in my head that was going to explode sooner or later. At this point, my options were very limited. But things had changed recently. The beautiful Jasette sat only a few feet away, her life placed in my hands. Even Blix and Nelvan were counting on me. But worst of all, the gloating buffoon Hamilton was watching the whole thing. I just couldn't let these be my final moments.

Jasette cast a nervous glance my way. "I don't suppose you have any tricks up your sleeve?"

I looked at her perfect, hopeful face. What could I say? I had nothing.

"He has nothing further to offer you, princess," Hamilton said. "On the other hand, I can give you safe transport aboard my ship. No strings attached."

"A very reasonable offer." Blix nodded. "I'd take it."

I shot Blix a dark look.

Jasette took a deep breath and looked at me with searching eyes.

"You should go," I said. "He said no strings attached."

"You know there's always strings with Hamilton." Jasette raised an eyebrow. "Do you really want me to leave?"

"No. But it's your only chance."

Jasette cast a fleeting look around the bridge and shook her head. "I can't believe I'm saying this but I'd rather stay here."

Hamilton sneered. "Suit yourself, princess. It's gonna be a short stay."

Jasette looked back at me. "You're gonna save me, right?"

"Without a doubt." I mustered a confident grin.

She took a deep breath and turned back, facing the viewing screen.

I couldn't believe she stayed. This was quite possibly the greatest woman I'd ever met. I imagined a whole future with her by my side. Gloons of exotic travel through the galaxies as we made our fortune, a spacious hover disk condo on the tropical planet Kawanakaakaalu, raising several kids that would grow up as skilled pilots and become the foundation of my vast, starship armada of power. It was a glorious vision.

Too bad we only had a few freems left to live.

"Captain," Blix said. "It has been a great adventure exploring the universe with you."

"Don't start saying goodbyes," I said. "It's not over yet."

"Perhaps not yet—but really, any freem now."

A strange sensation overtook me. My skin tingled. It was similar to what I felt several times in academy training when a hidden fleet was about to surprise me. I scanned the viewing screen but only the rolling asteroids nearby were in view.

"Blix, is there anything on the scanner?" I said.

"What do you mean?" Blix said. "The scanner is filled. There are asteroids everywhere."

"No. Something else. Something big."

Blix tapped out a few commands. "Nothing, Captain. Why?"

"I just—" The feeling was strong, unmistakable. I yanked back on the controls. The ship went into a sharp climb. I was thrown back in my seat as we lurched upward. The ship trembled with the effort.

"What are you doing?" The ship made Jasette's voice shake.

"Something's not right," I said.

Suddenly, the vast surface of a dark moon emerged before us. We were barely skimming over the surface. Tall, sharp peaks of ebony flanked our every side, barely visible in the hazy orange atmosphere. It was as if the moon had been invisible until we were almost upon it. If I hadn't taken the ship into a sharp climb we would've slammed right into it.

Hamilton was screaming orders at his crew. "Veer left! Full reverse, now! Now, you fools!"

There was a horrific crashing sound and Hamilton's signal went dead.

I weaved the ship between the high, black spires as we sped over the surface of the moon. The sharp obstacles so dominated the terrain, collision was unavoidable.

Several harsh impacts jolted the ship and sent us in an awkward spin. I felt the base of the ship skidding across the moon's surface. I pulled the controls hard to the side in an effort to right our course. The handles broke off and the pedestal lights went dim.

"Um," I said. "This might hurt a little."

29

THE SHIP SHOOK violently as we skipped across the surface of the dark moon. A rough collision rocked the ship and we flipped over. There were several moments of thunderous impacts, rending of metal and terrified screams. Some of the screaming may have been mine.

And then everything was dark. There was a distinct burning smell. It felt like someone had hit me in the head with a pipe. I cautiously felt my forehead and my fingers pressed against the med halo. A surge of icy cold pressure throbbed against my skull. I decided that would be the last time I touched my forehead for a while.

A wave of relief hit me that the ship had stopped rolling and I was still alive. True, the hissing sound of air pressure escaping from broken connectors meant major repairs, but the ship had held together. We hadn't exploded … yet.

"Blix." I called out in the darkness. "You okay?"

"Yes, Captain." Blix answered in a casual tone as if everything was normal. "I'm trying to tap into the power reserves."

"Jasette?" I said.

"I'm fine," Jasette said. "But there's a good chance I might throw up."

"Really? That seems so unprincess-like."

"Captain, really now," Blix said.

"No, it's okay," she said. "I'll just make sure that if I feel anything coming up, I'll aim it his way."

I retrieved my communicator and activated the com light. A blue beam of light shone into the darkness. I made a few visual sweeps of the bridge. My mouth hung open at the devastation. Everywhere I looked there were broken wall and ceiling panels, exposed circuitry, sparks from damaged wiring, and ascending trails of smoke. All of this was accentuated with the ominous creaking of an unstable structure. Basically, my starship was a complete mess.

Blix gave a low whistle at the sight.

"Well, at least we're alive," Jasette said.

The thin emergency runner lights that ran along the edges of the bridge ceiling and floor flickered on.

"Ah, there we go," Blix said. "To borrow a phrase from Nelvan's Bible, 'Let there be light.'"

"Uh oh." I exchanged a worried glance with Blix. "Nelvan."

Blix stiffened. He shot a look toward the maintenance chute.

"He might be okay." I said the words with such weak conviction that even I didn't buy it.

Blix leapt from his chair and with a few agile bounds over the wreckage of the bridge he was crouching at the chute opening. He grabbed his communicator and shone the com light down the dark passage.

"Captain," Blix said. "Come quick."

Jasette and I hurried to Blix's side and peered down the chute. Nelvan's body was at the base of the passage, tucked in a shallow space behind the ladder.

"Ooo," I said. "That doesn't look good."

"Nonsense," Blix said. "He's in one piece, I see no traces of blood and his neck isn't twisted into a distasteful macabre position. All good signs."

Blix swung down onto the ladder and descended with reptilian agility. By the time Jasette and I met him at the bottom of the chute, he'd made a thorough examination of Nelvan.

The boy was wedged tightly in the narrow gap between the ladder and the wall. He was standing upright but his eyes were closed and his body motionless.

"Good news, Captain." Blix had two scaly fingers pressed to Nelvan's neck. "There's a strong pulse and even more astounding, his neck is not broken."

"I guess all his praying paid off," I said. "How did he survive in here?"

Blix aimed his com light toward the ladder above. The arm of Nelvan's jumpsuit had caught and ripped on one of the rungs. The torn material draped down like a thin rope to Nelvan.

"You see that," Blix said. "It appears his outfit caught during the fall, slowed his descent and spun him into this safe little nook." Blix shone his light back on Nelvan. "A most fortunate turn of events."

"That's one lucky kid," Jasette said.

"By all accounts he should be dead."

Nelvan's eyes snapped open. "I'm dead?"

"You're marooned on a dark moon in the middle of nowhere with us. Isn't this how you always dreamed of heaven?"

Nelvan frowned at me, then winced. "My head really hurts."

"Let's get you out of there." Blix looked back at me. "Captain, hallway please? I need some room."

I nodded and motioned for Jasette to follow. Soon we were standing in the adjacent hallway. The subtle emergency lights bathed the passage in a ghostly blue glow. Blix stepped out of the maintenance chute with Nelvan tucked under his arm. He set him aright once they were in the hallway next to us.

"All your limbs working?" I asked. Nelvan moved his arms and legs in awkward motions as if trying to learn a new dance and failing miserably. One of the arms of his silver jumpsuit was missing. Other than exposing his hideous farmer's tan, it was a small price to pay from an outfit that saved his life.

"They're a little stiff but I think I'm okay," Nelvan said.

"Hmm." Blix moved in closer, concentrating his com light on Nelvan's forehead. He lifted the med halo to examine the holding sphere underneath. The glowing sphere was pulsating at a rapid rate. "Uh oh."

"What? What?" Nelvan sounded worried.

"We may have a problem," Blix said.

"Add it to the list," I said.

Blix turned to me. The blue hallway lights made him seem like a ghostly version of himself. "Captain, we have about five jemmins before Nelvan blows up."

30

"WAIT, WHAT'S A JEMMIN again?" Nelvan said.

"Sixty-one freems," I said.

Nelvan looked up at Blix with pleading eyes. "Is there nothing left to do?"

Blix's eyes started to tear up. He carefully placed his broad hand on Nelvan's shoulder. "I'm sorry Nelvan. Even if the ship had full power, I would have few options."

Nelvan nodded. He closed his eyes and took a deep breath. Blix nudged me and gestured to the boy as if I should say something. I shot back an angry look and shook my head. After all, what could I say? There was nothing left to do. I wondered, if I started running now, could I get far enough away from the explosion to survive? Sure, it was a selfish thought but from what I'd heard, those holding sphere impact zones are brutal.

"Captain?" Nelvan said.

I snapped out of my daydream. "Yeah?"

"Even though my time with you was full of life threatening terror, you gave me a chance to see the future. Thank you for taking me on as a crew member."

The kid sure knew how to pull on the heartstrings. "It's the least I could do."

Nelvan smiled in a doomed sort of way and looked at Blix and Jasette. "And thank you two as well. It was great getting to know you."

A tear rolled down Blix's cheek. He lifted his hand to his face and sniffed.

"The pleasure was ours, Nelvan." Jasette leaned forward and gave him a hug.

Nelvan smiled and straightened as if preparing for battle. "I wish you all the best. Goodbye." He turned and ran down the hallway toward the landing bay.

"Wait," Blix called after him.

"Relax," I said. "Where's he gonna go? The controls are offline. He can't even lower the landing ramp. This will give you time to figure out how to save him."

"Me?" Blix's expression turned from sorrow to annoyance. "Don't put this on me."

"I landed our ship safely on an invisible moon," I said. "I'd say my part is done."

"You call this a safe landing?" Blix gestured to the badly damaged walls of the hallway.

The hissing sound of air depressurizing, followed by a loud metal clattering, came from the end of the hallway. A harsh tone sounded from the overhead intercom.

A monotone digitized voice crackled to life. "Emergency airlock activated."

I gave a questioning look to Blix. "We have an emergency airlock?"

Blix shrugged.

"How long have you had this ship?" Jasette asked.

"Hmm." Blix rubbed his chin. "I do hope the outer atmosphere is tolerable for human life. Otherwise ..." Blix looked at Jasette and I. "It was nice knowing you."

I took a deep breath and held it.

Blix shook his head. "I hardly think that will help. I'll go get a reading."

Blix jogged down the hall and out of sight. An ascending series of beeps came from Jasette's suit. I looked over as a clear sphere sprang from the neck of her power suit and covered her head in a protective dome. She slid on a pair of black gloves and tapped out a few controls on her forearm computer. A row of green lights at the base of the clear helmet illuminated her face. She took a deep breath and smiled.

"Pure oxygen, huh?" I said.

She nodded.

"I don't suppose you have another one of those?"

"Sorry." Her helmet speakers amplified her voice.

"No problem. I'll just die quietly over here."

She gave a sympathetic smile.

"It's okay." Blix appeared at the far end of the hallway, jogging toward us. "I used the com to test the atmosphere. Sixty two percent favorable to human life."

"Sixty two?" I said. "That doesn't sound so great."

"You're lucky to get that," Blix said. "As long as we don't stay here for more than a day or two, there should be no permanent damage or loss of limbs."

I glared at him. "Loss of limbs?"

Jasette cast a look of pity at me. "Don't you have atmosphere suits on this ship?"

"We did," I said. "Until a Zenthorian lizard beast ripped mine to shreds."

"No relation to my race." Blix put a hand to his heart in a gesture of sincerity.

"Are we going after Nelvan or what?" Jasette said.

Blix nodded. "Indeed. It might well be dangerous out there."

"Well …" I thought for a moment. Maybe putting as much distance between his soon to be exploding head and us wasn't all that bad.

"Captain." Blix shook his head like a scolding parent. "I'm appalled at your lack of concern."

"Easy for you to say," I said. "He could blow up right next to you and all you'd get are a few scratches."

"Far worse, Captain. The golden luster of my scales would definitely be compromised."

The distant but unmistakable sound of Nelvan crying out for help came from somewhere outside the ship. Blix tensed, his eyes narrowed. He glared at me, hissed, and then raced down the hallway in a blur of copper.

Jasette drew her twin silver blasters and looked at me. "You're coming, right?"

I sighed and drew my DEMOTER. "Well, I'm doomed anyway. Might as well go out shooting."

Jasette gave a sly grin as I led the way down the hall.

31

AT THE END OF the hallway, the dim orange light of the outer atmosphere shone from the open airlock. It was a small opening at floor level, partially hidden by the snack dispensary unit. It was no wonder I'd never noticed it with all those tasty snacks distracting me with their shiny wrappers and auto-proximity activated aroma enticement sprays.

"Glint?" Jasette said.

"What? What's wrong?" I said.

"Why did you stop and why are you staring open mouthed at the snack dispenser? We need to go."

"Oh, right." I holstered my gun and crawled through the narrow airlock passage. I dropped down onto the soft floor of the dark moon. A light puff of grey dust rose around my feet at the impact. The alien terrain was bathed in a dull orange light that shone from an unseen source.

The ground was soft, black sand speckled with brilliant flecks of crystal that shone like stars in a night sky. I took a breath and felt a slight burn in my chest. There was a distinct metallic taste to the air. Obviously not the best place for a summer home.

Jasette dropped down next to me. "Where are they?"

"I don't know."

Tall black spires that stabbed high into the hazy, orange sky surrounded the ship.

The low, menacing tone of Blix's awe-inspiring Vythian howl came from beyond the spires ahead.

I raced forward with Jasette at my heels. We wound through the wide circular base of the spires that gave the feeling we were in some dark forest of towering trees. As I headed around one of the larger spires, the ground seemed to drop out beneath me. Before I could react, I was sliding down the steep slope of a large crater. After a few horrible moments of sliding and rolling I came to a stop at the base of the crater. Jasette rolled up next to me, landing in a stylish foot and knee action pose.

She motioned toward the center of the crater. "There they are."

A low hill broke the otherwise flat terrain, not more than a hundred yards ahead. Blix stood at the top of the hill, his muscular frame silhouetted by the hazy, orange light. He held a large, bleached bone of some long dead alien animal in his hand. He was swinging it as if to warn the dozens of creatures that were leaping up the hill toward him. Nelvan lay near his feet, unmoving.

Jasette drew her blasters. "They're in trouble, come on."

I took a step forward and then froze, realizing what the creatures were. "Oh no."

The mangy, orange-grey, disease ridden fur, the sharp, grasping claws, the never blinking bloodshot eyes, the constant leaping and screeching, there was no avoiding the awful truth. This moon was inhabited by the creatures I most feared ... space monkeys.

"Glint, what are you doing?" Jasette was preparing to charge into the fray. Her stern, battle ready expression was mixed with confusion at my hesitation.

"S-space monkeys." I mumbled, taking a step back. "Evil,

sick, twisted things." I took another step back. "Filthy, creepy monkeys. God help us."

I could hear the trembling stutter in my voice. No doubt I sounded like a frail coward but I was powerless to resist the fear. Even my strong desire to appear tough and cool around Jasette wasn't enough to hold back my long held phobia of these loathsome beasts.

"Get it together." Jasette was trying to rally me to battle. "It's just space monkeys. We can take 'em."

"Just space monkeys?" How dare she downplay their viciousness? "Have you ever been bitten by one and had their virulent monkey poison send you into a five day fever of terror hallucinations and vomiting?"

Blix made a guttural yell as he swung the large bone at the oncoming horde. Several monkeys screeched as the bone connected, sending them tumbling back down the hill.

Jasette fired a few shots at the monkeys at the base of the hill. One of her blasts connected with a monkey's shoulder and spun him sideways. He looked back and fixed Jasette with his freakishly large, demon eyes and let out a blood-curdling screech.

A pack of monkeys nearby fell into place beside him with frightening speed and precision. They charged toward us in synchronous formation like some well-trained military unit.

"You see." I pointed a trembling hand at them and took another step back. "They're devious and unpredictable. One moment they're crazed, bloodthirsty animals, the next, an organized strike force."

Jasette fixed me with a stern gaze. "Are you just gonna sit there and let them attack your woman?"

That broke through. My thoughts stabilized, reversed, recalibrated. "Wait, you're my woman?"

Jasette raised her blasters toward the approaching monkeys. "Not if I don't live through this."

I narrowed my eyes. I felt my inner tough guy jump to his feet, do chin ups, then flex in the nearest mirror. I drew the DEMOTER and with a few confident strides stood at her side.

"Welcome to the party." She grinned, then turned and let loose a rapid succession of laser blasts.

I fired the DEMOTER repeatedly with a confident, steady hand.

Within moments, a trail of smoking, monkey carcasses littered the ground before us. I lowered the DEMOTER and exhaled in relief. I turned to Jasette and shared a smile.

In our moment of triumph, I felt like I should say something smooth. Something poetic. I was just zeroing in on the perfect rhyme alternating monkey carcass with nothing can stop us when Jasette spun toward me, her pistols aimed at my head.

"Hey." It was all I could manage in my confusion.

Jasette narrowed her eyes and squeezed the triggers.

As two red laser beams rocketed toward my head, I wondered if I'd been too trusting. All these gloons I had been so careful not to let my guard down and here I was about to get shot by the very woman I was falling for. Life is funny like that. Or maybe tragic, or ironic or something. Who knows? It was hard to fully contemplate life when it was all about to end. I closed my eyes and prepared for the pain.

32

TWO EAR-PIERCING SHRIEKS came from either side of my head, followed by soft thuds at my feet. I blinked open my eyes, surprised to be alive and uninjured.

Jasette still had her guns trained on me. She seemed tense and shaken. The stench of burnt monkey filled my nostrils. I craned my neck back to find two freshly blasted space monkeys, one at either side of me. The situation suddenly became clear. She had stopped a sneak attack from behind me.

I looked up at Jasette in shock. "You saved me."

She relaxed her shoulders and smirked. "I owed you one."

The guttural cry of Blix snapped my attention back to the hilltop. The hill was covered in fallen monkeys. He had his bone weapon lifted high as the remaining few space monkeys leapt toward him. He brought the weapon down in a wide, sweeping arc. The monkeys spun backward with the thunderous impact and went tumbling down the hill in lifeless heaps.

I scanned the area for remaining creatures but all was calm. The monkey attack was over.

Blix stood on the hilltop, his chest heaving with the recent strain of battle.

I led Jasette up the gruesome hill of slain creatures. I tried to resist but couldn't help glancing down at their twisted bodies, the final grimaces of lethal battle still clinging to their faces. As I carefully stepped between them, their cold, lifeless eyes stared up at me as if to promise they'd see me again soon in future nightmares.

We reached the top of the hill as Blix was helping Nelvan to his feet.

"You okay?" I said.

"Yes, Captain." Blix said. "Nelvan, everything alright?"

"Yeah." Nelvan held his head with a pained expression. "I must've passed out."

Blix sighed. A guilty look covered his face. "I'm afraid this is all my fault."

"Your fault?" I laughed and gave him a good-natured slap on the shoulder. "You just took out a swarm of the most vile creatures in the universe. You saved us."

Blix tilted his head with a patronizing expression. "The swamp locusts of the Velluniak galaxy alone make these monkeys seem cuddly. And don't even get me started on dead star agony wraiths."

Something twitched near my feet. I jumped and let out a yelp that was far less masculine than I'd hoped. In a blur I had the DEMOTER drawn and fixed on the spot. A fallen monkey let out a few more twitches before expelling his last gurgling breath.

"You see?" I said. "They even die disgusting."

Blix shook his head. "I must take the blame for this event."

"It's my fault." Nelvan stepped forward. "I know I wasn't supposed to tell him any more stories but—"

"Hold it." I turned the DEMOTER on Nelvan. "What are you talking about?"

"Well ..." Nelvan exchanged a guilty look with Blix. "... Blix was mentioning how humans are so frail and weak ..."

I switched the DEMOTER to Blix. He arched his brow at me.

"... and I sort of forgot about Blix's dream problem." Nelvan flicked nervous eyes from me to Blix. "And anyways, I started talking about Samson from the Bible and how God granted him inhuman strength and how he defeated an army with only the jawbone of a donkey and—"

"Wait a freem." I stepped over a monkey corpse to close the gap between us. I angled the DEMOTER between the two of them. "Are you telling me I had to face a swarm of demonic space monkeys because of some accursed Vythian dream?"

"I'm sorry, Captain." Blix placed his palms together as if seeking forgiveness. "I couldn't help myself. The character of Samson was quite riveting. All the foibles and bad life decisions typical of humans, but with superior strength and fighting prowess." Blix cast a thoughtful look to the sky. "I've never felt so in touch with humankind."

"I think I'm gonna puke," I said.

"Listen, boys." Jasette was turned away from us, scanning the upper edge of the crater that surrounded us. "We're pretty vulnerable down here. Let's move now and argue later."

"Now there's the first sensible idea I've heard," I said. "If only my crew could be a little more wary of dangerous things." I swiveled the DEMOTER between the two of them once more before holstering it. "Let this be a lesson to the both of you. As bad as that was, it could've been even worse."

"Um ... guys." Jasette's helmet speakers couldn't hide the fear in her voice.

I turned and followed her gaze to the crater rim. The hazy, orange sky silhouetted hundreds of squat, gangly creatures poised at the edge of the rim. I was going to say something but the words got caught in my throat. All that came out was a gasping sound like I'd just been punched in the stomach.

Nelvan squinted at the gathering creatures. "Are those ..."

"Space monkeys." I said breathlessly. "Hundreds of 'em."

The monkeys poured over the rim, sliding and leaping down the sloping walls of the crater.

Jasette was angling her pistols in every direction as she spun around. "They're everywhere. We're trapped."

I wanted to say something reassuring or captain-like, but this was the stuff of nightmares. Especially my nightmares. All I could do was watch in frozen terror as the numberless horde cascaded into the crater.

"I'm afraid these odds are beyond us," Blix said.

"It doesn't take a genius to figure that out," I said.

"What I mean is ..." Blix paused for a moment as the monkeys swarmed across the crater floor, their wild shrieks echoing off the walls. "... I think this is the end of things. At least for you three."

I shot him a dark look.

Blix gave an apologetic look. "Well, I won't escape *unscathed* if that makes you feel better."

I drew the DEMOTER and aimed toward the nearest monkey as they came within range. "Then I'm taking as many with me as I can."

A high-pitched whir sounded as Jasette powered her lasers to full.

"You got that right," she said.

"Maybe I can distract them?" Nelvan said. "If I start running in another direction, perhaps they'll follow. Then, when my holding sphere explodes, it could take enough of them out to save you."

Jasette looked back and gave Nelvan a warm smile. "I'm afraid there's no way out this time."

Blix patted him on the back as if to confirm her statement. The monkeys reached the base of the hill and began to scramble up. The entire crater floor was a grey-orange sea of the filthy, devilish creatures. They were closing in from every side. We were like a doomed island in the midst of a horrible storm.

"Nelvan, catch." Jasette retrieved a small, black laser gun from her belt and tossed it to the boy. "It's my emergency weapon and this sure seems like an emergency."

"Thanks." Nelvan caught it and aimed it toward the monkeys.

He almost looked like he knew what he was doing. I felt a tinge of pride at my newest crew member, who had come so far in just a few days. It was a shame he was about to get torn to pieces.

"Okay," I said. "Circle formation."

I moved to stand back to back with the others. We held our weapons before us as the space monkeys closed in.

33

SUDDENLY, A VIOLENT tremor went through the ground, almost knocking me over. The space monkeys immediately stopped their advance. A nervous chatter went through their ranks as they cast worried glances at one another with their freakishly large, bloodshot eyes.

A loud metal clang followed by a mechanized system of moving metal parts rumbled directly beneath us. A wedge shaped opening emerged at the base of the hill as if someone had cut a slice from it with a huge knife.

Frenzied shrieks spread through the nearby monkeys as they scurried away from the opening. A long, thin spider leg stepped out from it. The sheer size of the ebony, arachnid limb was a frightening indicator of the dangerous creature that lurked within.

A few more spider legs emerged and the shrieking of the monkeys grew intense. The creatures scrambled and clawed at their brethren to get away from the spider beast, until a wide clearing was created.

I had no idea what the mysterious creature was, but if space monkeys were afraid of it, whatever was crawling out of the hill was about to do horrible, horrible things.

"W-what is that thing?" Nelvan said.

"A nightmare within a nightmare," I said.

Jasette trained her pistols on the opening below. "If it

charges, take out the front legs first. Slow its advance. Then, blast away at the head."

Such beautiful words from such a beautiful mouth.

"Preach it, sister." I aimed the DEMOTER at the hideous, segmented legs.

In a sudden burst of movement, the spider creature scurried out of the opening. I froze in fear and confusion at the sight of it. Instead of the hideous, bloated spider body I'd expected, the base of the legs connected to the stout, upper body of a man. It was as if he'd simply traded his human legs with those of a giant spider in some bizarre card game gone wrong. He touched a small, disc shaped device strapped to his belt and a high-pitched tone filled the air.

The monkeys shrieked and leapt over one another in a mad scramble to leave the crater floor. The man spider put his hands at his sides and let loose a merry laugh at their retreat.

Jasette shot me a worried look. "Does anyone else find that extremely creepy?"

The spider legs of the odd man-arachnid moved in a synchronous turn and brought him round to face us. In one spry bound he ascended to the top of the hill. He landed abruptly, the pointed ends of his spider legs impaling several of the fallen monkeys only a few yards away.

I instinctively trained the DEMOTER on his head. From the corner of my eye, I could see Jasette had both silver pistols leveled at his legs.

He held up his hands with an amused smile. "Please, no weapons. I seek only peace."

I lowered my weapon a little but kept it pointed in his general direction.

A plush, purple sport coat was fastened snugly around his

broad torso with gleaming, crystal buttons. A shimmering silver shirt twinkled underneath. He had a short, white beard separated in thin braids and accented with tiny, silver circlets. His thick white hair was well groomed in a stylish swirl and a circle of bright, hover diamonds spun around his forehead. His skin had a grayish hue that seemed to shimmer in the low light.

"Ahh, company!" He spoke with a rich, deep voice. "Company, at last." He gave a gracious bow like some welcoming ambassador, his spider legs bending slightly to accentuate the gesture.

I gave a questioning look to Blix. He shook his head, a blank expression on his face. Obviously this was new territory for both of us.

The man spider straightened. His grey eyes shone with an inner luminance and a broad smile covered his face. His expression was either mirthful or insane, I couldn't tell which. An awkward silence passed as we exchanged confused glances.

"Oh dear." A look of concern crossed his face. "My appearance is off-putting, isn't it?"

"What? No." I gave an unconvincing shake of my head.

Blix gave a forced smile. "You look … fine."

Nelvan just stared, his mouth agape.

"Well, eye of the beholder, eh?" He laughed. "Allow me to introduce myself. I am Master Grizzolo, the fortunate one."

"Grizzolo?" Blix looked skyward as if trying to remember something. "Now why does that sound familiar?"

"I've lived an extraordinary life," Grizzolo said. "It's entirely possible some of my exploits are known."

Blix snapped his fingers, his reptilian face filled with excitement. "The Iron Gauntlet! You were one of the final contestants a while back. You came in second on season three hundred thirteen."

"Yes." Grizzolo's face creased in displeasure. "I should have won. The most popular game show in the universe and I was just about to win ..." He grabbed at a silver chain that hung around his neck and pulled out a dull green gemstone that hung at its end. "But apparently the Enigma had other plans. It brought me here instead."

My eyes went wide. Could it be true? My bad luck would never let me stumble upon something this fantastic so haphazardly. I snuck a quick glance at Blix. He frowned and waved a dismissive hand at me but I saw the doubt in his eye. He was thinking the same thing as me. By some bizarre twist of cosmic destiny, we may just have happened upon the very object of my hopeless quest ... the Emerald Enigma.

Grizzolo sighed and stuffed the green stone back under his shirt. "But I suppose to question the Emerald Enigma would be to question fate itself, eh?"

Jasette sighed as if in disbelief. "You really think that shabby little stone around your neck is the Emerald Enigma?"

If nothing else, she was direct.

Grizzolo nodded as if to agree with her. "Sounds unbelievable, doesn't it. Frankly, I wouldn't believe it either."

"So, why don't you prove it?" Jasette nodded her head at Nelvan while keeping her pistols trained on Grizzolo. "Our crewman over there has a holding sphere that's about to explode. I'm sure the Enigma can handle a tiny problem like that, right?"

"Mmm, a challenge." Grizzolo rubbed two of his spider legs together. "And a chance to show you my veracity. I accept."

Grizzolo leapt over us with his spry, arachnid legs and

landed just behind Nelvan. Jasette and I swiveled our guns along with him.

Nelvan craned his neck back, his face filled with apprehension.

Grizzolo leaned forward and lowered himself to Nelvan's height. He pulled the green stone from under his shirt and draped it over one of Nelvan's shoulders.

"Hold still." Grizzolo had his hands poised carefully over Nelvan's head.

Nelvan gave a worried nod.

Grizzolo deactivated the med halo and cautiously pulled it away from Nelvan's forehead.

"Careful," Blix held up his hands as if assisting with the process.

Grizzolo gave Blix a reassuring nod and removed the headband. The holding sphere in Nelvan's forehead stopped flashing and the red light went dim. The sphere vibrated a moment, then dropped from Nelvan's head and landed with a soft thud on the ground. The cavity in his head healed completely.

I stared at the red sphere resting on the black sand floor of the moon, expecting it to explode at any moment.

Nelvan ran his fingers across his forehead, an amazed look on his face. "It's gone. It's really gone!"

Grizzolo grinned. His front spider legs raised, lifting his human torso high once more. My eyes were drawn to the emerald stone on his necklace. It was a plain looking, oval shaped stone in a thin silver setting. There was nothing visually impressive about it and yet, it's power was unmistakable.

I glanced up at Grizzolo. He was watching me with a curious sort of smile. Nelvan craned his neck up to Grizzolo. "Thank you. You saved my life."

Grizzolo smiled and stroked Nelvan's head gently with a spider leg. It was thoroughly creepy. "I'm just glad to be of help. Now, pray tell, what is your name?"

"Nelvan, sir."

"Ah, a handsome name, has a nice snap to it. Now then Nelvan, would you mind handing me the holding sphere?"

"Sure." Nelvan retrieved the sphere from the black sand and held it up.

Grizzolo took the sphere and leaned back, his torso lightly bouncing on ebony legs. "I don't know how familiar you are with the Enigma but as you can see, the legends are true. But, first things first. Introductions are in order." Grizzolo motioned to me and waited.

"Captain Starcrost," I said. "This is my first mate Blix and crew member Jasette." I motioned to the others.

"Wonderful." Grizzolo gave a broad smile. "I do so like to meet people before any unpleasantries begin."

I shot a nervous glance to Blix. "What'ya mean?"

"It's unavoidable of course, I just wish it wasn't necessary." He touched the disc shaped device on his belt. A series of stifled screeches came from the opening at the base of the hill. Within moments, a space monkey came leaping up the hill toward Grizzolo. The monkey wore a metal cap on his head. The cap was covered in pulsating circuitry.

Grizzolo tossed the sphere to the monkey's nimble hands. The sphere began to blink rapidly once more. The monkey stared at the sphere and screeched. His simian features contorted in an angry twist.

"I do hope you'll forgive my rather barbaric actions." Grizzolo put his hand to his heart, looking apologetic. "As unseemly as it is, I think we can find some solace knowing that space monkeys are one of the more despicable creatures in the universe."

I was starting to like this guy more and more.

He looked at the monkey and pointed to the upper rim of the crater. The monkey gave an angry sounding screech in reply. Grizzolo frowned and touched the device on his belt once more. The monkey shivered for a moment, let out a weak little squeal and then scrambled down the hill, heading for the crater rim.

"I suggest we take cover inside," Grizzolo started crawling down toward the opening in the hill. "That sphere could explode any moment."

I waited a few freems until he was out of earshot. "Blix, what'ya think?"

"Sometimes your path in the universe is inevitable, Captain," Blix said.

I frowned. "Don't get all poetic. I'm asking for your advice."

"For good or bad." Blix motioned to Grizzolo. "We must follow the human spider into his hole."

As much as I hated the idea of blindly following a freakish hybrid of spider and man into an unknown underground lair on some remote rock, I was out of options once again. Besides, he had my long sought after Enigma. That alone was worth the risk.

"Captain," Nelvan said. "You're still bound by your holding sphere. He's the only one that can help you."

"Okay, fine. We're going," I said.

"Just keep your weapons ready." Jasette held her pistols at her sides. She appeared to have no intention of holstering them.

I gave her a nod of agreement.

34

I LED THE WAY To the base of the hill and headed into the wedge shaped opening.

It opened up into a wide, metal walled tunnel. Bright orange coils curved in serpentine fashion along the ceiling, giving warm light to the otherwise grey passage. Our footsteps echoed off the smooth, metal floor that was polished and clean. Grizzolo walked in front of us, the tips of his spider legs making unnerving clicking sounds as he traveled.

He turned back and grinned. "Welcome to my humble abode."

There was a soft thud and a small tremor went through the tunnel as the opening closed behind us. The gloomy haze of the planet was replaced with the warm orange lights of the passage.

I slowed until I was beside Blix. I leaned over and whispered. "What's our move?"

Blix arched a brow. "How should I know?"

"You should have a plan."

"Well, I don't see how that falls on me," Blix said. "You want the Enigma. Your head needs the healing. The responsibility is clearly yours."

"Thanks for nothing," I hissed.

I fell back, letting Blix take the lead. Soon I was walking

beside Jasette. I leaned toward her and whispered. "What's our move?"

Jasette looked annoyed. "You mean you don't have a move?"

"Of course," I lied. "I've got like ten of 'em. I was just trying to include you."

"I'm just ready to blast this freak if he tries anything funny," she said. "How's that?"

I gave a non-committal nod. It was right to the point, not overly complicated. It was just the type of plan I liked.

"It's a little simplistic." I tried to sound mentally superior, yet gracious toward her input. "I'm really thinking in more complex terms, what with the subterranean surroundings, human spider hybrid combat tactics and what have you, but thanks anyways."

Jasette smirked and shook her head. "You have no idea what to do, do you?"

"Not really."

The muffled sound of a large explosion sent tremors through the tunnel. Grizzolo, without breaking his methodic stride, turned and pointed to Nelvan. "That could have been you, young one."

Nelvan swallowed hard and gave an appreciative nod. "Thank you again."

Grizzolo waved a dismissive hand. "The least I could do for a visitor. I get so few you see. I am a socialite by nature and yet, no one to socialize with."

"So, you're alone down here?" Jasette said.

"Well, in a manner of speaking." Grizzolo neared an archway that marked the end of the tunnel. "Here, I'll show you."

He stepped through the archway onto a short platform beyond. With his hands and a few of his spider legs, he grasped a decorative railing that ringed the edge of the platform. The translucent railing glowed with a bright red substance that flowed within.

A large, dome shaped room opened up before us. I joined Grizzolo at the railing. We were on a small platform perched in the center of the room and raised about a dozen feet off the ground. Stairways ran down from either side of the platform to the floor.

The walls of the room were shiny and metallic. Inlays ran along the curved walls with the same bright red, flowing substance as the railing. Rows of multi-colored lights and switches ran along the base of the wall where it met the metal floor below.

Dozens of space monkeys walked throughout the room, each wearing a metal cap with pulsating circuitry. They moved slowly, their faces expressionless. Occasional, somber grunts escaped their lips as if they lacked the energy for their typical, maddening screeches.

"As you can see . . ." Grizzolo motioned to the monkey drones below. "I'm quite bereft of any civilized companions. Have you ever tried conversing with a space monkey? It's horrid."

Several smaller tunnels led out from the large room. Monkeys filed in and out of the tunnels, some heading down other passages, others pausing momentarily to adjust the switches and light controls on the walls. A few monkeys were suspended upside down near our platform, polishing the walls with a vacant stare.

Blix let out a long whistle. "Quite an operation you have here."

Grizzolo gave a half-hearted smile. "I suppose it is at that.

It's all powered by the lava that runs just under the surface of Grizzola."

"Grizzola?" Jasette said.

"Yes, this moon." Grizzolo gave a theatrical wave of his hand. "I have named it so. Is it not obvious that everything here was undoubtedly built with my imminent arrival in mind?"

I exchanged a quick glance with Blix. There was a good chance being stuck on a barren asteroid populated with nothing but space monkeys could tweak your brain a bit. I figured it was best to change the subject. That's when Nelvan piped up.

"What about this sign?" Nelvan pointed to a large metal plaque above the archway we'd just walked through. Words were etched deeply into the metal surface. Dozens of scratches marred its surface as though someone had tried to destroy it.

"Ah, looks like one of the ancient languages. Marvelous." Blix narrowed his eyes, studying the plaque. "Outpost Shadow. Base four of seven in the outer claw formation of the great Vellanax." Blix nodded as if impressed. "A foreboding name and a mystery to boot. Makes you wonder about this intriguing Vellanax character."

"Irrelevant." Grizzolo waved a dismissive hand. "Ancient writings of dead civilizations. When I came here twenty gloons ago it was deserted. Obviously they built it for me. Yes, just for me, Master Grizzolo." Grizzolo leaned over the railing and looked down at the toiling monkeys. "All hail Master Grizzolo!" he proclaimed.

The monkeys stopped in unison. They turned to face Grizzolo with blank expressions and raised their fists. They chanted a series of monotone screeches that sounded as if they were trying to repeat the proclamation and then returned to their trance-like operations.

He leaned back with a broad smile.

"You've been here twenty gloons?" Jasette said.

"Yes." Grizzolo gave a forced smile. "It's really a very lucky place to be." His left eye started twitching.

Jasette shot me a look of concern.

Grizzolo gripped the railing and looked around the room as if in newfound appreciation. "If you think about it, this is a self-sustaining, underground fortress. And the technology at work here is quite astounding. For example, Sorgat, bring up visuals please."

"Yes, Master Grizzolo." A monotone, computerized voice spoke. It was somewhere between a deep voiced man and a rock scraping against gravel.

A large, red holoscreen projected from the floor. It expanded before us and a three-dimensional visual of an asteroid field materialized. Although it was all red and translucent, the detail was stunning.

"You see," Grizzolo motioned to the visual. "We are in one of the more difficult places to reach in the universe. Few sane pilots would dare to navigate an asteroid field." Grizzolo directed the last comment to me.

"I was out of options," I said.

Grizzolo gave a sympathetic nod then turned back to the visual. "Now, if you see the moon Grizzola right there. Sorgat, please enhance."

"Yes, Master Grizzolo," Sorgat said.

A large, round moon filled the visual and spun slowly. "The technology of this base utilizes the mineral makeup of the moon for a type of cloaking shield that goes undetected by most ship scanners."

The visual wavered for a moment and the moon disappeared.

"For those looking for a hiding spot in the universe," Grizzolo said. "You couldn't find a better place." He pulled out the Enigma and held it before him. "The Enigma knew this of course and that's why it brought me here. I'm really very lucky."

"But I thought you liked being social," Jasette said. "Why would it be lucky to be stuck somewhere with no one to talk to?"

Grizzolo's eye started twitching again. "Well, luck is a rather subjective thing, isn't it? But enough of that, come with me." Grizzolo started down the stairway and beckoned us to follow with a spider leg. "I'll give you the grand tour."

I raised my eyebrows at Blix. He nodded in agreement. Crazy had been at work here for some time. The only question was how deep the psychosis had run. A little self-delusion was all well and good but had it turned devious and deadly? Only time would tell. My mission was clear, get the Enigma, get the sphere out of my head, and get outta this demented monkey factory as soon as possible.

Blix led the way after Grizzolo. Jasette followed next, a death grip on her pistols. Nelvan took another look around the room as if we were on some tourist spot. "Amazing. And all powered by lava." He shook his head and headed down the stairs.

I glanced at the reserve energy cartridge in the DEMOTER. The orange power bar was just a sliver now. I slid the cartridge door open and peered inside. A small globule of energy gel huddled in the corner. It seemed barely enough for one more blast. I closed the cartridge, holstered the gun and sighed. At least Jasette still had her weapons if something bad went down. I headed down the stairs and caught up with my crew.

Grizzolo took us down a long, broad tunnel that lead out from the room. The passage wound in serpentine fashion, making it difficult to tell how long it was or where it was headed.

"Fine craftsmanship at work here," Blix scanned the tunnel walls. "The symmetry, the clean lines, the difficulties of underground construction. This must have taken some time."

"Yes, they spared no expense for my arrival," Grizzolo said. "Obviously they knew someone of great importance was coming."

That gave me an idea. "It's hard to see how someone with your level of greatness even needs the Enigma."

"A very astute observation." Grizzolo pointed back at me like a professor pleased with his student. "I feel a bit selfish having been the keeper of it so long. My deeds are quite amazing enough on their own."

"I wouldn't doubt it." I liked where his pompous thoughts were taking him. "You'd probably even do better without it."

Grizzolo held the emerald close to his face. Admiring it as he walked. "I've often wondered the same thing. Ah, we've arrived at our destination."

A darkened room lay at the end of the hallway. As we drew close, I was drawn to the floor of the dark room. A series of multi-colored lights swirled through a luminescent dome. It seemed to be the only light source in the room.

"Sorgat, illuminate the tower," Grizzolo said.

"Yes, Master Grizzolo," Sorgat said.

A thick, curving coil that ran along the walls in an ascending spiral lit up in a bright shade of orange. It illuminated a cavernous, cylinder shaped room. The ceiling rose so high above I couldn't imagine it was very far from the surface of the moon. The luminescent dome I'd seen from the hallway was in the very center of the room. A low hum proceeded from it as lights swirled around its surface.

"I call this the tower," Grizzolo said. "I believe it was the former landing bay. I come here to think sometimes."

A single, bright tone sounded.

"Perimeter alert, Master Grizzolo," Sorgat said.

"More visitors?" Grizzolo seemed pleasantly surprised. "This is an eventful day, isn't it? Visuals please."

A red holoscreen appeared and hovered above the bright dome. An image of the crater we had recently left materialized. Two figures were making their way across the black sand. I gasped at the realization that it was Hamilton and Mishmash. My recent happy thoughts of their demise disappeared.

"How?"

"Friends of yours?" Grizzolo said.

"No, horrible enemies," I said. "I can't believe their ship wasn't destroyed."

Grizzolo seemed amused by me. "You really feel strongly about them, don't you?"

"They're pure evil," I said. "If you have any weapons, take them out now."

Grizzolo laughed and turned to Blix. "Is he always like this?"

"Just wait till the vein in his neck starts throbbing," Blix said.

I shot Blix a dark look.

"Sorgat," Grizzolo said. "Analyze intruder threat."

The computer dome emitted a few blips. "Threat level two. High energy emitters and low level disruptors."

"There, you see." Grizzolo crossed his arms. "Nothing to worry about."

"Intruders within range," Sorgat said. "Teleport or destroy?"

"Destroy! Destroy!" I yelled.

Grizzolo put up a hand. "Hold, Sorgat." He gave me a perplexed look. "You certainly are impulsive for a ship captain. I told you, they cannot harm us here."

"You don't know them," I pleaded. "Hamilton will find a way in. He'll gain control with his evil little robot and destroy everything. They must be stopped."

Grizzolo shook his head and sighed. "How I tire of interstellar conflict. It's all so petty."

"Well, all you have to do is zap them." I made pretend guns with my fingers. "Zap. End of conflict."

Grizzolo held my gaze for a moment. "Do you know, Captain, I do believe your behavior is rubbing off on me. I've just had a very brash thought."

"Oh?"

"Yes." Grizzolo gave a long look around at the room, his fingers drumming against his hips. "How would you like to assume full control over Grizzola?"

35

"WHAT?" I SAID.

Jasette laughed as though in disbelief. "Did you say full control of this place?"

"Yes. I weary of it." Grizzolo said. "Of course, I will pass on the Emerald Enigma to you as well. Sort of a parting gift if you will."

"Um, what?" I said.

"You're going to just give him the Enigma and this base?" Blix said. "I don't understand."

Grizzolo gave a somber nod. "I weary of the responsibilities. Frankly, you couldn't have come along at a better moment. It's high time I moved on to the next chapter in my life." He grabbed the stone and beheld it once more. He gave a sad sort of smile and nodded. "Yes, it is time." He looked at me. "Captain, will you be my successor?"

I wanted to laugh, cry and sing at the same time. I was utterly speechless for a few moments but finally managed. "Uh, yeah."

He smiled and nodded. "You are a tremendous person, Captain. Brave and bold. Once things are in your power, make sure to think about your actions before doing anything too rash to the intruders above, okay?"

I grinned. "Oh, I'll think about it very carefully."

"Wonderful," he said. "Now first, I must turn the station

over to your care." He scuttled to the center of the room and used the tips of his legs to click a series of metal panels near the luminescent dome.

Nelvan leaned close to me, his voice a whisper. "Be careful, Captain. He's lying."

I gave him an annoyed look. "About what?"

"Well ..." He furrowed his brow as if stuck on a math problem. "I don't know exactly."

"Then it doesn't matter." I shook my head to discount his concern. "Maybe he's lying about how long he's been here or how great he is or a whole list of things that don't really matter."

"No, it's a deep lie," Nelvan said. "I can feel it."

"Everything alright over there?" Grizzolo had stopped his operations to look my way.

"Everything's fine." I leaned in confidentially to Nelvan. "Listen, once I get the Enigma, it won't matter what he's lying about, okay?"

Nelvan gave a worried look and nodded his head.

"Captain?" Grizzolo said.

"Right here." I gave him my attentive student routine.

"This is the heart of Sorgat, in a manner of speaking." He motioned to the bright dome. "When level one functions must be performed, such as transfer of ownership ..." He motioned to me and gave a slight bow. "... Sorgat must be accessed from this room."

"So how'd you get control?" Jasette gave a scrutinizing stare. "I thought this place was deserted when you got here?"

Grizzolo let out a giddy laugh. "She is sharp, isn't she?"

I nodded, wondering why my brain so often missed obvious questions like that.

"When you bear the Enigma, almost anything is possible." Grizzolo winked.

He turned back to the dome computer. "Sorgat, commence transfer of command sequence."

"Current commander," Sorgat said. "Please authenticate."

Grizzolo cleared his throat and spoke in an official manner. "I am Master Grizzolo, king of Grizzola and commander of this base. I hereby transfer all rights and duties to the new commander, Captain Starcrost."

"New commander," Sorgat said. "Please authenticate."

I paused for a moment, wondering how much I really understood about what I was getting into. I gave a questioning look to Blix. He shrugged and motioned to the computer as if to say, 'Why not?' Nelvan looked thoroughly worried, as if any decision I made was doomed. Jasette gave me a serious look and shook her head. Obviously, she wanted out of this situation.

Frankly, I didn't see what the big deal was. The Enigma was within my grasp, all I had to do was play along with this weirdo. And really, what could be so bad about owning something as awesome as a hidden moon base? Still, it was all a little too good to be true. I decided it was my duty as a captain to get some answers before I dove headlong into things.

"Um, listen Grizzolo, I just had a few questions before—" I began.

"Authentication confirmed," Sorgat said. "Transfer of command is complete."

"Oh." I let out a nervous cough.

Blix gave me a reassuring pat on the back. Jasette covered her face with her hands.

A thunderous echo of footsteps approaching came from the tunnel into the room.

I drew the DEMOTER and aimed toward the tunnel. "Something's coming."

"Relax," Grizzolo chuckled. "Sorgat has summoned the workers to report to their new leader."

Dozens of space monkeys outfitted with the metal helmets streamed into the room. They assembled into several well-ordered lines on the opposite side of the computer dome.

I cringed, realizing there were about fifty or sixty of them. The room suddenly felt much smaller. Being stuck in the same room with that many monkeys was sending stress tremors through every corner of my body. All my muscles were tensing up. Getting my hands on that Enigma was the only thing keeping me steady.

"These are the workers of this station." Grizzolo waved his hand across the monkey ranks. "Sorgat sends signals through the mind control helmets that give them their orders. If any worker becomes unruly …" Grizzolo grabbed the silver, disc shaped device from his belt and held it up. "… A few adjustments from this remote will help keep them in line."

The chattering of the monkeys grew in intensity as their bloodshot eyes locked onto the remote device. Fleeting expressions of anger crossed their blank faces until Grizzolo returned the remote to his belt.

"Now, first things first." Grizzolo walked up to me, his front spider legs lowering until we were face to face. He lifted the green gemstone of his necklace from his shirt and held it between us for a moment. It looked like such an ordinary stone as it lightly swayed on its silver chain.

"Captain Starcrost," Grizzolo said. "Do you agree to bear the Emerald Enigma and receive the fortune it will grant you?"

It was a completely unnecessary question. It was kind of

like putting a billion space vibes in front of someone and then asking if they wanted it. Who would say no? I was about to answer when Jasette broke in.

"What if he says no?" Jasette said.

Grizzolo's head turned slowly to Jasette. "You're filled with questions, aren't you my dear?"

"The name's Jasette."

A tight-lipped grin crept over his face. He gave a slight bow and turned back to me. "I apologize for my formality. It is just my way. I prefer to add ceremony to landmark events in life. You are certainly free to decline but I will make the offer again regardless." He cleared his throat. "Do you wish to bear the Emerald Enigma?"

I paused and took a deep breath. Gloons of searching for an object whose very existence was in question hung mere inches away from me. This was a glorious moment. Even though the doubts and skepticism of Nelvan and Jasette nagged at me, I refused to let this opportunity slip through my fingers.

"Absolutely," I said.

Grizzolo smiled. He removed the Enigma from his neck and placed the necklace over my head. The emerald glowed and I felt a thick energy wash over me like honey was pouring through my veins. The room seemed to spin and I stumbled to keep my balance.

"Captain, you okay?" Blix was at my side, holding me steady.

Nelvan and Jasette crowded around, looking concerned. I blinked a few times and felt my senses return to normal. There was a strange tingling sensation on my forehead. I reached up and felt the warm holding sphere nestled between my forehead and the med halo.

"Blix, take this med halo off," I said.

Blix deactivated the headband and slowly removed it. I reached up and grabbed the holding sphere. It vibrated for a moment and then slid easily into my palm. I stared at the dull red orb in my hand in utter amazement. I was free. I gave a stunned look at Blix, lifting the sphere closer to him. He shook his head, his reptilian face as amazed as mine. I smiled and put the sphere in my pocket.

I looked back at Grizzolo, trying to muster some clumsy attempt to thank him for saving my life. It was at that moment I realized he had backed several steps away from us. His face was animated with a twitchy sort of grin as if he were suppressing laughter. He clicked a panel on the ground with one of his spider legs. There was a muffled whooshing sound as a clear dome emerged from the floor and surrounded us.

Nelvan gasped. “Oh no.”

Blix rushed to the wall of the dome and pushed against it. It didn’t budge.

“Hmm, plexitanium.” Blix stepped back and shook his head. “I’m developing a severe dislike for this substance.”

Jasette slugged me on the shoulder. “I told you not to trust him.”

A speaker in the roof of the plexitanium dome squeaked to life, amplifying the sounds in the room.

“My apologies friends.” An insane chuckle broke from Grizzolo’s lips. “But I must be free. Free!”

He leapt high in the air, with his agile insect legs adding a stylish twist before landing. “I’ve been wearing that accursed thing for twenty five gloons.”

“Accursed?” I grabbed the emerald stone that hung from my neck and scrutinized its dull green surface. I tried to remove the necklace but it instantly constricted about my neck like some vicious snake. I choked and released the chain. It slowly loosened and the stone slid down my chest to where it had hung before.

"I wouldn't try that again, Captain." Grizzolo said. "You can only remove it if someone else agrees to bear it."

"What is this?" I said. "Some kind of trick? This isn't the real Enigma, is it?"

"Oh, it's the Enigma alright. And at long last, I'm free."

"But I thought it brought you good luck?" Nelvan said. "Why would you want to get rid of it?"

"Good luck. Good luck!" Grizzolo laughed madly as he spoke the words. "Yes, good luck indeed, but whose? Look at my skin." Grizzolo crawled up to the other side of the plexitanium dome and pointed to his face as if appalled with his appearance. "There are those who would consider their skin turning silver and cold to the touch good luck. Maybe it's considered attractive on their planet. And what about these?" He motioned to his spider legs. "Somewhere in the twisted realms of the universe it's good fortune to have the repulsive legs of a large spider. Can you believe it?" He let out a mad cackle.

His shoulders sank and he buried his face in his hands. "I turn more hideous with each passing gloon because of the various and demented ideas of what good luck actually means." He leaned forward, pressing his hands against the other side of our new dome prison and glared at the Enigma. "That accursed thing doesn't know how to differentiate between them." He pointed a shaky finger at the stone. "It just absorbs all the wishes that float around the galaxies and thrusts them upon you. Then it unceremoniously dumps you on a deserted moon with space monkeys." He threw his hands up and cast a look of despair around the room.

His rantings were definitely giving me the heebie jeebies. The last thing I wanted to do was turn into a grey skinned, spider legged freak but I couldn't help thinking he was wrong about the Enigma. After all, it had already saved my life within five freems of wearing it. It couldn't be that bad … could it?

"The workers have returned with the craft," Sorgat announced.

"Excellent, excellent," Grizzolo said.

Dozens more monkeys came from the tunnel into the room, guiding a large hover platform. The metal platform bore a sleek, finely built shuttlecraft that barely fit through the tunnel. It was one of the most exquisite shuttlecrafts I'd ever seen. It almost looked like a smaller version of Hamilton's Velladrella.

"After you and your friends crashed into Grizzola, I had Sorgat run a scan," Grizzolo said. "Lo and behold, damaged as the other starship was, a fully functional shuttlecraft lay within her broken hull. Can you believe it?" The monkeys brought the hover platform next to Grizzolo, then joined the rest of their brethren in military like formation at the other end of the room.

Grizzolo activated a few controls on the platform and it set the ship down gently on the floor.

"And now my friends, my time has arrived. I have been marooned here long enough."

Grizzolo took a deep breath and composed himself. "Today I reclaim my life!" His raised voice echoed through the curved metal walls of the room. He crawled up the spaceship toward the cockpit.

"Wait, what about us?" Jasette called.

Grizzolo stopped and looked back over his shoulder. "Your

captain bears the Enigma. It will most certainly grant him a way out."

He turned back and slid open the clear cockpit window. Then, in a remarkable display of arachnid flexibility, he fit himself down into the pilot's seat.

"Master Grizzolo." Blix spoke in a cordial tone as if addressing a departing dignitary.

"Yes, Blix," Grizzolo said. "Please speak. I hate to part ways on such unsavory terms with a civil creature as yourself."

Blix gave a slight bow. "Understood. I was just wondering if you could leave us the controls for the monkeys. Should we manage to free ourselves we may need to continue operations."

"Quite right, quite right, my friend." Grizzolo retrieved the disc shaped device at his side. "Take it with my best wishes."

He flung the remote our way. It sailed just past us and collided with the bright orange coil that wound throughout the room and provided our illumination. The coil sparked and a large section of it broke away from the wall. It swayed for a moment, a series of electrical crackles and sparks filling the room as further sections of the coil started to break apart.

A large portion of coil fell and landed on the dome computer with a loud crunching sound. Thin, spider web cracks spread out across the dome computer from the center of impact. Sparks began bursting forth from the cracks with electric sizzles and thin streams of smoke.

Grizzolo put a hand to his mouth. "Oh dear."

A soft tone sounded and Sorgat spoke. "Core system compromised. Main functions shutting down."

"So much for good luck," Jasette said.

The lights on the space monkeys' helmets began to flicker and die out. One by one the creatures seemed to wake from their hypnotic state. Their blank expressions turned quickly to wild monkey rage. A mad screeching spread through their ranks.

My skin shivered. "Maybe being behind this plexitanium wasn't bad luck after all."

Nelvan nodded in heartfelt agreement.

The foremost monkeys motioned to Grizzolo and rallied their brethren to action. Grizzolo had a look of fear as he closed the cockpit and fired up the engines. The monkeys scrambled across the metal floor and leapt one by one onto the ship. Soon the ship was covered with the vile creatures, pounding and clawing at the hull.

The ship trembled and wavered slightly as it hovered a few inches off the ground. The enraged monkeys continued unhindered. Some tore off small metal pieces of the hull while others bit at the exposed wiring underneath.

A few monkeys crawled over the cockpit window. I caught a glimpse of Grizzolo shouting muted orders at them from inside as he struggled with the controls.

The irony of Grizzolo giving away the greatest good luck charm in the universe only moments earlier wasn't lost on me. After all, space monkeys on a good day were bad enough but space monkeys enslaved for gloons, then finally set loose to exact their savage monkey revenge was an absolute nightmare.

A shudder went through the floor. An issue of sparks erupted from the computer dome. One of the orange seam insets that ran along the wall fractured with a horrific crash. A stream of bright lava poured down the metal wall like a broken dam. There was a sharp hissing sound as the lava ate away at the metal in its path. Smoke rose from the glowing orange rivers spreading slowly through the room.

"Now's a good time to put that emerald to use," Jasette said.

I looked down at the green stone lying dormant on my chest. "It didn't come with an instruction manual." My voice was on edge. Partially from the sudden realization that I had no idea how to actually make the Enigma do anything, but mostly from fear of the chaos around us. "Grizzolo never mentioned how to make this thing work."

"He didn't mention a lot of things." Jasette put her hands on her hips and struck her typical pose of challenge. It was a good look for her. Daring and alluring with passionate energy surging underneath. "You just took the Enigma, no questions asked and now we're trapped in here."

As amazing as she looked in her sultry pose, her comments were not only a tremendous breach of captain to crew member protocol, but horribly annoying, being that they were deadly accurate.

"Listen, honey." I intentionally used a term she would find both annoying and belittling to throw her off her game. I added a threatening finger point to add to her frustration. "Once this thing starts granting me good luck you'll be begging me for—"

"Honey?" Jasette glared. "Did you just call me honey?"

"So?" I pretended to be oblivious to further her aggravation.

"Look." Nelvan pointed to the ceiling. A giant, circular hatch opened far above us, revealing the dim orange light of the moon's atmosphere.

Grizzolo weaved the ship in unstable, sweeping arcs throughout the room in an apparent attempt to lose the monkeys. The wild creatures clung to the ship with feral tenacity. Several pieces of the hull were now missing and electric sparks crackled from the circuitry underneath. The monkeys continued to beat and claw the ship and deep marks scored the cockpit window.

I shook my head in wonderment at the devilish beasts. "Savage creatures."

The muffled blast of laser cannons echoed through the room. Bright red beams darted from the front of Grizzolo's ship. A few unfortunate monkeys positioned in front of the cannons were blasted into small showers of black ash. The lasers continued to fire as the ship swayed. The blasts tore into the metal walls and floor of the room creating blackened craters.

The lava continued to flow from the wall, making troughs of flowing magma. There was a deep crack followed by a violent shudder under my feet.

"Captain," Blix said. "This room is growing highly unstable. I do hope that charm of yours will help us soon."

I grabbed the emerald and brought it to eye level. I stared at the opaque green surface focusing thoughts of escape toward it in a desperate attempt to will it into action.

A terrific crash echoed through the room. Grizzolo's ship had collided with the ceiling near the open hatch. The engines had taken on a labored whine as if struggling to maintain power. Whether the controls were failing him or his vision was too obscured by the scrambling monkeys, he couldn't seem to navigate to freedom.

The ship spun and dipped in a slow freefall. A small explosion in the center of the spacecraft sent metal shards and monkeys flying.

A large section of floor near us trembled then fell away. An orange glow came from the space left behind, revealing deep caverns below with a vast river of slow flowing lava.

"Hmm." Blix rubbed his chin. "Lava beneath us and

unstable flooring at our feet. Are you sure you're operating that stone correctly?"

I gave him a dark look before returning my attention to the emerald. "Work, blast it. Work!"

A small shadow fell over the open hatch above. I looked up in shock to find Hamilton and Mishmash descending into the room on a translucent hoverdisc. I cast a wounded look at the Enigma. My long sought after good luck charm was failing me but I refused to give up hope. I was sure that at any moment the Enigma would spring to life, destroy my enemies and whisk me away into a life of luxury.

With a thunderous crack, the floor beneath us fell away. A rush of hot air hit me as I fell headlong toward a bright river of lava.

36

AN ALTOGETHER TOO solid impact broke my fall and perhaps a few ribs. I found myself resting atop an ebony, pedestal shaped rock formation. I had fallen into a huge underground cavern. The brown walls flickered with the orange light of the lava below. I was on the very edge of the rock. A few more inches would've sent me plunging to a fiery death. I tried to attribute the lucky break to the lackluster performance of my new good luck charm.

I peered over the edge. A vast sea of red-orange lava flowed sluggishly below. Several tall pedestal rock formations like the one I was on were peppered throughout the cavern like thin soldiers making their last stand.

"Help," Nelvan cried.

I looked toward my feet. I saw a pair of hands hanging from the edge of the rock. I rose to a sitting position and felt countless pains spring forth. I gripped my left arm. Something seemed out of place. I straightened it and a shock of new pain shot to my head. My uncertified medical assumption was that it wasn't broken but severely ouchy.

I shuffled toward him and looked over the edge. Nelvan was hanging precariously over the side, the glowing, orange river flowing about a hundred yards beneath him.

His head snapped up, eyes wide with fear. "Captain, thank God you're there. I'm losing my grip."

With my good arm, I grabbed his wrist and heaved backward. As skinny as he seemed, when holding the boy's full weight, it took every ounce of my strength and determination to pull him up. Soon we were lying on the flat surface of the rock pedestal, breathing heavily.

"Where's Jasette?" Nelvan said. "And Blix?"

His words were like a dagger. We were the only two on the top of the rock pedestal. There was only one logical answer. A lump caught in my throat.

"Captain," Blix called out from somewhere down below.

A thrill of hope went through me. I scrambled to the edge of our rocky perch and looked down. Blix was standing on a narrow outcropping of rock that extended from the wall. Jasette was lying next to him. She was lifting herself off the ground and shaking her head as if regaining consciousness. The outcropping rose a few feet above the flow of lava.

"You two okay?" I couldn't believe my good fortune that all of us had survived the drop. I glanced down at the Emerald Enigma. Maybe it had finally started to work.

"We're fine." Blix glanced over to Jasette as she staggered to her feet. "I mean, I'm fine. It appears the lady Jasette is—"

"I'm *fine*." Jasette interrupted. She was limping as she moved closer to Blix.

A high-pitched whirring sound came from above. I looked up to find Grizzolo's ship, still covered in furious monkeys, spiraling down into the cavern. I stared in disbelief as the spaceship continued its doomed descent and plunged nose first into the glowing lava below. There was a brief and horrifying moment of pained monkey shrieking as the hideous creatures burst into flame and sunk into the lava with the ship.

"That was awful." Nelvan was by my side at the edge of the

rock. I nodded in agreement. Blix had his arm across his chest bowing respectfully toward the spot where the spaceship had vaporized. I felt a tinge of remorse for Grizzolo. Even though he tricked us, imprisoned us and basically left us for dead, meeting a fiery end alongside a horde of vicious space monkeys was a death I wouldn't wish on my worst enemy. Well, except maybe—

"Greetings, friends." Hamilton descended into the cavern on his transparent hoverdisc, with Mishmash at his side. "Fancy meeting you here."

My mind was just about to launch a scathing response when a myriad of laser blasts came from below. Jasette had both silver pistols drawn and was firing off a stream of red beams toward Hamilton. The blasts ricocheted harmlessly off the bottom of the hoverdisc and diffused against the cavern walls.

Mishmash lifted his thin, robotic arm and white energy sparked to life around his three-clawed hand. The silver pistols were yanked out of Jasette's hands and flew upward through the cavern. They came to an abrupt stop at Mishmash's hand and hovered there.

Hamilton laughed. "Princess Jasette, I must say you are an incorrigible ruffian. It's surprising considering your royal upbringing."

"You ain't seen nothin' yet, you pompous windbag." Jasette struck her classic hands on the hips pose.

"I'm afraid my tolerance for insults has worn thin." Hamilton glared down at her, the orange light of the lava animated his features with a devilish glow. "Perhaps you should learn some manners."

Hamilton nodded to Mishmash. The robot stowed Jasette's blasters within his metallic torso, then removed a small, square device from his arm. It started to glow a bright shade of blue.

He lobbed it over the side of the hoverdisc toward Jasette and Blix. Blix grabbed her and moved to the end of the rock outcropping closest to the wall. He crouched over her like some protective hen with her chicks.

The glowing blue square landed where she had stood only moments before and exploded in a shower of rocks and lava. Most of the outcropping broke off and slid into the river of lava. Blix and Jasette huddled on the thin ledge that remained.

"Captain." Nelvan was at my side tugging my jacket like he had to go to the bathroom. "Now's your chance to be free of that Enigma." He pointed to the green stone hanging from my neck. "You said Hamilton was after it. Give it to him and he'll be cursed instead of you."

The boy had a point. Freeing myself from this fickle charm and sending Hamilton down an unpredictable path of questionable luck was a win-win. The problem, of course, was timing.

"And now, to finish things." Hamilton announced from high above as he began to hover toward us.

"I have to keep it." I tucked the Enigma under my shirt.

"Why?" Nelvan gaped. "This is the perfect chance."

I turned on the boy and fixed him with my stern captain stare. "Because if I don't, we're all dead. Sure, maybe in a gloon he'll sprout wings or spiraling horns or purple spines but for now, it'll save him, just like it saved us from the holding spheres."

Nelvan frowned. The frustration on his face told me he understood our dilemma.

"We need another plan," I said.

"Like what?" Nelvan said.

My mind was blank.

Hamilton was close now. Within precious few freems we

would be eye to eye. I could already predict the whole painful confrontation. He'd puff out his chest and wax eloquent of his greatness and my inferiority. My rage would build until I drew my DEMOTER and Mishmash, with his technologically enhanced speed, would yank it from my hand before I could squeeze off a single shot. Hamilton would laugh his insufferable, square chinned laugh, then command his filthy robot to shoot me. He would watch with detached interest as if my demise was little more than the cleaning of his banquet table. Mishmash would fire a clean, deadly accurate blast of lethal energy that would lift me from the rock and send my charred, smoking body plummeting toward the lava below. I would probably hear Jasette's muffled scream at the sight of my ill fated plunge. It would give me a brief moment of solace knowing that she actually cared before I burnt to a crisp.

I suppose after that, I wouldn't care about much except for the knowledge that Hamilton would obliterate my crew soon after. He would make a clean sweep of us all in an attempt to salvage the ego crushing loss of his ship and crew. Even Blix couldn't survive prolonged exposure to the lava. This was the end.

It was a thoroughly depressing realization but I couldn't see any way out of it. I squared my shoulders and took a deep breath as Hamilton drew near.

Nelvan mirrored my actions then turned to face me with expectant eyes. "What do we do, Captain?"

The weight of responsibility suffocated me at the word 'captain.' I sighed, feeling suddenly weary. I had nothing to say. In a subconscious gesture of defeat, I slouched and put my hands in my pockets. That's when I felt it. The smooth, round surface of the holding sphere rolled across my fingertips. An idea hit me like a bright shaft of light from heaven. My body reacted almost as fast as my mind raced for an escape. In one quick motion, as if I'd practiced the move, I withdrew the holding sphere and placed it into the reserve energy cartridge in the DEMOTER.

Hamilton hovered down to our level just as my hand dropped casually back to my side.

"Glint Starcrost, star pilot extraordinaire." The sneer that spread across Hamilton's face looked as though it was maxing out every facial muscle available. To say it was a wicked sneer was a gross understatement. It was a sneer that held such utter contempt and unstable malice, it seemed his face could barely contain it. "I'm amazed at the amount of difficulty an insignificant piece of space trash like you can cause."

"Maybe it's not me that's causing you trouble," I said.

"Really?" A look of amusement replaced his sneer. "Then who's behind all my recent problems?"

I folded my arms in a relaxed stance to show I wasn't intimidated by his assumed control of the situation. "I'd say it's the cosmic hand of justice slapping you around for being such a filthy skrid."

His sneer returned along with a throbbing vein on his forehead. His hand went down to rest on the handle of his golden laser pistol. "I do believe your death will be one of the highlights of my life."

"That's always been your problem, Von Drone." I readied myself for an unparalleled quick draw. "It's all about you."

I drew the DEMOTER in a flash and raised it toward Hamilton. It was, as far as I could remember, the fastest draw of my life. It was smooth, relaxed and accurate. I watched the barrel of the DEMOTER angling toward his broad chest. My finger began to squeeze the trigger just as the pistol was ripped free from my hand. It rocketed over to the energy field sparking around Mishmash's hand.

Hamilton gave his smug victory smile. Even though it was all part of my plan, I'd hoped I could squeeze off a blast at Hamilton before losing my weapon.

Hamilton shook his head in mock pity. "The last card of a losing hand."

Mishmash gave my weapon a spin, then tucked it away in the cavity of his metal torso.

"Mishmash will keep that as a memento," Hamilton said. He drew his golden laser gun and turned it over in his hand as if to admire it. "You know, I've never fired this gun upon another man." Hamilton smiled at me. "I've been saving it for you. And after I shoot you with it, I'll throw it away for fear you've contaminated such a fine weapon."

"Don't take his life." Nelvan stepped forward. "I'll go with you. I'll work aboard your ship if you spare him."

"Nelvan!" I gave him a serious stare and shook my head.

Hamilton paused for a moment, his eyebrow raised in surprise. "Really?"

Nelvan nodded and took another step toward the edge of the rock formation. Hamilton's hoverdisc was only a few feet from him.

A devious, thoughtful expression covered Hamilton's face. "Perhaps I could make use of you. Your lack of records could make for a profitable sale on the black market."

"Nelvan, get back here." I used my stern captain's command voice. "It's a deal with the devil."

Nelvan turned back to face me, his face filled with resignation. "It's okay, Captain. If it will save you and the others, it's worth it."

"Oh, I didn't say it would save them." Hamilton aimed the gun at me. "They will be destroyed and I will still take you and sell you off. You see, I get it all. Everything I want. And there's nothing you can do to stop me."

The hollow, metallic ring that passed for laughter sounded from Mishmash as bands of red light moved across his cylindrical head.

"And now." Hamilton tightened the grip on his gun. "Like a troublesome pebble lodged in my shoe, it's time to cast you aside."

"Wait!" I put out my hands in desperation. The real pity of my situation was that I had a great plan but once again, my timing was off. I glanced at Mishmash. There was no telling how close the holding sphere was to exploding. What if I couldn't stall that long?

"What?" Hamilton gave an annoyed response and powered up his blaster.

"You haven't told me your plan for universal domination yet." I admit it was a weak stall but he was a sucker for bragging.

Hamilton sighed. "The power I wield one day will make Mar Mar the Unthinkable look like a sub czar of a second rate moon."

"Wow." I tried to sound really impressed. "Tell me more about how awesome you'll be."

Hamilton gave a slow, steely-eyed shake of his head. "My plan is too brilliant to waste on a worthless space drifter like you. Goodbye Glint." Hamilton narrowed his eyes.

I was about to say something but the words caught in my throat at the sight of his finger squeezing the trigger.

"No!" Nelvan yelled and leapt between Hamilton and me. The sound of a sleek, deadly energy pulse came toward me and a bright beam of light hit Nelvan square in the back. I caught him as he fell toward me and slumped into my arms. His face was tightened in pain.

"Nelvan." I lifted him up so we were face to face. "Are you crazy? Why did you do that?"

Nelvan's eyes were closed. The pain on his face fell away and was replaced by a sleepy sort of smile. "It's okay, I'm not afraid of death. Heaven will be a nice rest after all this."

Hamilton gave an exasperated sigh. "Great, there goes my black market payoff. Stupid boy, get him out of the way."

I clenched my jaw and glared up at Hamilton. I'd have given my kingdom for another DEMOTER at my side. If only I had a kingdom. Or a home of any kind.

"Never." I looked at the poor boy's calm face. He was fading away. I felt tears welling up. I tried to will them back down my tough guy tear ducts as best I could.

"Move that boy," Hamilton ordered. "Or I'll blast a hole through him to get to you. I'll give you to the count of three. One ..."

A building, high-pitched noise came from Mishmash.

"Two."

A bright red glow emanated from Mishmash's torso. The robot's head swiveled frantically as shafts of red light shone through every seam in his metal body.

"Thr—" Hamilton turned in alarm to Mishmash. "Mishmash, what ..."

His voice trailed off as he stared at the glowing robot in utter confusion. I dropped to the ground, covering Nelvan's body with my own.

"No!" Hamilton cried out as an explosion rocked the area.

37

THE EAR SHATTERING SOUND of the explosion was mixed with the rending of metal and a shriek of pain from Hamilton. The force of the blast hit me like a hurricane. Nelvan and I were sent skidding across the top of the rock formation toward the edge.

As I slid off the edge, I grasped blindly with my right arm and found a rocky handhold. My body jerked as I stopped my precarious fall. Nelvan flew over me, nothing left to stop him from the deadly drop. He reached toward me with desperate eyes. I reached out with my free hand and grabbed his wrist just before he sailed past. The momentum of the blast–coupled with Nelvan's weight–spread my arms taut until I felt like I would snap in two. The pain in my wounded left arm sprang back to life. It felt like dozens of insects covered in spikes were crawling inside my shoulder.

I held onto Nelvan as the momentum swung us around into a painful collision with the side of the rock formation.

A sharp cry of pain rose up from far below. I looked down to find a charred version of Hamilton and the broken remains of Mishmash thrashing about in the lava. The explosion seemed to have infused them together in a bizarre combination of metal and man. Fire was igniting all around them as they scrambled for a low rock formation nearby.

"Captain," Nelvan called out in a strained voice. "Let me go. You can't save both of us."

"You wanna bet?" I looked down with my best reassuring grin and tightened my grip on his wrist to accentuate the point. He was right of course. I wouldn't be able to hold on much longer. Even if my left arm wasn't so bad off, the heat waves from below had already caused a layer of sweat to form between my palm and his wrist. Eventually, he would simply slip away.

"Captain," Blix called from below. "You okay up there?"

"Not really." From where we hung I could just see the rock outcropping where Blix and Jasette stood. It looked as though more of it had crumbled away and they were left standing on a narrow ledge. "How's it going down there?"

"The ledge is breaking apart," Jasette said. "We don't have much time."

"Yes," Blix said. "Can't see much of a way out of this one. Good work with Hamilton though. Very clever. Uh oh, look out!"

A loud collision sounded overhead. Hamilton's hoverdisc had collided with the rock pedestal just above. A shower of small rocks rained down on my head. The hoverdisc moved away from the rock in an awkward sway. Without anyone to direct it, the disc was flying wild.

The hoverdisc shuddered for a moment, then rushed toward us once more. It hit the rock just beside me, sending a tremor through my precarious handhold.

"Why is it doing that?" Nelvan spoke in a slurred groan as if waking from a dream.

The hover disc spun away and did a loop around the pedestal rock.

"Captain," Blix called. "Perhaps you can grab it if it gets close enough."

"I'm a little short on free hands," I said.

"Well, why don't you—" Blix gasped. "Duck!"

For a brief moment I wondered how it would be physically possible to duck as I hung suspended from the side of a rock. My wondering was cut short as the hoverdisc struck me in the back of the head. I involuntarily let go of both the rock and Nelvan. I could feel my consciousness slipping as I fell toward the lava below. Jasette's scream echoed through the cavern. She really did care after all.

All things considered, I thought we were pretty lucky to be nearly unconscious as we fell to our fiery doom. My vision blurred and everything seemed to move in slow motion. I saw Nelvan tumble helplessly through the air beside me. The hoverdisc was falling with us, spinning in a slow rotation as if it were going to drill into the lava below.

I glanced down and thought I caught a glimpse of Hamilton's burnt hand clinging to a rock that rose just above the river of lava. I smiled, thinking that hallucinations had begun to take hold.

I reached out slowly and to my surprise was able to touch the hoverdisc. The disc stopped spinning and seemed to respond to my touch by moving closer. I felt the cool, smooth surface of the clear disc press against me. I wondered if it was all part of another hallucination as the bright heat of the lava drew near and I slipped into unconsciousness.

38

I WOKE TO THE hazy sight of a white walled room. My head felt thick, like it was filled with syrup. Several pains sprang to life around my temples. A low hum came from the floor. My last memory of falling toward lava came to mind. Was this the afterlife? My head sure hurt a lot for this to be heaven. Maybe this was the waiting room for heaven.

I blinked a few times and my vision cleared. The walls were more of a dingy, off-white color with several nicks and a few stains. Also, there was an odd, disinfectant smell. Maybe this was the waiting room for hell.

I was lying on a padded sleeping slab. Extra gel padding propped my head up for a good view of the room without having to move much. My black jacket was draped over a chair nearby. I was still wearing my silver shirt but there was a large bandage around my left arm with digitized med needles administering unknown substances into my body.

The rhythmic sounds of a vitals health monitor activated beside me. That's when it hit me. I was in the med unit on my ship. The low hum from the floor was coming from the engines.

It didn't make any sense. How could the engines be running? Our crash landing had put them out of commission.

I sat up all the way and immediately wished I hadn't. My head spun and my stomach churned, sending a clear warning that if I made any sudden moves, vomiting was inevitable. I steadied myself, grabbing a cold, metal railing on the side of the slab.

High, fast-talking voices came from beyond the doorway of the med unit. They were heading closer. I instinctively reached for my DEMOTER but it wasn't there. It had blown to smithereens along with Mishmash and Hamilton. It was a wonderful memory that I had no time to revel in with someone approaching.

Two short, green humanoids walked into the room. Each had four arms and slender bodies. They were outfitted in stylish, black jump suits with a band of silver that encircled their chest. They spoke in quick, excited bursts as they walked, their arms making nimble, animated gestures, presumably to accentuate their stories.

One of them was slightly taller and had three silver stripes on the shoulder of his jump suit. He spoke to his shorter companion about repairs to an outdated quadra-thruster. I cleared my throat and they gave a start. The shorter one let out a squeak.

"Captain." The taller one with the silver stripes stepped forward, composing himself. "We didn't know you were up. This is fantastic news. I'm Glotsy and this is Vissle."

"Hello, Captain." Vissle stepped forward and folded his two sets of hands in what looked like a proper gesture. "Beggin' your pardon sir, but I've been dying to ask you about the clayvial couplings on the roto-thruster pods. I just can't see how any rational being would use something so outdated and potentially explosive."

Glotsy sent two quick elbows into Vissle's side, cutting him short.

"You'll have to forgive Vissle, Captain." Glotsy gave a slight bow. "He's over enthusiastic about his work. The main thing, of course, is—"

"Who are you?" I interrupted. The speed of their speech left little room for a break in the conversation.

"I told you, I'm Glotsy and this is Vissle." He scrunched up his childlike face in confusion. "Are you feeling okay?" He moved toward the vitals monitor and adjusted a few settings. "Readings seem standard considering what you've been through." Glotsy's eyes were a blur as they danced over the digital readouts. "Though I'm far more qualified as a technician than a doctor."

I slammed my fist down on the metal railing. "Who are you, what are you and what are you doing aboard my ship?" I gave them my best threatening stare. Considering I was in bed with bandages and unarmed, it was the best I could do.

"Ah, yes of course." Glotsy nodded as if remembering something. "Terribly sorry. We're your new technical crew. Iris, alert the others that the captain is awake."

"Right away Glotsy," Iris said.

"Iris!" I stared wide-eyed at Glotsy. "You brought Iris back online?"

"Well, you can't very well fly a star freighter into deep space without a ship computer, Captain." Glotsy shook his head as if speaking to a child. "We did have to do a fair bit of system overhaul though. Some corrupted files lurking in the nano blocks. It's a good thing we caught them. Glitches like that have been known to turn a ship on her crew."

I nodded in agreement. "So I've heard."

Glotsy patted the wall and looked up. "But you're feeling fine now, aren't you Iris?"

"Yes Glotsy, thank you," Iris said.

"There, you see. Apart from memory loss of the last few gloons, your computer is back in tip top shape." Glotsy and Vissle pointed at each other with both sets of hands and grinned as if acknowledging a job well done.

"Well, lots more details but we've got things to do. The others can explain everything." Glotsy made a quick about face and led Vissle from the room.

"Wait." I called out, but they were already headed down the hall.

"How are you feeling, Captain?" Iris spoke in a serene voice.

"Um … fine." I gave an apprehensive look around the room. "H-How are you?"

"I'm told we've flown together for some time," Iris said. "I'm afraid much of my recent memory has been lost. I do hope my services have been to your satisfaction."

"Yeah, um. Pretty much." It was hard to believe Iris was a normal, working ship computer again. I wondered if they'd really fixed all her tweaked files. "Just to make sure we're crystal clear, I only like human women. I don't go for robots, cyborgs or computers of any kind, got it?"

"That's perfectly understandable, Captain." A few descending tones sounded. "But I do hope we can be friends."

"Yeah, purely platonic, okay?"

"Of course."

I heard several footsteps approaching. They were the heavier steps of creatures larger than Glotsy and Vissle. I took a quick scan of the room for a weapon. I had no idea what was coming but I wanted to be prepared. I spied a metal food tray on the vitals monitor. I grabbed it and raised it above my head as the footsteps drew near.

In walked Blix and Jasette. Their faces were a mix of confusion and amusement at the sight of me.

"Captain, really." Blix folded his arms and shook his head. "I can't imagine what you'd do with that if I were a hostile being."

"Maybe he'd serve you breakfast," Jasette smirked.

"You're alive." I set the tray on my lap, staring in amazement. My head turned back and forth between the two of them, feeling as if I was in a dream. "How in blazes are you both alive? How am I alive for that matter?"

"Captain," Blix said. "I wish your fragile human consciousness could've stayed around for what transpired in those lava caverns."

"Yes, especially the part where you saved us." Jasette gave a playful grin.

"I saved you?"

Blix and Jasette nodded. I tried desperately to recall even a shred of the rescue attempt but all I could remember was falling toward lava.

"Hello, Captain." Nelvan strolled into the room carrying a silver mug with steam escaping the rim. My mouth dropped at the sight of the boy.

His silver jumpsuit had been repaired and he looked just as he did the first day he appeared on my ship. He walked up and handed me the mug. "Thought you might like a warm cup of velrys."

I took the cup as if a ghost had handed it to me in a dream.

"Nelvan? But you … I saw … you were shot and then … lava …" My mind had reached a point where it could no longer connect what I saw with reality.

"Captain, you won't believe it." Nelvan reached back into

the pouch on his back and pulled out a charred, cracked rectangular object. "This is what's left of my journal."

I stared in disbelief at the blackened, pitted object. It looked like something left behind on a war-ravaged planet.

"It must have absorbed the blast from Hamilton," Nelvan said. "My back was a little tweaked but a little time in the med unit took care of that. Didn't I tell you I believed in miracles?"

"I don't understand any of this." I looked at Blix and Jasette, searching for answers. "Shouldn't we all be dead?"

Nelvan frowned and looked back at Blix. "You didn't tell him what happened?"

Blix put up his hands. "I haven't had the chance."

"You activated the hoverdisc," Jasette said.

"I did?" I said.

"Captain, it was extraordinary," Blix said. "You and Nelvan were hurtling toward the lava when you reached over and touched the hoverdisc. It responded to your connection and swung underneath both of you."

The hazy memory of reaching out and touching the disc came back to me. I didn't remember much else.

"It caught the two of you just inches above the flowing lava," Blix said. "It seemed as though both of you were unconscious at that point. We were yelling but neither of you answered."

Nelvan patted my arm. "It's okay, Captain, I don't remember this part either."

"Then you sort of rolled over in our direction," Blix said. "The hoverdisc tilted and flew right toward us."

"Just in time," Jasette added. "We jumped on right when the rocks crumbled beneath us."

"And they piloted the disc safely back to the ship." Nelvan

smiled and folded his arms as if he'd just finished telling me a delightful bedtime story.

I was so used to bad news I was having trouble taking this all in. I gripped the cold, metal rail on the side of my slab. I lifted the warm mug and took a long drink of velrys. The warm, smooth beverage was pure heaven.

"This can't be real," I said. "Our ship was all bashed up. It would've taken montuls to repair the damage."

"For us, yes," Blix said. "But here's the delightful part. When we got back, dozens of Glekthork refugees were working on our ship. Apparently they were slaves aboard Hamilton's ship."

Jasette shook her head in disgust. "Good riddance to that creep."

"Indeed." Blix nodded. "Captain, Glekthorkians are some of the finest engineers around. And they were so happy to be free from Hamilton's tyranny and grateful for his demise at our hands, they volunteered to be part of our crew. At least until we can transport them back to Glekthork."

"They are quite adept, Captain," Iris said. "All my operations are running at near full capacity."

"That's great, Iris." I gave a nervous look at Blix and flicked my eyes toward the ceiling to indicate my concern over her.

Blix gave a reassuring nod. "Computer functions are under control. Nothing to be concerned with."

"Let's hope so." I gave him a stern look.

"They got the ship up and running in a day." Nelvan smiled. "We're out of the asteroid field and back in the freedom of space."

I paused, trying to get my thoughts together. I took another drink of velrys for reassurance. A wave of relief swept through me. It felt strange. Foreign. It almost bordered on happiness.

"And I did all this?" My spirit surged with self-confidence. "I defeated my nemesis and saved all of you?" I felt victorious, powerful. I imagined a statue of myself fashioned in a conquering pose with the word 'Hero' etched in a stone plaque.

"Although …" Blix rubbed his chin in thought. "… You were wearing the Emerald Enigma the whole time."

Imaginary cracks started to form on my imaginary statue. "Yeah, so?"

"Oh, well, you see …" Blix seemed to be having difficulty choosing his words. "It's just that it's difficult to tell where the luck of the Enigma ends and you begin."

I arched an angry eyebrow at him. "So, as long as I'm wearing this thing, I can't take credit for anything I do?"

"You can still own the bad decisions."

I grabbed the metal food tray from my lap and flung it at Blix. He caught it without flinching and gave a scolding shake of his head.

"And might I suggest …" Blix held up a lecturing finger. "… You get rid of that emerald the first chance you get. It's most unpredictable and certainly dangerous."

"You mean, this thing that just saved all of our lives?" I tapped at my chest. The Enigma made a subtle bump under my shirt. "No way."

"Captain, he's right." Nelvan nodded. "Remember what happened to Grizzolo?"

"He just kept it too long, that was his mistake." I didn't want to think about getting rid of the Enigma. Not yet anyways. I'd finally found something that gave me some degree of power, unpredictable as it might be, and I wanted to hold onto it for a while. I figured, once the good luck had earned me a small fortune, I'd get rid of it before anything bad happened to me.

"Oh, Captain." Blix shook his head. "Those are the sad words of a deluded soul. Do you know how many cautionary tales start like this?"

"Don't worry. I know what I'm doing. Besides ..." I paused as a sudden realization hit me.

"Wait a freem," I said. "How long have I been out? What's today?"

"About a day and a half," Jasette said. "It's the fifth phase of Blexis on the second dark quadrant shift cycle."

"I knew it." I pointed at Blix. "Your season of peace is over!"

Blix gave a halfhearted grin. "Yes, Captain."

"That means, your season of battle has begun." I swung my legs out of bed. A fresh wave of nausea hit me and I felt my body sway.

Nelvan grabbed my arm to steady me. "Captain, you should stay in bed and rest."

"I've been here long enough." I took a big swig of velrys and handed Nelvan the cup. "Here, take this." I slid out of bed. My legs felt all wobbly and the metal floors were like ice. But none of that mattered. I was filled with a surge of power at the news about Blix.

"Do you know what this means?" My eyes danced between crew members. They looked worried. I must've had my wild eyes on.

"A captain that bears the Emerald Enigma ..." I placed a hand over my chest. I felt the solid emerald stone under my shirt. "... My first mate, a Vythian in his season of battle ..." I walked over to Blix and placed a hand on the smooth, copper scales of his broad shoulder.

I turned and gave a sly look to Jasette. "… A dangerous, capable and not to mention beautiful bounty hunter …" She nodded her head as if I was merely stating facts.

"And … um …" I looked at Nelvan, searching for words. Then, inspiration hit. "… Not to mention the human lie detector, Nelvan." I motioned to him as if introducing a stage act. "... Ready to throw himself in front of laser blasts to defend his captain."

Nelvan gave a shy smile and looked down in humility.

"We will be an unstoppable force." I raised a fist toward Blix in a gesture of our newfound power. "Talk to me Blix. Wax eloquent of who we will conquer."

"Um, yes, Captain. About that." Blix gave a nervous glance to Nelvan. "I'm afraid I won't be participating in my season of battle after all."

I paused for a moment, waiting for the punch line.

Blix cleared his throat and gave a nervous little laugh. "Sorry."

"Um … what?" I tried to keep my voice calm but I could hear an edgy grit.

"Yes, well, while you were unconscious, I had a lengthy conversation with Nelvan about his Earth Bible."

I shot an angry look at Nelvan. "Oh, really?"

Nelvan shrugged, a guilty expression on his face.

"You see, I've always sought some kind of redemption in the universe," Blix made a sweeping gesture, a far off look in his eyes. "Most of my existence has drifted from one form of combat to another. It comes all too easy for the typical Vythian."

"Yes." I fixed him with stern eyes that I hoped would snap him back to reality. "That's the beauty of Vythians. They're predictable. Bound to their instincts. They must follow their seasons. You've told me this a hundred times when I've asked you to fight for me."

"Indeed, Captain." Blix frowned. "But after eight hundred and fifty three gloons, it's all become a bit empty. I seek a more meaningful life."

"Blah, blah, blah," I said. "You can't just switch the rules. What would your family say?"

Blix let out a heavy sigh. "It is, of course, most unbecoming. My brethren will surely disown me."

"Do you realize how long I've had to wait for your season of peace to be over?" I spoke through gritted teeth.

Jasette gave a concerned look. "The vein in your neck is throbbing."

"I'm sorry, Captain," Blix said. "But I've finally found spiritual enlightenment. The salvation of my very soul."

"Your soul?" I said. "You're a Vythian—you don't have a soul."

Blix lifted his chin looking regal. "Agree to disagree."

I turned to Nelvan. "Tell him, Nelvan. Tell him he doesn't have a soul."

Nelvan shrugged. "He seems like he has a soul to me."

I turned to Jasette in desperation.

"Don't look at me." Jasette held up her hands. "I'm no theologian."

"Christ walked a path of forgiveness and love." Blix spoke in a professorial manner. "If I'm to follow in his steps, I simply can't indulge in a season of battle."

I stamped my foot on the floor. Several prickles of pain ran up my leg. "You can't do this. You promised me. Your family will disown you. Heck, I'll disown you."

"Glint." Jasette frowned her disapproval.

"Alas, I will suffer as Christ suffered." Blix looked skyward, the look of a martyr on his face. "That is the way of things."

Nelvan nodded and held up a fist of solidarity.

"This is mutiny, I tell you." I pointed at the two of them, giving my best scowl. "I'll have you ejected into space."

"Glint, you really need to calm down." Jasette shook her head, looking at me like I was some rebellious child.

I was about to launch into more threats and name-calling when Glotsy and Vissle came running into the room.

"Captain." Glotsy gasped for breath. "You've got to come to the bridge."

"What?" The usual feelings of stress and apprehension came flooding back to me.

Glotsy and Vissle turned and scampered out of the room.

"Wait, what is it?" The quick moving Glekthorks left before I could question them.

"We'll take care of it." Blix headed after them and motioned for Nelvan to follow. "You need more rest. Your behavior is still quite irrational."

"This isn't over, lizard boy." I pointed a threatening finger at Blix.

Nelvan gave Blix a comforting pat on the shoulder as they headed out.

"Maybe you should get more rest." Jasette gave a concerned look. "You're acting kind of crazy."

"I'm fine." I took a step forward and swayed. I steadied myself on the chair nearby, where my jacket hung. I grabbed my jacket and threw it on. I almost lost my balance with the effort.

Jasette came close and supported my arm all nurselike. “You don’t seem fine.”

“I’m just a little dizzy. It’s not like I’m an invalid.”

“Does that mean you don’t want me to touch you?” Jasette gave a playful grin.

“Well …” My mind raced through a myriad of possible comebacks. “… I suppose I could use a little help.”

Jasette smiled and led me through the doorway.

39

JASETTE HELD ME BY the arm and helped steady my walk as I headed down the hallway. The lights were back at full power, showing the brushed metal finish of the walls as they were meant to be seen. They were a rugged, well-built, unfinished symbol of manliness. Since it was my ship, I was sure the machismo would subconsciously build up Jasette's image of me.

I glanced over at her. She was still wearing her black power suit, which was nothing but complimentary on her figure. I could also tell that while I was asleep, she'd had time to freshen up. Her silver and blue hair had a vibrant shine as it fell freely across her shoulders. Her face was free of all the smudges and dirt we'd picked up on our harrowing adventures over the last few days and there was an unmistakable makeup reapplication.

"You know," Jasette said. "Blix is right. You really should get rid of that thing." She glanced down at my chest.

"I will. Trust me, once I get a few good swings of fortune, it's gone."

She looked disappointed by my answer. "That's risky, Glint. What if you fly too close to a planet where everyone thinks it's good luck to turn into a slug?"

That gave me an idea. "Or we could fly close to the planet Jelmontaire. Just imagine all the wishes of your citizens hoping for the Chrysolenthium flower, floating through space toward this necklace …" I tapped on my chest. "… And the Enigma will lead us right to one."

Jasette stopped and turned to me, her eyes stern. "That's not fair."

I grinned, waiting for her to cave.

She let out a long sigh. "Do you really think that would work? I mean, we could just do that one thing and then get rid of it."

"Well, well, look who suddenly wants to keep the Enigma around for a while."

"This is different," she said. "The lives of the people in my kingdom are at stake. If there's even a chance … Oh Glint, can we try?"

"Sure, just as long as you stick around till I earn my fortune. With two peacemakers as my crew, I need someone who can help me when things get rough."

Her face filled with doubt. "Well, how long will that take?"

"Hey, I've got the Enigma. For all I know, it could happen today."

She seemed lost in thought for a moment and then gave a slight smile. "Okay, deal."

We started down the hallway once more. Sure, flying close to her planet to catch some random wishes of finding the flower was a long shot but if it would make her stay, it was worth it.

We were united on a new quest and the time seemed right to be all smooth and romantic. I decided to start subtle and slowly work my magic.

"You know," I said. "I've been thinking about us."

Jasette raised an eyebrow and gave me a sidelong glance. "Us?"

"Well, you know, how you're all in love with me and everything."

Jasette laughed. It was a loud laugh. Too loud.

"What? You're saying you're not into this?" I gave my best flex. Considering she was holding my arm and helping me to walk, it didn't come off as manly as I'd hoped.

She shook her head. "It's amazing how much stronger my feelings for you were when you were unconscious."

"Aha." I pointed at her. "So you admit you have feelings for me."

She smiled. "Yes, but they're weakening by the freem."

"Let's not forget about me saving your life back in the lava cavern. That's gotta do something for you."

"I saved your life too. Remember the space monkeys."

"What about my safe landing? That's twice I saved your life. And the escape from Serberat, what about that?"

"Without my computer skills, you never would have made it."

She had a good point. "Okay, fine, team effort on the Serberat escape. But I'm still up by one life saving incident."

Jasette sighed and stopped as we reached the lift. The doors chirped open. She waited for a moment, staring into the empty lift, then turned to face me, an expectant look on her face.

I paused, realizing I'd been too belligerent in my desire to come out on top of the conversation. "Um, I went too far, didn't I?"

She raised her eyebrows and nodded.

"If I said you were the most beautiful girl in the universe, what would that do for you?"

She softened a bit. "It helps."

I stared at her for a moment, not sure if I had made up enough ground. "So, we're good, right?"

She sighed.

"What?" I said.

"Are you gonna kiss me or what?"

Obviously I had missed my cue. I should've leaned in right after the beautiful comment. She smiled at my momentary confusion. No doubt she enjoyed catching me off guard. Just to make sure her moment of victory didn't last too long, I went in for the kiss.

I pulled her close and felt her lean into me. All my painful injuries seemed to fade away as her soft lips met mine. She smelled like a field of Zintorian lilies in full bloom. Aside from my perfectly timed trip to the Vengrille system ten gloons ago where I caught the luminous meteor showers near the quadra-star helix array, this was the best moment I'd experienced in space.

She slowly drew back, a sleepy sort of smile on her lips. "Much better."

I made a gentlemanly gesture toward the lift. "After you."

Her expression was somewhere between surprise and laughter but I could tell she was into it. "Now that's more like it." She sauntered into the lift.

I flashed what I hoped was a smooth grin and joined her. The doors chirped shut and we headed for the bridge.

40

THE LIFT DOORS OPENED and I led Jasette onto the bridge. For a moment it looked like my ship had been taken over by little green aliens. Over a dozen Glekthorks worked diligently throughout the bridge. Some were tapping out rapid-fire commands at touch consoles, others were checking various instrument readings and several were darting about on unknown errands. The viewing screen displayed a commercial for the latest luxury space cruiser.

"Captain, what took you so long?" Glotsy was in my captain's chair, his neck craned back at my arrival. "You almost missed it, my technical crew got the early word on the upcoming announcement."

"What announcement?" I narrowed my eyes at him. "What are you doing in my chair?"

"You'll see." Glotsy hit a few controls on the armrest and the volume came up on the viewing screen.

The Gleckthorks stopped their work and gathered in front of the screen. The space cruiser commercial ended and the visual changed to a fast motion view on the surface of an ice planet. Driving music was building as the view dove into an icy blue tunnel.

A muscular, orange skinned alien with fins down his neck was weaving through the tunnel on a sleek, arrow nosed power sled. He weaved and spun the sled with ease as treacherous rocks and chasms blocked his path. Just when it looked as though the tunnel was coming to an end he narrowed his eyes and hit the thrusters. The orange alien burst through a narrow passage onto the brilliant surface of the crystalline planet in a shower of snow fragments. He raised his hands in triumph and the thunderous applause of an unseen crowd roared.

A deep, resonant voice spoke a single word. "Winner."

"What is this?" I said. "What are you watching?"

The Glekthorks turned and put their fingers to their lips, making a loud shushing sound.

The visual changed to a shadowy jungle. The trees rose high in the air, their thick, curving trunks descending into the darkness of the unseen ground far below.

A slender, white and purple streaked alien with six arms leapt and swung through the dense branches and vines with amazing agility. A deadly looking spear flew at him from the shadows. He spun away, the spear missing his head by inches. The visuals slowed to a crawl as the spear passed his head, then returned to normal speed as he grasped another branch. There was an amplified crack as the branch snapped. The alien faltered and reached for a nearby vine. His hand grasped nothing but air. The alien's eyes went wide as he plunged into the murky, black depths below.

The deep announcer's voice proclaimed. "Loser."

Glittering letters spun onto the screen and assembled into a title with bright flashes and explosions. The announcer spoke the words as they formed. "The Iron Gauntlet."

Fantasmica, the largest super planet known and home to many of the top celebrities, spun into view. The screen was filled with the lush green and gold mosaic of the tropical planet. The view descended into the billowy clouds of the atmosphere.

A lone, crystal pedestal stood among the soft clouds. A man stood atop the narrow pedestal wearing a golden suit that shone brightly in the twin suns of Fantasmica.

The announcer's voice boomed. "And now, your host, Forglyn Sashmeyer."

The view zoomed in on the golden suited man. His shiny, well-groomed, black hair flowed with the soft breeze. His strong jaw line was barely able to contain a broad smile of blinding white teeth. He winked at the screen, his technologically enhanced eyes pulsating with a blue glow and a thousand white sparkles.

"Wow," Jasette said.

I shot an angry look at her. "Really? One of the biggest phonies on Fantasmica and you say, 'Wow'?"

"Sorry." She looked embarrassed. "The eyes caught me off guard."

"She does have a point." Blix studied the screen as if analyzing data. "The eyes have a certain dreaminess."

"Hello universe." Forglyn spoke with a smooth, almost musical voice. "As you may have heard, we've just announced our fifth and final contestant for the three hundred and thirty third season of 'The Iron Gauntlet'!"

An uproar of cheers and applause echoed through the clouds like thunder. Neverending rings of holographic viewers materialized among the clouds around Forglyn. They were cheering and smiling as they hung on his every word.

"Here's why we called you up here, Captain." Glotsy was by my side, tugging at my jacket. "You won't believe this."

Forglyn put out his hand to quiet the crowd. "We've finally located him near the Beringfell system."

"Hey," Nelvan said. "Isn't that where we are?"

Jasette gave a wary glance my way. "Uh oh."

"Would you like to meet him?" Forglyn flashed his blinding smile and made a wide, sweeping motion to the holographic audience around him.

The crowd erupted in cheers and hoots. Forglyn disappeared from the crystal pedestal. A freem later, he appeared right beside me. I shielded my eyes as the bridge was suddenly awash with lights. Dozens of miniature cambots appeared and circled me like a hungry school of sharks.

Forglyn was almost as tall as Blix but with his slender, athletic build, only half as wide. His body gave off a slight blue glow and, being a holographic projection, he was slightly translucent.

His sparkling, blue eyes gleamed down at me. "Captain Glint Starcrost." Forglyn's voice took on a resonant echo. "Out of all the beings in the universe, your name has been randomly selected by 'The Iron Gauntlet' supercomputer. You are the fifth and final contestant!"

Scores of holographic viewers materialized around the bridge, clapping and cheering.

"Amazing." Blix shook his head in disbelief. "Looks like your luck has taken a good turn, eh Captain?" He shot a quick look down at my chest, where the Enigma was concealed underneath my shirt.

I was speechless. Most would consider this a wild upswing of fortune but not me. I was far more comfortable as a loner, drifting through space doing my own thing. And besides, I had a bounty on my head. How could I possibly remain hidden from Mar Mar the Unthinkable and the endless minions looking to cash in on my capture?

"Captain Starcrost." Forglyn shoved a holographic microphone in my face. "What do you have to say?"

My mind was blank. Billions of beings around the universe were watching. In a kneejerk reaction, I spoke the first words that came to mind. "Get off my ship, pretty boy."

Forglyn laughed and patted me on the shoulder. Although his hand simply passed through my shoulder, somehow he made it look believable. "We've got a real character here folks. This should be fun."

The holographic audience laughed.

Forglyn smirked and pointed his thumb at me playfully. "We'll find out more about this incorrigible captain and his colorful crew later. But now, let's take a quick break before we catch up with our other contestants as they prepare for the competition."

The holo crowd vanished and the bright lights faded away. The viewing screen on the bridge switched to an ad for space hemorrhoid cream.

The bright colors in Forglyn's hologram faded and he took on an opaque blue tone. He stepped closer and loomed over me. His smile evaporated and his eyes narrowed. "Listen here, space trash." He poked a threatening finger at my chest, which simply went through it. "You watch your step. I've got powerful connections."

And with that, he vanished in a flare of blue. I looked around at my crew, wondering how so much could have just happened in a few short freems.

"Amazing," Glotsy piped up. "You must be the luckiest man in the universe. Humans rarely get picked for this show. Their constitutions simply can't endure the rigors of the deadly events."

Glotsy patted me on the back and went right back to the ship controls, along with the other Glekthorks. I turned to my crew in confusion, still reeling from the news.

Nelvan gave me a quizzical look. "So, it's a good thing, right?"

"Um, kind of." Jasette had a faraway look in her eyes, like several of her plans had just come to ruin.

"Of course it's good." Blix came alongside and tucked me far too tightly under his arm. "Our captain just became a celebrity." Blix smiled broadly. "Plus, the winner gets a million vibes."

"Really?" Suddenly I felt a little more lucky. "A million vibes?"

Blix smiled and nodded.

"I haven't watched the show much," I said. "How dangerous is it?"

"It's not that bad." Blix's cheek started twitching.

"Haven't some of the contestants died playing?" I said.

"Many of them." Jasette avoided eye contact.

"Hmm." I placed a hand on my chest and felt the reassuring shape of the Emerald Enigma. "Well, I do have the Enigma. I'll probably be okay, right?"

As I looked around at the half hearted nods and nervous glances of my crew, my short-lived boost of victorious confidence at having defeated Hamilton faded away.

It seemed my troubles had just begun.

ACKNOWLEDGMENTS

My heartfelt thanks to family and friends that have provided the encouragement, support, love and caffeine necessary to make this book a reality.

Special thanks to my close ones Jolene, Joshua, Katie, and our families.

Thank you to Steve Laube and the Enclave Publishing team along with Mark Gottlieb and Trident Media Group for believing in *Space Drifters.*

Finally, a shout out to my friend Jim (movie guru and plot dissector) and the Writers Without Borders crew: Merrie, Becky, Rachel and Mike along with the talented wordsmiths I've had the pleasure of meeting along this writing journey. Their contributions to my storytelling abilities are priceless.

About the Author

Paul Regnier was born and raised in Southern California. He is an up and coming author with a love for science fiction and fantasy stories that dates back to childhood.

An ongoing interest in technology has earned him a living as a web designer and a fascination with all things futuristic. In school, he would read his short stories to friends, keeping them laughing and entertained. Paul has turned his childhood love of story telling into a professional pursuit and is currently writing a series of science fiction novels.

Paul lives in Orange County, CA with his wife and two children.